SO-CMS-510

"Wayne, why did you vote the way you did?"

"Maybe I don't like to be rushed into things."

Maggie straightened and shoved stray bangs out of her eyes. "That's something, anyway. Something I can work with."

The muscles of his jaw rippled along one side. "I'm not sure I like the idea of being the object of one of your campaigns, but I guess it comes with the territory."

"It won't hurt," she said with a smile. "Not much, anyway."

A silence fell between them, the pale wisps of their breath mingling and dissipating in the moonlit air. He pushed away from the truck. "What exactly is it you want from me, Maggie?"

"I want your promise to consider my proposal with an open mind."

"I'll consider that proposal of yours, if you'll consider the possibility that my mind was open to it in the first place."

She squelched the urge to argue his last point. "All right," she said, extending her right hand. "I will."

He slid his hand against her palm. It was wide and warm and rough with calluses.

His long fingers slowly closed around hers. "That's something, anyway," he said. "Guess I'll find out whether or not it's something I can work with."

Dear Reader,

When I began work on *The Rancher Needs a Wife*, I didn't intend to write a story about stage fright. But as I sat at my keyboard and struggled with my writing fears—the doubts that appear every time I place my hands on the keyboard and whisper that I won't be able to pull off the trick this time—I realized I could transfer some of my feelings to my characters. Not a nice thing to do, perhaps, but torturing characters is one way writers create stories.

In this second book of my BRIGHT LIGHTS, BIG SKY series, Wayne and Maggie face their fears of public exposure in surprising ways. I hope you'll enjoy their triumphs over their struggles as much as I enjoyed writing about them.

I'd love to hear from my readers! Please come for a visit to my Web site at www.terrymclaughlin.com, or find me at www.wetnoodleposse.com or www.superauthors.com, or write to me at P.O. Box 5838, Eureka, CA 95502.

Wishing you happily-ever-after reading,

Terry McLaughlin

THE RANCHER
NEEDS A WIFE
Terry McLaughlin

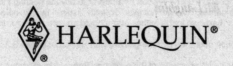

HARLEQUIN®

TORONTO • NEW YORK • LONDON
AMSTERDAM • PARIS • SYDNEY • HAMBURG
STOCKHOLM • ATHENS • TOKYO • MILAN • MADRID
PRAGUE • WARSAW • BUDAPEST • AUCKLAND

If you purchased this book without a cover you should be aware
that this book is stolen property. It was reported as "unsold and
destroyed" to the publisher, and neither the author nor the
publisher has received any payment for this "stripped book."

ISBN-13: 978-0-373-71400-1
ISBN-10:   0-373-71400-9

THE RANCHER NEEDS A WIFE

Copyright © 2007 by Teresa A. McLaughlin.

All rights reserved. Except for use in any review, the reproduction or
utilization of this work in whole or in part in any form by any electronic,
mechanical or other means, now known or hereafter invented, including
xerography, photocopying and recording, or in any information storage
or retrieval system, is forbidden without the written permission of the
publisher, Harlequin Enterprises Limited, 225 Duncan Mill Road,
Don Mills, Ontario, Canada M3B 3K9.

All characters in this book have no existence outside the imagination of
the author and have no relation whatsoever to anyone bearing the same
name or names. They are not even distantly inspired by any individual
known or unknown to the author, and all incidents are pure invention.

This edition published by arrangement with Harlequin Books S.A.

® and TM are trademarks of the publisher. Trademarks indicated with
® are registered in the United States Patent and Trademark Office, the
Canadian Trade Marks Office and in other countries.

www.eHarlequin.com

Printed in U.S.A.

ABOUT THE AUTHOR

Terry McLaughlin spent a dozen years teaching a variety of subjects, including anthropology, music appreciation, English, drafting, drama and history, to a variety of students from kindergarten to college before she discovered romance novels and fell in love with love stories. When she's not reading and writing, she enjoys traveling and dreaming up house and garden improvement projects (although most of those dreams don't come true).

Terry lives with her husband in Northern California on a tiny ranch in the redwoods. Visit her at www.terrymclaughlin.com.

Books by Terry McLaughlin

HARLEQUIN SUPERROMANCE
1348–LEARNING CURVE
1372–MAKE-BELIEVE COWBOY*

*Bright Lights, Big Sky

Don't miss any of our special offers. Write to us at the following address for information on our newest releases.

Harlequin Reader Service
U.S.: 3010 Walden Ave., P.O. Box 1325, Buffalo, NY 14269
Canadian: P.O. Box 609, Fort Erie, Ont. L2A 5X3

For Karin, who wondered what happened next.

CHAPTER ONE

WAYNE HAMMOND FIGURED two factors were responsible for the standing-room-only crowd at tonight's school board meeting: a visiting celebrity and the rumor of a big donation. He doubted it was a sudden curiosity about educational policy or campus maintenance that was filling the high school auditorium's dented metal chairs as fast as they could be unfolded.

Most of the folks who'd turned out on this cold September night in Tucker, Montana, had likely come to gawk at the man seated opposite Wayne's chairman spot on the board's makeshift dais. Hollywood superstar Fitz Kelleran slouched in his boneless style on a front row seat, his long, jeans-clad legs crossed at the ankles. One arm was slung across the back of his wife's chair, where he toyed with the tail of her thick reddish braid with casual and absentminded affection.

Ellie Harrison Kelleran was a very lucky woman, and it wasn't only because the widow had lassoed a marriage proposal from the handsome actor who'd arrived at her family's ranch for a summer location shoot three months ago. It was because she'd deflected a potential proposal from Wayne.

He frowned down at the meeting agenda, remembering how he'd been easing his way into a courtship. He'd figured he'd keep things practical at first, pointing out the logic of a match between two longtime friends and neighbors, a match that would remove some of the fence line between their spreads. Ellie would gain a new daddy for the young daughter Tom Harrison had left behind when he died, and Wayne would get a head start on the family he'd always wanted.

Not the most romantic approach, maybe, but then he hadn't thought Ellie was the kind of woman who needed it. That was before Kelleran had arrived at Granite Ridge Ranch and swept her right off her feet.

Wayne had been wrong about a woman before, and his own marriage's failure was a painful testament to that. He'd thought fun-loving Alicia would settle into life on his ranch and quit her pining for the round-the-clock social whirl of Las Vegas. Looking back on it all, he could see what a fool he'd been to toss aside his usual caution and rush headlong into a relationship with a woman who craved the kind of attention he couldn't provide.

But like most of the single men in Tucker—and likely some of the married ones, too—Wayne had taken one look at Alicia and fallen head over heels in lust. When he'd regained his balance, he'd found himself married to a woman who didn't care for life on a ranch, wasn't in a hurry to start a family and didn't want to stay through another Montana winter. He didn't intend to lose his footing again.

At the moment, however, he was thinking he might have slipped into a mess of a different kind. The audience continued to swell in a shifting, murmuring mass with dozens of staring faces, and a familiar discomfort had him hunching in his seat and poring obsessively through the thin stack of paperwork before him.

Stage fright. It unnerved him enough to keep him from the spotlight, but, on occasions such as this, he hunkered down and refused to let the panic prevent him from participating in community events or taking advantage of business opportunities. Tonight he'd force himself to sit with his fellow board members and remind himself, over and over, that no one had come to ogle him. He'd concentrate on the business at hand and the familiar faces in the front row and ignore the ocean of bodies beyond.

"Here comes trouble." Board member Trace Bardett shoved a knobby black microphone into a short plastic stand under Wayne's chin and jerked his head toward the woman striding down the crooked center aisle. "Ms. Hell-on-Heels."

Maggie Harrison Sinclair. She had her mother's blond hair and blue eyes, and her father's rangy height and angular build, but her agile mind and uptown attitude were all her own. Throughout their high school days she'd made it clear that she was aiming for bigger landscapes and broader horizons. Plenty of classmates had dreamed of similar, exciting futures, but only Maggie had scrounged up the gumption and the guts to make her dream happen.

And now she seemed as out of place in this Stetsoned and Wranglered crowd as a Lotus at a stock car race, sleek and exotic and meant for something other than circling a dirt track.

She'd come back to Granite Ridge in June for her niece's birthday celebration, and she was still there, camped out in the guest cabin. Rumor had it she was lying low, licking the wounds of a nasty divorce—some unfortunate tangle of infertility and infidelity, though Wayne hadn't paid much attention to the gossip over which ex-partner had been guilty of which. Still, no one in Tucker had expected Maggie to stick it out this long, and even after she'd agreed to fill a temporary teaching vacancy at the high school, the local consensus was she'd head back to Chicago at the earliest opportunity. Exactly what that opportunity might be had been the source of lively conjecture.

Ignoring the curious glances cast her way, she aimed her fancy leather briefcase through the crush, marched to the front of the room and slid into the empty seat beside her former sister-in-law. Wayne caught himself staring and lowered his eyes, but a pair of flirty pink bows on sexy black heels hovered within his peripheral vision. And a few seconds after one endless leg lifted gracefully to cross over a shapely knee, the scent of some richly seductive perfume flowed over the papers lying below his unfocused gaze.

"Lordy." Charlie Simms, seated to his left, leaned in with a gravelly whisper, and the extra-onions-on-the-burger smell riding on his breath went a long way toward banishing Maggie's spell. "Legs like that should be locked up for inciting a riot."

A few moments later Shelby Ingersoll and Alice Landry took their seats next to Charlie and Trace at the board table, and Trace reached over and flipped on the microphone. Everyone groaned as the sound system squealed abuse through the speakers tacked up near the stage curtains behind the dais, and Wayne waited for the worst of it to subside before calling the meeting to order. The crowd shuffled to its feet for the flag salute and then shifted back to wait through the routine of roll call, agenda adoption, minutes approval and reports.

At last the time arrived for new business. Wayne stared at his papers and cleared his throat, and then winced when the speakers whined in protest. "The board is pleased to announce," he said, "that the newest member of our Tucker community, Mr. John Fitzgerald Kelleran, has generously pledged the sum of twenty-five thousand dollars to the local school district, specifically for improvements to the high school campus."

Several whistles punctuated the applause that followed, nearly drowning out the feedback squawking in sync with the din. Kelleran shot Ellie a rueful glance before rising from his chair to face the audience and nod a brief and modest acknowledgment. She rolled her eyes to the ceiling and tugged him back into his seat.

Wayne smiled at her reaction. Marriage to a millionaire would never change Ellie. He only wished he could feel equally confident about Tucker. He was as grateful as any of them to have the money for the school, but a bit worried about the effect such largesse—and the deep pockets of its source—might have on the local economic balance.

He waited for things to settle down a bit before he continued with the business end of the proposition. "Mr. Kelleran requests that his donation be applied toward one specific purpose, whether that be for academic, athletic or structural use. The board is to consider the proposals presented to it, and to make its recommendation to Mr. Kelleran for his approval no later than the first of the coming year."

"Shouldn't take three months to figure out a way to spend the money," Boot Rawlins called out from the back row. "I can think of a dozen ways between now and next week."

Laughter and a buzz of conversational commotion followed Boot's interruption, and Trace tugged the microphone closer. "Since there aren't any other items of new business," he said, "I move that we proceed to the next item on the agenda—communication from the floor."

"I second that motion," said Charlie.

The ladies of the board agreed, and Wayne settled back into his chair, coasting along with the political maneuver and preparing to consider the one proposal he expected to hear tonight. News of Kelleran's offer had leaked the moment he'd made it, and it hadn't taken long for a groundswell of support to rise in favor of one particular use for the windfall. It wasn't a purely democratic system, but it seemed to work just fine for the folks in and around Tucker. No one liked to rock the boat—unless enough of them thought it should be capsized and sent to the bottom.

He reclaimed the microphone to recognize Frank Guthrie, father of two Tucker High students—a varsity lineman and an all-county first baseman—and president of the athletic boosters' organization.

Guthrie strode to the front of the room and hitched up his silver rodeo-prize belt buckle before turning to face his fellow parents and community members. "In anticipation of a certain amount of money being suddenly made available to the high school," he said, "it just so happens I have here a list for some equipment and materials, along with bids for the construction and labor required for setting things up."

He raised a handful of papers. "I propose that the board approve the purchase of a new football and baseball scoreboard for the high school field, along with new metal stands to seat a crowd of two hundred."

More whistles accompanied the cheering for Guthrie's speech, and he bobbed his head and clapped with the others, crushing the edges of his list. "And it just so happens," he continued, "that the total for these improvements is only a tad bit over twenty-five thousand dollars. The members of the booster club figure they can cover the excess amount with the proceeds from a barbecue dinner served up as part of the halftime celebrations during this season's home-coming football game."

With a flourish, he turned and handed Wayne the wrinkled papers and moved back down the aisle toward his seat.

"Are there any other proposals this evening?" Wayne asked as Guthrie's copies were passed to everyone at the board table. He glanced down at a shopping list that seemed a little short on the details and a touch optimis-tic on the math.

"Oh, hell," said Trace.

Wayne's head snapped up, and he smothered a groan as one of the people in the front row raised her hand. "The chair recognizes Maggie Sinclair."

She stood and began to pull thin, colored folders from her briefcase.

"Lordy," Charlie whispered. "What the hell do you think she's up to?"

"This better not take long," Trace murmured none too quietly. "I told Janie I'd finish up here in time to fetch her mother home from bingo at St. Veronica's."

Maggie stepped to the front and angled herself to face the audience and the board. Her long, slim form, outlined in a snug pink jacket and skirt of some kind of lumpy burlap-like fabric, was no-nonsense straight.

"In anticipation of Frank's anticipation," she said, inclining her head toward Guthrie and his cronies on the other side of the room, "I've come here tonight prepared to make an alternative proposal for the use of the funds pledged by my brother-in-law."

"Pushing the family connection," Charlie muttered as Maggie handed some of her folders to Alice. "Playing hardball."

"She's got the balls for it," said Trace.

His comment crackled faintly over the speakers, and sniggers spread in a wave through the room. Kelleran coughed behind his fist and sank lower in his chair, and Ellie glared at the three men at the board table.

Maggie flashed a cool smile at Trace and stepped closer. "Ladies and gentlemen of the school board," she said. "Please take a good look at the stage behind you."

Wayne swiveled with the others to gaze at the darkened area. He saw what he'd always seen there: wine-red curtains, a bedraggled backdrop and scraps of lumber tilted against cobwebby corners. He turned back in time to see Maggie hand Kelleran one of her neat packets.

"If you were to look more closely," she continued, "you'd see curtains so threadbare they're on the verge of disintegration. Lighting so old and damaged it poses an electrical hazard. Mice nesting among the flats and a questionable supply of costumes and props that should be hauled to the nearest landfill. As for the sound system, well, that's the one thing that isn't in a state of disrepair."

"Thank God for that," said Boot.

"That's because there isn't one," she said when the audience had quit laughing at Boot's remark. "Nothing beyond this one miserable excuse for a microphone and two poorly wired speakers." She plucked the microphone from its little plastic stand. Right on cue, a painful squeal bounced off the auditorium walls.

Several members of the audience shifted uncomfortably as the feedback died with a strangled echo. Wayne noticed Kelleran paging through his packet with a frown.

"As you'll see when you've had a chance to examine the paperwork I've given you," said Maggie, "I've outlined and prioritized a list of purchases to replace broken and outmoded equipment, along with some basic necessities that would make the stage area both safe and useful for any number of school and community purposes."

She flipped the switch on the microphone, set it back on the board table and shifted to face the crowd. "A functional school stage can be used and enjoyed by the entire student population, not only those involved in football or baseball. Students who participate in sports and students who don't. Students who wish to appear before an audience and those who prefer to stay behind the scenes. Students who are male *and* female," she added with a meaningful glance at the two female board members.

"I propose," said Maggie, "that the school board use

the funds so generously provided by actor Fitz Kelleran to promote the performing arts here at Tucker High School. I propose that the board repair and refurbish the high school stage area."

When she took her seat, the kind of debate Wayne had hoped to avoid began in earnest. One audience member after another took the floor, arguing the value of gate receipts at sporting events versus box office income, or pointing out the numbers of students involved in athletics as opposed to those who might be tempted to try out for a play, or measuring the benefits of physical fitness against the development of talent off the playing field.

His unease intensified as the people he knew so well began to label and categorize and count each other as either pro or con, with the sum of twenty-five thousand dollars highlighting the differences.

Beside him, Trace pulled a cell phone from his pocket with a frustrated sigh and mumbled something about arranging transportation for his mother-in-law.

When the audience's arguments began to spread throughout the auditorium and to grow a touch heated, Wayne called for order. "I'll remind you all that the board has until the first of the year to make its final recommendation."

"But if we get moving on this," shouted Guthrie, "we could have the bleachers in place and the scoreboard ready for the homecoming game next month."

"I move that we vote on both proposals tonight,"

said Charlie. "No one has come up with anything else, and it's obvious plenty of folks feel mighty strong one way or the other about this."

"I second that," said Trace.

Shelby and Alice straightened like stiff bookends on each side of the board table, tight-lipped and solemn, looking to Wayne to take the next step.

Damnation. His stomach twisted into a taut, queasy knot. This was the moment he'd been dreading since Maggie had pulled those little colored packets out of that briefcase of hers. He could feel the crowd's attention closing on him like a vise. He stared at the chipped veneer on the table, trying to block the image of dozens of eyes staring at him, and his head pounded.

"It has been moved and seconded," he said, knowing he couldn't do anything else, "that the board vote tonight on the two proposals for allocating the donation pledged by Mr. Fitz Kelleran. All those in favor?"

Charlie and Trace quickly renewed their support.

"All those opposed?"

"Nay," said Shelby.

"Nay," said Alice.

It was up to Wayne to break the tie.

Logic pulled him one way; his conscience tugged him the other. And his hesitation over the matter only prolonged the panic playing havoc with his thought processes. At the edges of his vision he could see Charlie's head shake in disbelief and Trace shift in an impatient move. And he could just make out a sassy pink bow on a pointy black shoe dangling from a long, slim foot attached to a spectacular ankle.

He surrendered to the inevitable and released the breath he'd been holding. "Nay."

CHAPTER TWO

A HALF HOUR LATER, Maggie wobbled on her heels as she crossed the gravel lot toward Wayne Hammond's pickup. She knew her fashion choices were impractical for the ranch lands of southwestern Montana, but she was unwilling to abandon this one small link to the sanity of city life. "Hey, Wayne! Wait up a minute."

He turned to face her, his dark brown hair and Marlboro Man features nearly obscured by the wide brim of his black Stetson. As she crunched and lurched her way closer, he shot out an arm to steady her, and she was reminded just how tall he was. She was the same height as many of the men she knew, but even in her heels she had to tilt her head back to meet his gaze.

And since this was Wayne, his gaze immediately dropped to the ground at his feet. The man was as bashful as ever.

"Thanks," she said.

He released her arm. "You should get yourself a good pair of boots."

"I've already got some."

"I meant some real ones."

"I know what you meant." She wedged her hands into her tiny jacket pockets and wished she'd thought to pull on her wool duster before heading his way. "I have a pair of 'real boots,' too. But they don't exactly coordinate with raspberry bouclé."

"Raspberry bouclé." One side of his mouth quirked in a half smile, and his eyes flickered up to meet hers for a second before lowering again. "Sounds nearly good enough to eat."

She suspected, for a moment, that he might be flirting with her. But since this was Wayne, she figured the teasing tone in his voice was simply that—a mild and friendly poke for old times' sake. "Look," she said, "I didn't come out here to exchange fashion tips."

"I'm relieved to hear it." He toed the gravel with a worn leather boot. "Wouldn't want folks around here to get the wrong idea about why I've suddenly taken up such an interest in raspberry bouclé and the like."

He shot her another one of his shy glances, and she got the distinct impression he was enjoying some mysterious private joke at her expense. "No, I don't suppose you would," she said.

"Why did you come out here, Maggie?"

"To tell you that I'm surprised you voted the way you did," she said. "And to thank you for doing it."

She heard his deep intake of breath and his quiet, resigned sigh. "I didn't do it for you," he said.

"I know that."

"Then why are you thanking me?"

"Maybe I'm trying to be neighborly."

"Is that why you made your proposal?" His glance this time was as sharp as the frosty air. "To be neighborly?"

"Are you implying my proposal isn't?"

"There's nothing wrong with your proposal."

"With my methods, then."

"I'm not implying anything."

"So you're coming right out and saying it."

He shoved his hands into his pockets and cocked one hip against the truck door in a casual pose. "If you're looking for a fight, Maggie, you're going to have to look somewhere else."

She flashed him one of her sweetest smiles. "Now, why would I want to pick a fight with one of the very people I need to convince that my proposal is the right choice for Tucker High?"

"I don't know," he said in a maddeningly reasonable tone.

He stood there, as solid and steady as ever, waiting with the kind of long-suffering patience that always seemed to ratchet up her frustration level, and she fought back the temptation to stalk away. She reminded herself that she needed his goodwill if her plan was going to succeed, and that she'd have to learn to deal with his special brand of stubborn passivity.

He'd lowered his head until his hat brim hid most of his face, but she could still see the slow curve of his lips.

"What are you grinning at?" she asked.

"I can nearly hear the wheels spinning in that clever head of yours," he said. "Figuring all the angles, all at the same time. Probably looking to find the weakest link on the board and work on it until it snaps."

"Is that what you think I'm doing? Working on you?"

His grin disappeared and his chin came up, the merest fraction of an inch, enough for her to see the faint glint of his eyes beneath the Stetson's brim. Shadow and light slid over his features, highlighting the rugged arrangement of skin and bone. He'd been a good-looking boy. And he'd grown to be an extremely attractive man.

A strong man, a man who had refused to follow his mother's desertion, who had dug in and struggled through his alcoholic father's abusive decline and early death. A man who had battled to hold on to his family's ruined ranch and then slaved to rebuild it. A man who would never be a weak link by any stretch of the imagination.

"I'd like to see you try," he said in his deep, quiet voice.

"I'll bet you would," she answered.

"Could be interesting."

"Could be at that."

Something hovered and snapped in the cold space between them, something that had nothing to do with the echoing past or the current situation. And then his hat brim lowered like a blind to shut her out, and her tension floated away on a tiny cloud puff of a sigh.

"Guthrie did a lot of working of his own on that

proposal of his," said Wayne. "Talked up his idea with a lot of folks around here. Hammered out a kind of informal agreement on how things should be."

"He never considered any possibility other than something connected to sports."

"I s'pose there's a bit of truth to what you're suggesting. Guthrie's mighty proud of those big boys of his. And he's got another one coming along that promises to be every bit as big and fast and tough." He settled back more comfortably and crossed his feet at the ankles. "And maybe nothing else came to mind because sports is something most everyone in town can relate to."

"Maybe that's because there's nothing else to do."

"Maybe so. It's hard to find a variety of things to do when there aren't more than a few thousand people in this and the next three counties put together. And most of them are busy with making a living off the land." His shoulders lifted in a shrug. "And maybe sports are what most folks like to watch. And if they don't, they can talk about how their neighbors' kids did in the game the night before."

"There's more to life than ball games."

"That's right," he said. "There's rodeo."

She folded her arms and glared at him. "You obviously agree with Guthrie."

"I do?"

"And because you do," she said, brushing aside his question, "why did you vote the way you did?"

"Maybe I don't like to be rushed into things."

"All right, then." She straightened and shoved stray bangs out of her eyes. "That's something, anyway. Something I can work with."

"If you say so." The muscles of his jaw rippled along one side and then the other. "I'm not sure I like the idea of being the object of one of your campaigns, but I guess it comes with the territory."

"It won't hurt," she said with a smile. "Not much, anyway."

A silence fell between them, the pale wisps of their breath mingling and dissipating in the moonlit air. He straightened away from the truck, and his dark eyes gleamed down at her. "What exactly is it you want from me, Maggie?"

"I want your promise to consider my proposal with an open mind."

"I'll consider that proposal of yours, if you'll consider the possibility that my mind was open to it in the first place."

She squelched the urge to argue his last point, deciding it would be better to let it go and close the deal. "All right," she said, extending her right hand. "I will."

He pulled his hands from his pockets and slid one of them against her palm. It was wide and warm and rough with calluses.

His long fingers slowly closed around hers. "That's something, anyway," he said. "Guess I'll find out whether or not it's something I can work with."

"TEAM CAPTAIN and two-time All-County quarterback, Wayne Hammond!"

The dull roar of the homecoming crowd in the stands drowned out the electronic echo of the voice blaring from the speakers, and he throttled back the fear so his feet could move. He aimed for the straggly group of his senior class teammates arranged around the fifty-yard line and started across the field.

The jounce of the padding, the salty stink of his sweat, the hot puffs of breath shredding in the knife-cold night air as his uniform shirt shoved through them—he took it all in, every crystalline sensation, to crowd aside the swelling lump of panic. Trampled grass, slippery mud, the ground so hard beneath cleated feet, jarring his aching knee with every step.

It didn't hurt, not really, not enough to be taken out of the game. He didn't favor the leg, didn't show the pain.

Didn't let them know it hurt.

He used the pain. Focused on it—that's what he always did. He pulled tight, pulled in, shut out the rest and went through the motions. Shook hands, Jed's and Grizzle's and Trace's. Faced the stands, nodded and raised a hand. Stared into the lights, the icy white glare. Let the lights blind him to what was beyond—the faces, the people.

This was what he'd worked for, and waited for, and dreamed of and dreaded. All those practices, all those hits, all those sweet, sweet moments of release, of the *ball taking flight, sailing toward the target on an invisible thread of energy connecting perfect motion with victory. Bones and muscles and imagination and will. Physics, just like the words on the tattered pages of the fat textbook resting in his locker.*

He craved the quiet pleasure of that success and all the other victories, craved the dark silence of the room at home as he tucked another paper memento into the box beneath the bed. But it didn't matter. Not really.

It wasn't real, not any of it.

This moment wasn't quiet, this sensation wasn't pleasure. This was public—whistles and yells, the slap of fleshy palm to palm, the smell of popcorn oil and spilled beer, the staring eyes. Too many eyes, all aimed at him.

"Wayne!" The drink-slurred voice rose above the others. "Wayne!"

The old man. Drunk, as usual. But not too drunk to climb into a truck and get himself out here. He'd have to rush out of the locker room after the game, find a way to get his keys, make sure he didn't kill himself—or someone else—getting home.

If he made it home tonight.

He pulled back, pulled deeper inside. Stared into the lights, focused on the pain, kept his chin high. He held, held.

It didn't bother him, it didn't matter. Not his fault, not his doing. It wasn't real.

"Wayne!"

Someone laughed. The noise shifted. The crowd, the many-bodied, fickle, vicious thing in the stands, wavered in the dark shadows beneath the lights. A groan, a hush—the mangled-play, bad-call, missed-pass kind of noise.

His focus slipped, and he lost his way in the darkness, and the scene came into view, indistinct, a nimbus of cold, electric-white sparks at the edges. His father stumbled down the stands toward the fence at the edge of the field.

The faces, the stares. Horror, embarrassment, curiosity, pity.

The pity sliced at him, cut away bits and pieces of his resolve.

The panic clawed at him, ripped through him, tried to drag him away from the torture, away from the pain.

He stood and held, chin up. He didn't move. Couldn't move.

Couldn't let them know how much it hurt.

"Wayne!"

"Wayne!" Someone in the crowd echoed his father's loose-jawed, calflike bellow. "Wayne!" Someone else laughed.

He turned and saw...

No.

It doesn't matter. It's not real.

It's only a dream.

A dream. Only a dream, nothing real. Only a memory. Too long ago to matter.

None of it mattered, not anymore.

Wayne groaned and kicked away the covers, rolling to sprawl on his back in his empty lake of a bed. Boone, his elderly yellow Lab, whined and padded across the floor and lifted his head to fit beneath his master's waiting hand. Wayne stroked the dog's fur, finding comfort in the contact with another living being as he lay waiting for the sweat to cool, waiting for the slick, queasy tremors to subside. They always did, after a while.

He stared at the shadows cast across his ceiling. His ceiling, his room, his house. Thick, sturdy lengths of roughhewn pine stretching to the lofty peak above him, dotted with familiar knots. *There's the one that curves like an Egyptian's painted eye. There's the one with the crack like a fishhook.*

He inhaled deeply, settling, and scratched Boone's ear the way the old dog liked it. In another moment or two he'd head down to the kitchen to start up the coffee and then climb back up here to shower. It didn't matter what time it was. He'd begin the day, begin his routine.

He always did, after the dream. The work helped to sweep away the dregs of lingering shame. The dream didn't matter when he had chores to do.

He rose and moved through the familiar motions, grateful in these predawn moments for the silence and solitude of his big, empty house. He ran his palm along the satiny surface of the long oak handrail to the ground

floor and passed through dim rooms of richly grained
wood and stacked rock, rooms done up in the tans and
greens that reminded him of the forests at the eastern
edges of his land.

The loneliness faded into the background for a while
on nights like this. It took too much energy to pull in,
to pull tight, to shove things back inside the shadows
he'd fashioned for himself. He was relieved he didn't
have to hide his midnight pain from anyone else.

He measured coffee and poured water, while the
bright lights of his kitchen banished the afterimages of
the nightmare. He supposed those moments at the
school board table the evening before—that replay of
the old panic, when the sweat prickled on his skin and
his voice box locked up and refused to move—he
supposed it had been a kind of trigger. Most of the time
he could control his fear of appearing in a public way.
He'd faced it down, often enough, dragging himself
behind any number of microphones, forcing himself to
take on the presidency of the Cattlemen's Association
and settle into his supervisor's seat at the county court-
house.

But when the shower spray hit him, hard and hot, the
last bit of his dream came back to pummel him like the
water. That last moment, before he'd struggled to full
consciousness—that last moment had been a new
torture, something he'd never before experienced.

Maybe he'd never dreamed that part because it
hadn't happened. Maybe he'd invented it—maybe the

panic of the evening before had added some new layer to trick his mind and tease at his self control.

All his calm rationalizing and logical explanations deserted him, sliding and trickling like water down zigzag paths, swirling in a maelstrom as if to disappear down the drain.

It was no dream. It was a memory, something so painful he'd never revisited it.

He'd turned and seen…*her.*

Maggie Harrison, the most beautiful girl in the senior class. Tall and boyishly slim, cool and self-contained, supremely confident in her brains and her beauty and her close-knit, loving family. She'd held the kind of powerful popularity bestowed on those who let the world know they didn't care whether or not they possessed it. And the fact that she never used it carelessly only increased its gravitational pull on her captivated friends.

He, too, had been caught helplessly in her orbit, too attracted to ignore her but too pulled back within himself, too locked away inside his problems to match the ease of her manner or respond to the effortless flash of her smile.

Even in those rare and precious times her smile had been aimed in his direction.

He tipped his head beneath the water and closed his eyes as it ran down his face like tears, remembering now in agonizing detail how she'd stood to one side of the game field, moments before accepting the homecoming queen crown, dressed in her sapphire-blue gown, leveling her sapphire-blue eyes on his. There'd been no pity or disgust in her expression—none of that for Maggie Harrison.

Maggie Harrison *Sinclair.* She'd always been out of his league, beyond the limits of his possibilities.

Unlike Ellie, the girl Maggie's mother had taken in a few years before. Wayne had always suspected he shared a secret, silent kinship with Ellie. They'd been two lost souls longing for family and tied to the land. While he'd labored to rebuild the ranch his father had left in ruins, he'd dreamed of the day he'd call on her and invite her for a ride, to head out toward the aching beauty of the mountains and discuss…something. Possibilities of some kind or other.

He hadn't known how to talk to a girl, how to make that first move toward a first date. He'd never figured he'd had a good opportunity, not with schoolwork and ranch chores and sports schedules eating up his time, not with his father sick or staggering around or passed out on some convenient horizontal surface. He'd never believed he had the right, not with the family finances edging near disaster and the future looking like a mighty flimsy enterprise. He wasn't even sure he wanted to make a future with Ellie. But he figured he'd better start somewhere, or he'd end up alone.

But then old Ben Harrison had fallen ill, and his prodigal son Tom had come back to help out. Tom had taken one look at Ellie—all grown up, confident and capable—and he'd won the race for Ellie's hand in marriage before Wayne had had a chance to stumble out of the starting block.

Suddenly restless, Wayne dressed and prowled through the silent house, past shapes graying in the dawn, rooms waiting for family and spaces wanting womanly touches. His ex-wife hadn't cared about putting her own mark on this place. Maybe that was a good thing, since her personal style had never meshed with his. He knew his friends had been surprised when he'd proposed. They'd warned him that Alicia didn't seem the type of woman to put down roots or to consider her man before herself.

But they didn't understand his gnawing need for someone to move through the spaces of this house with him, someone to share a meal at his table or to visit with at night. Someone to give him the children he wanted, children who'd learn to tend the land beside him and inherit it when he was gone.

Someone who didn't come from Tucker, someone who didn't know the hurting, frightened person he was in his dream. Someone who'd see only the man he'd learned to pull from the deep, still, secret center of himself.

Battling back the torment of this waking, yearning dream and the ache of desires that chased him through the sleepless nights, he walked into his office and forced himself into the leather chair behind his desk. Now that his cattle had been brought down from summer's mountain pastures and spread along the valley, it was time to turn his attention to preparations for hunting season. He tapped a command on his keyboard and waited for the computer file listing the first group of lodge guests to appear on the monitor screen.

And he ignored the loneliness squeezing him in its iron fist.

CHAPTER THREE

MAGGIE FINGER-COMBED her short, layered hair in the Granite Ridge guest cabin Friday morning and then paused, staring beyond her reflection to the log walls and beamed ceiling that had once seemed to press in on her. She gripped the edge of the dresser, remembering last summer's plunge into failure and anxiety, the dizzying spiral drop that had left her gutted and clumsy with a case of the shakes.

Her first panic attack had sent her scurrying from Chicago. Her second had tempted her to extend her stay in Granite Ridge indefinitely. But Harrisons didn't cry or crumble. And now her life had purpose again.

No more shakes, not today, not tomorrow, not next week or next month. "I'm back," she told the Maggie in the mirror.

Behind her, one of her grandmother's quilts spread across the tarnished brass bed, and a braided wool rug lay over pine plank floors. She smiled at the comforting familiarity and the sense of timeless belonging. The snug place was earthy and warm, and as different from the bedroom in her Chicago condo as it was possible to get while remaining on the same planet.

Her former Chicago condo, that was.

She pulled a cashmere sweater over her silk camisole top, adjusting the neckline to let a bit of lace show in the front vee. The ache of loss seemed duller this morning, and the fingers fastening a string of beads around her neck were steady.

Now she could admit that her rush to sell her share of the furnishings to her soon-to-be ex-husband during the divorce proceedings had been a mistake. At the time, all she'd wanted was to get clear and get out, but she missed her French mantel clock and the wide-mouthed majolica vase, the art deco bronze and the signed Konopacki print. When she'd quit her job and fled the city, she hadn't known where she'd land. And her things certainly wouldn't match the decor in this cabin her brother Tom had built for his wife and their baby girl.

A ripple of sorrow caught her by surprise. It seemed she'd done more grieving for her brother in the three months she'd spent here at Granite Ridge than she'd done three years ago, when the pain of his death was fresh and raw.

Her widowed sister-in-law had recovered and remarried, and her niece seemed delighted with the development. Even her mother, Jenna, had found herself a new husband. Now it was Maggie who was on her own, who was taking her turn to make a fresh start.

She intended to make the most of it. She believed in making the most of everything.

"Everything," she said with a nod. "I'm back, and soon I'm going to be back on top."

She smoothed her slim wool skirt over her hips and stepped into snappy heeled pumps with contrasting oxford-style topstitching. Dressing as if she were heading to her former position at a private college-preparatory academy gave her the illusion of normalcy, even if she was about to climb into a mud-splattered sports utility vehicle and travel narrow county roads toward her temporary job teaching English classes at Tucker High School.

She collected her leather briefcase, slung a tweed overcoat over one arm and stepped into the knife-edged chill of a Ruby River valley morning. Sticky-fingered yellowed leaves clung to the willows edging Whistle Creek, and the serrated mountain peaks that seemed to hang close above wore a dusting of early snow. Overhead, geese called in their nasal tones, and underfoot the frosted ground crackled beneath her heels.

Memories floated about her like field haze as she bumped along the track leading to the creek bridge. She supposed it was the sharp bend in the gravel road that made her think of her first kiss with that fast-moving preacher's boy behind the snack stand at the barrel racing tournament. And it must have been the faint scent of alfalfa in the cargo section that brought back the night she'd had one beer too many and let a

Sheridan shortstop feel her up in the back of his daddy's horse van.

Or it could be the eleven-month stretch of sexual deprivation that had her system keyed up over reruns of adolescent experiments in foreplay. Sentiment didn't usually kick up her pulse rate and warm her from the inside out.

And dwelling in the past wouldn't solve the problem of her future. There wasn't a simple or convenient method to fill in the blanks, but she wouldn't let that fact trigger another episode of shaky self-doubt. The divorce settlement had provided enough money to get her settled in the next place—wherever that might be. In the meantime, she had a roof over her head and time to spend with her family. Time to find a challenging placement, in an academically focused school in a stimulating urban setting.

Time to plot her steps and strategies, to win the battle she'd set in motion at the school board meeting.

She tightened her grip on the steering wheel, ready to transform all her frustrations into motivation and to focus her energies on her goals for the school theater. When she'd accomplished all she intended, sleepy little Tucker High wouldn't know what had hit it. If there was one thing she knew how to stage, it was a campaign.

Around the last bend in the creek, perched on a knoll above the stumps of cottonwoods charred by last summer's fire, she glimpsed the tall, white house where she'd spent her childhood. Constructed in the Victorian era responsible for its jutting angles and fanciful trim, the house had sheltered Harrisons for one hundred and twenty-five years. She loved its rambling wings and wide porches, the gables and bays, the nooks and crannies that still held her girlhood secrets and dreams.

She parked on the graveled side yard path and climbed the back porch steps, wincing when the screen door slapped the mudroom jamb. The aroma of the coffee kept fresh and waiting on a brightly tiled counter beckoned from her mother's cheery kitchen. Beyond yellow-checked curtains at the sink window, puffy hydrangeas fading to mauve and the autumn-tinged leaves of hardy lilacs framed a view of freshly painted outbuildings and pasture land rolling on a grassland carpet toward the Tobacco Root mountains.

"Morning, Maggie." Will Winterhawk, the Harrison ranch foreman, entered from the dining room and poured a mug of his own before settling at the oversize kitchen table. It still seemed odd to see him take his place there so casually, though he'd been an unofficial part of the family for over twenty years. Last month he'd made it official with a wedding, and he'd moved his small bundle of clothing and his dozens of boxes of books into Jenna's lavender-scented bedroom suite at one end of the second-floor hall.

The fact that her mother had received a marriage proposal from a younger man—a certified hunk of a younger man—was deeply satisfying.

"Morning, Will."

"You're up early."

She turned to face him and leaned back against the counter. "You know what they say about the early bird."

"It catches the school board's approval?"

She lifted her mug in acknowledgment. "You heard about that, did you?"

"News travels fast around here. You should remember that."

She cocked her head. "Was that an observation or a warning?"

One of Will's slow smiles spread across his dark features. "Take it any way you choose."

Fitz Kelleran, barefoot and damp around the edges, jogged down the narrow service stairs and dropped a grade-school spelling text on the kitchen table. Even in worn work clothes, the man was ridiculously handsome. His golden-boy features and devilish charm had given him his start in the movies; his talent kept him on Hollywood's A list. "Morning, Will."

Will nodded a greeting.

Fitz headed for the coffee and nudged Maggie aside with his hip. "Morning, Margaret."

She narrowed her eyes. "Margaret?"

"Oops. Sorry. I forgot that's what your ex calls you."

"You didn't forget. You don't forget a thing. In fact, you seem to have an annoyingly efficient instant recall of most conversations, word for word."

"It's not instant," he said with one of his dazzling grins. "It's permanent."

"Except when it suits you."

"That's the annoyingly efficient part."

"Children." Jenna carried a laundry basket piled high with bath towels past the table, headed toward the mudroom. Her gold hair was threaded with silver, but her features and figure were still youthful. "Please. If you must bicker, take it outside."

"It's too cold to bicker outside," said Fitz. "May we bicker in the office? How about whispered taunting? Only the tauntee would hear it, I swear."

"Can it, Kelleran." Maggie finished her coffee and turned to rinse the mug. "I don't have time for any of your nonsense."

"I could make it fast." He leaned in and lowered his voice in a sample whisper. "Come on, Maggie. One good insult, to start the day right."

"Can it, or I'll tell Ellie you're bugging me again."

That shut him up fast. There was something oddly endearing about the way the man pretended to live in abject terror of her pint-size former sister-in-law.

Maybe that's what had gone wrong in her own marriage. Not enough playful pretense or genuine concern. At least, not on her husband's part. Alan was the premier member in their unequal partnership, the one with the blue-blooded background, the one with the ivy-league education and the finely tuned sensibilities. Recently she'd realized that his expectations weren't so much a subtle tutoring as a smothering burden.

But it was too early in the day for regrets and recriminations. And she'd already spent too much time this morning indulging in memories. She needed to concentrate on the business she'd intended to discuss with Fitz when she'd headed to the house this morning.

"That was a nice offer that was announced at the board meeting last night," she said. "Very generous."

"Thank you." He sipped at his coffee. "And that was an interesting proposal you made."

"Interesting?"

"Very interesting." He saluted her with his mug. "And well prepared."

"Two compliments in one morning." She waved her hand in front of her face. "I'm all aflutter."

"I wouldn't let the local males know you're such an easy mark, if I were you."

"Don't worry about it. And don't worry about my plans for the theater." She settled back against the counter and crossed her arms. "I did my research."

He nodded. "And plenty of it."

"So…"

"So?"

"So, what do you think, Will?" she said, turning to the ranch foreman for a little extra support. "Don't you think improving the stage area would be a good use of those funds?"

"I think I'm going to have to think long and hard on this whole situation."

"How long?" she asked.

"Until it's over." Will gave her a wink and sipped at his coffee.

"Then it's a good thing you don't have a part in making the decision," she said. "But *some* people do. *Some* people have a serious responsibility."

Fitz donned a suitably sober face. "Responsibility."

"Yes. A very serious one." She shook her head with a sigh. "Making the right decision is a heavy burden. It can impact the future in countless ways."

"Hmm," murmured Fitz. "I suppose I could deal with that burden by offering another donation next year."

"Yes, you could." She unfolded her arms and checked her manicure. "Or you could double this year's."

"Yes, I could." Fitz's serious frown slowly dissolved into a wicked grin. "But I won't."

She raised one eyebrow. "You won't even consider the option?"

"Nope." He rocked back on his heels. "I want to see you try to get people to change their minds. Ten bucks says you can't do it."

"I'm not going to bet on something this important."

"Ten bucks, and the loser takes out a full-page ad in the *Tucker Tribune*. Winner chooses the wording."

She choked back a laugh. "No."

"Afraid you'll lose?"

"It's not a competition."

"No one said it was."

"It's going to turn into one," said Will. "I hope you realize that. Both of you."

Before Maggie could respond, Jody, her twelve-year-old niece, bounded down the stairs. "Morning, everyone. What's for breakfast?"

"Your gran mentioned something about French toast," said Will. "I'm hanging around to see if she meant it."

"Jenna's making her French toast?" Fitz looped an ankle around a chair leg and snagged a place at the table. "Sorry to give such late notice, Will, but I won't be helping you repair the south well house this morning. I quit."

"You can't quit," said Jody as she dropped into her seat. She pulled a napkin into her lap and tucked hair the same reddish hue as her mother's behind one ear. "You're the boss."

"Explain that to your mom," said Fitz. "Please."

Fitz may have purchased the ranch after the fire's destruction pushed Granite Ridge's shaky finances to the edge of bankruptcy, but Ellie remained in charge, managing the day-to-day details as she had since Tom's death.

"You knew what you were getting into when you married her," said Jody. "I warned you."

"You did not."

"Yes, I did. I said, 'Fitz, watch out.'"

"That had nothing to do with marrying your mother. That was before I stepped in that pile of shit out behind the barn and ruined my dress loafers."

"It could be the same thing, only different. Like a metaphor." Jody shot him a smug smile. "We studied similes and metaphors in English this week."

"And you obviously paid close attention." Maggie decided to join the breakfast crowd and squeezed in beside Will. "That was a wonderful comparison. Slightly abstract, but loaded with meaning."

Ellie strolled in from the dining room. She'd probably been up since dawn, working on the books in the office off the front entry. "Morning, everyone."

Fitz caught her hand as she passed him on her way to the coffeepot. Maggie noticed the quick squeeze he gave her fingers before he released them, and the way his hot and hungry gaze followed her across the room.

Had Alan ever looked at her like that? She couldn't remember. And surely a look like that would be something a woman would never forget.

"Time for the spelling review." Fitz picked up the text and flipped through the pages. "Ready, Jody?"

"Ready."

"*Satellite.*"

Jody dutifully spelled out the word as Jenna came back into the room and began to assemble breakfast supplies on the counter.

"*Reception,*" said Fitz.

Ellie selected a large skillet from the overhead rack and turned to adjust the flame under a burner. Jody spelled the word.

"*Remote.*"

Will tipped his chair back against the wall with the hint of a smile as Jody continued the exercise.

"*Control.*"

"Hold it right there." Ellie spun around with the skillet in her hand.

"Oh-oh," said Jody. "Bad timing."

"Satellite reception?" Ellie glared at Fitz. "Remote control?"

Jenna's shoulders shook with silent laughter, and Will's smile spread across his face. Fitz's innocent expression was a testament to his skill as an actor.

"It's an experiment, Mom," said Jody. "We're studying subliminal advertising in English this week."

"Subliminal," said Fitz. "S-u-b-l—"

"I know how it's spelled," said Ellie. "And I know what the two of you are up to. And it's not going to work."

"I told you." Jody glanced at Fitz with a sigh.

"You did not. You said it was a good idea."

"The satellite TV hookup, not the spelling stuff. That was Fitz's idea," she told her mother.

"I can tell when something is Fitz's idea," said Ellie. "It's usually harebrained and half-baked, and comes at me from every point on the compass for weeks at a time."

"Got to give the man points for trying," said Will.

Ellie aimed the skillet at him. "You stay out of this."

"Thanks, Will." Fitz gave him a comrade-in-arms nod. "I appreciate it."

"I'm not risking my health on your account," said Will. "I kind of like the idea of a couple more channels to watch late at night."

"Since when do you watch TV at night instead of reading?" Ellie asked.

"Well, now...I've changed my habits of late," said Will. "I thought it might be nice to watch some of those nature shows, but I guess there are plenty of other things I could find to do instead of reading."

At the sink, Jenna made a strangled sound.

"Oh, for crying out loud." Maggie rose from the table and began to crack eggs into Jenna's big mixing bowl. "Get the satellite hookup, Ellie. Better yet, get Wes to drag cable out here. Hell, have him dig a ten-mile-long ditch and put it all underground so you don't have to look at it. It's not like your husband can't afford it."

"That's not the point." Ellie didn't sound too sure of the point any longer, but that wouldn't pry her stubborn grip from it. Once she'd dug into something, it could take a few sticks of dynamite—or an extra-strength dose of Fitz's charm—to shake her loose.

"While you're at it," Maggie continued, "I'd like to have a hookup at the cabin. There are lots of educational shows I could be recording for school."

"Hundreds of them," Jody added.

Fitz stood and carefully removed the skillet from Ellie's hands. He set it on the counter and wrapped his arms around her waist. "We missed one of my old movies last night. The one where I played a downhill racing skier."

Ellie smiled and softened against him. "That was Robert Redford."

"It was? I get myself mixed up with him sometimes."

"In your dreams, Kelleran."

"That's my favorite cue." He bent and scooped Ellie over his shoulder. Ignoring her shrieks, he headed toward the stairs. "And I'm suddenly in the mood to continue this discussion in private. Jenna, kindly save some French toast for two. The missus and I will have our breakfasts later."

Jody shook her head with a worldly sigh. "Looks like I'll need a ride to school again, Aunt Maggie."

"Sure, kiddo." She watched with a smile as her brother-in-law toted his bride up the stairs. "I'd like a chance to discuss this subliminal advertising concept with you."

CHAPTER FOUR

MAGGIE SAT IN A lumpy booth at the Beaverhead Bar & Grill Friday night and stared at her best friend from her school days, Janie Morgan Bardett. "You've got to be kidding."

"Wish I was," said Janie as she shoved her empty beer glass to one side. "And on top of mistaking a grizzly for a brown bear, the idiot fumbled his load and the bear got within twenty paces before he finally got a shot into him."

"At least it got so close there was no chance of missing a second time."

Another autumn, another hunting season. Another round of tracking lore and venison recipe exchanges. Nothing much had changed in Tucker, it seemed, including the primary topic of conversation each year at this time.

Certainly nothing much had changed in Tucker's only bar. The music in the jukebox, the beaver profile on the cocktail napkins, the ugly brown felt on the pool tables, the smudged walls and blue-hazed atmosphere, the aroma of hot grease and cold brews was all just as she'd left it fifteen years ago. Even the stale peanuts in the battered plastic bowls looked suspiciously familiar.

A loud *crack* behind their booth signaled the start of another round of pool. The betting was nearly as impressive as the bragging, if a woman had the kind of heart that fluttered over cowpoke paychecks and poorly disguised sexual analogies involving cue sticks and pockets. Apparently a pair of twentysomething coeds who'd hiked down from the Continental Divide found it all, like, totally fun.

"Speaking of fumbling loads…" Janie drummed her short-nailed fingertips on the table. "Why was Alan letting you investigate fertility treatments when he was…well…"

"Busy proving he *wasn't* infertile?" Maggie sighed and took a fortifying sip of wine. Her personal life was a source of unceasing fascination, and Janie claimed her right, as former number-one confidante, to have first crack at the best and juiciest details. "Which he accomplished by knocking up one of his grad students."

"I don't understand." Janie leaned forward. "I mean, all that effort with all those doctors, and then he goes and pulls something like that?"

"I don't think it's something anyone understands, including Alan. He had a history of risky behavior with grad students." And as one of the most popular professors and academic advisors in the English Literature department of a Chicago university, he'd had a steady supply of fresh, young, poetry-adoring fans. "That's how I met him."

"Yeah, but he wasn't married when you were dating him."

"That only makes it slightly less unethical," said Maggie with a weary sigh. "Although I did drop the class after I started sleeping with him."

"Why were you the one most at fault in that scenario?" Janie asked with a frown. "He's the one who was hitting on students."

Maggie's mouth twisted in a wry grin. "He didn't have to hit very hard."

"I hate to admit it, but he was a handsome bastard."

"You don't have to talk about him in the past tense. He's still alive."

"Yeah, well, he's still a bastard, too." Janie shook her head. "What did you see in the guy, anyway?"

"You mean, besides the incredibly good looks?" Maggie spun her glass in a slow circle. "He was everything I wanted to be. Sophisticated, refined. Knowledgeable about things like art and good food. He socialized with interesting, important people."

"The one time I met him, he seemed like he had a stick stuck so far up his butt it would pop out his nose if he sneezed."

Maggie grimaced. "He didn't enjoy visiting here."

And he'd elaborated on every reason why not. He hadn't been able to find a common point of reference with any of the members of her family, so he couldn't relax at the ranch. He was unable to comprehend Tucker's ambiance, so he felt handicapped when trying to communicate with its citizens. He apologized for everything with genuine regret, and he made it all sound as if the root of the problem was his inability to appreciate things from a different perspective, but there was a simpler way of expressing the truth.

Alan was a snob.

"Well," said Janie, "I don't suppose I can blame him for that. Tucker doesn't exactly compare to Chicago."

"No, it doesn't." The soft thunk of a ball in the pocket was followed by a triumphant howl. "But then, Chicago doesn't compare to Tucker."

Maggie raised her glass and stared at the pale amber wine. "You and Trace have a good life here," she said, "and you're raising a couple of wonderful, beautiful girls."

"They're special, all right." Janie sat back with a smug grin. "And I have to admit, I can't imagine them being happy anywhere they didn't have plenty of room to ride their horses."

"I missed riding like that, when I moved away." The homesickness for wide open spaces and the freedom to move through them on horseback had been a physical ache those first few weeks in her cramped college dorm room with its stark view of boxy high-rises.

"And now I bet you miss Chicago." Janie sighed and leaned an elbow on the table. "All the things to do, the shows and the museums and the shopping."

"Sure." Maggie caught the eye of the bartender and signaled for refills. "I miss it every day."

Janie straightened and waved as Trace sauntered into
the room. He waved back at his wife, tossed a scowl in
Maggie's direction and stopped by the long, curved bar
to engage in what appeared to be a serious conversation
with Wayne.

"Wonder what that's all about?" asked Maggie.

"You can't guess?" Janie folded her arms on the
table. "I have to warn you, you've landed on Trace's shit
list for that stunt you pulled at the school board meeting
last night."

"It wasn't a stunt. Not exactly, anyway."

"Damn," muttered Janie. "Looks like girls' night out
is ending early. Here comes a double dose of man."

Wayne and Trace approached the table, carrying
their own drinks and the refills.

"Mind if we join you ladies?" asked Trace. He slipped
in beside Janie and gave her a quick peck on the cheek.

"If you promise to behave." Janie flicked a finger
against the edge of his hat. "No school board business."

Maggie shifted to the side to make room for Wayne.
He handed her a second glass of wine and then slowly
folded his lanky frame into the tight space.

"We were just talking about how much Maggie
misses Chicago," said Janie.

"Figures," said Trace. "Things around Tucker aren't
half as lively as goings-on in the big city. Not without
stirring something up. *Umph*."

He jerked slightly and glared at his wife.

"So," she said, "what do you miss most, Maggie?"

"The shopping, I guess." She sipped her wine. "About this time of year, I started looking forward to the holidays. All the lights, the crowds. The parties."

"Parties." Janie leaned forward. "What were those like? Nothing like the ones around here, I'll bet."

"No." Maggie shook her head, comparing the colorful, stomping, free-for-all fun of a barn dance to the little-black-dress formality of a college reception. "Not the same at all."

"We can make our own kind of party," said Trace. He cocked his head toward the dance floor, where a couple of cowhands were shuffling to and fro with the hikers. And then he swiveled out of the booth and turned to face his wife. "Dance with me, Janie," he said. "Come and rub up against me like you used to."

"How can a gal resist an invitation like that?" She shot a grin at Maggie and wiggled her way along the long bench seat. "That's just about the hottest offer I've had in weeks."

Maggie watched them walk to the dance floor, hand in hand, and flow into each other with the practice of a couple that knew each other's every move. She smiled at Trace's awkward bear hug of a dance hold and the way Janie's eyes laughed up at him.

She held on to her smile, floating on her own sentimental mood. And then her smile died, bit by bit, when she glanced at Wayne and found him staring at her.

Those big brown eyes of his could be unsettling when he turned them on something other than the floor.

Deeply set, filled with secret shadows, they seemed to bore right into her and probe at her sensitive spots. She waited in vain for the corners of his mouth to gradually tip up in one of his shy smiles to ease the intensity of his expression.

She leveled a challenging look at him, daring him to break away first, willing him to cut her loose so she could suck in the air she suddenly needed so badly. But he pinned her in place with that soul-deep gaze, held her absolutely still as he angled his big frame to the side and slid along the bench to straighten and stand over her, long-limbed and wide-shouldered and blocking out the room behind him, one big, tough hand extended toward hers where it rested on the table.

She hesitated to take it, and in the next moment grasped it to prove that his silent invitation didn't unnerve her. And then he was slowly leading her toward the other pairs of bodies swaying in the smoke and the music, and guiding her just as slowly toward him, and pulling her smoothly into his arms.

She knew he was a working man, but it was still a shock to feel granite-hard muscle beneath the worn cotton of his shirt. She knew he was tall, but it was still a surprise to feel him rest his chin on top of her head. The feel and the fit of him was an alien thing, so different from the softer, shorter partner she'd grown accustomed to.

Tonight was filled with foreign sensations—the tacky floor clutching at her heels, the tang of pine and leather and yeasty malt, the powerful shoulder beneath her fingertips, the rasp of calluses against her palm, the heat of a wide, long-fingered hand spread low across her back. Foreign, and somehow familiar. A strangely intoxicating blend.

"Are you missing Chicago enough to be thinking about going back?" he asked. His voice rumbled through her.

"I'm not going back." She lifted her chin and looked at him. "I don't believe in going back—or backward. I'll give some other city a try."

His hand shifted to her waist, pulling her close as Trace and Janie swung into their path. Her chest brushed his shirt front, and her breath backed up in her lungs.

This was crazy. This spine-tingling reaction to a dance with an old school friend was pure foolishness. It was all these strange sensations—they were too much for her to process at once. It was the second glass of wine that was making her a little light-headed, and the thud of the bass from the jukebox that was making her pulse throb. And it might be the fact that she was out of practice with this kind of contact with an adult male. Other than a few brotherly hugs from Will and Fitz, she hadn't been this close to a man in nearly a year.

He raised his hand again to the spot above her waist, and she was aware of the press of each of his fingers. She tipped her face back to find those deep, dark eyes of his trained on hers. They drifted slowly down to her mouth, and she realized that she'd let him kiss her, that she wanted him to kiss her. It was the light-headed, out-of-practice part of her that willed him to do it, begged him to do it.

With a final twang the music ended, and they parted from each other by slow and reluctant degrees—the subtle retreat of a shoulder, the slight shift of a leg, the long slide of his palm down her back, the soft tug of her fingers from his hand.

"Thank you, Maggie."

She wanted to speak, to snap off the odd thing sprouting between them with a flip remark, but all she could manage was a nod.

He settled his hand again at her waist and guided her back to the booth where Janie was collecting her jacket and purse.

"I'm heading out," said Janie with a quick, one-armed hug. "Got to hurry and get the sitter home before time runs out on the hot offer I got out on the dance floor."

Maggie squeezed her back and promised to call soon to make a date for another girls' night out.

When she turned, intending to invite Wayne to join her for another drink, she discovered he'd disappeared without a word.

Since it was Wayne, she should have expected it.

What surprised her was the quick, hot slap of disappointment.

CHAPTER FIVE

THEA GASTINEAU, the icy-gray and ramrod-stiff principal of Tucker High School, straightened her glasses on her thin nose and studied Maggie across the faculty room table during Monday's lunch break. Maggie met her gaze with her most confident smile.

Thea tapped a clawlike finger on the proposal Maggie had slipped into her office mailbox that morning. "You're sure you want to do this."

"Absolutely sure."

"A theatrical production of the sort you have in mind is going to take a lot of work. Especially on the tight schedule you've planned."

"I have plenty of experience with extracurricular projects. I know what I'm getting into. And there are several reasons for choosing an early performance date."

"Yes," said Thea. "I can see that it would be good to have a project like this in motion before the next board meeting."

Maggie's smile widened. "That's one of the reasons."

"It's going to be expensive."

Maggie pulled one of her mother's molasses cookies

from a brown lunch sack. "I've developed quite a talent for soliciting community business donations."

"This isn't Chicago." Thea set aside the proposal and picked up her plastic fork. "Folks here don't have as much money to spare."

"And because this isn't Chicago, they're going to be more generous with what they've got."

The principal poked at a piece of limp salad lettuce in a small plastic container. "Tucker hasn't been your community for a number of years."

Thea's matter-of-fact tone soothed the sting of her words. And Maggie was finished with feeling defensive about her long absence from her hometown. "This project will provide me with an excellent opportunity to get involved again."

Thea glanced up. "You sound very certain of yourself."

"I was hoping I sounded convincing."

"That, too." Thea pressed her thin, colorless lips together in a slight frown. "What is it you hope to gain from your time here at Tucker High, Maggie?"

"Besides a few paychecks?" Maggie broke off a bite-size piece of the cookie. "Precisely that—time. Time to decide what to do next. Where to go."

"There's no secret agenda here? No ulterior motives?"

"I'm planning a theater revue, Thea," Maggie said with a reassuring smile, "not a coup."

"It might be seen as one and the same."

"And by some of the same members of the community I'm hoping to tap for donations and assistance."

Maggie washed the cookie down with a sip of milk. "It's going to be quite a challenge. One I'm looking forward to."

"At least you're aware of the complications." Thea finished her salad and reached for the container's lid. "I see you've thought things through."

"I always think things through. I like to know what I'm getting into before I take the first step." Maggie brushed a few stray cookie crumbs from her slim black wool skirt. "Things may not always work out quite the way I'd planned, but at least I'm prepared to deal with any problems that might arise."

"I appreciate the fact that you've already outlined several you may encounter." Thea glanced again at Maggie's preliminary paperwork. "And I don't think those problems would have any negative impacts."

"So…do I have your permission to proceed with my plans?"

"Yes, you have my permission." Thea swept the papers into the folder Maggie had provided and set it aside. "But give me until the end of the week to get back to you on the budget items."

"All right. And thank you."

Maggie helped herself to another cookie and offered the last one to the principal. "What I'd really like, Thea, in addition to your permission, is your blessing."

Thea lifted one thin, grey brow above the rim of her glasses as she accepted the cookie. "Wouldn't they be one and the same?"

"Not necessarily."

There was a long pause as Thea studied her again. Maggie tried not to squirm beneath that cool, assessing gaze.

"No, they wouldn't be the same thing," Thea said.

Maggie folded her hands on the table and leaned forward. "I'd like to secure as much faculty support as possible, or at least build a consensus before I start this project. I'll begin meeting one-on-one with the other staff members this afternoon."

"Ah, yes. The all-important communal consensus." Thea smiled her wintry smile. "You may go through the motions of doing things the way we do them here—the way you must have learned things are done when you lived here before—but you still manage to put your own spin on them."

"Is that a bad thing?"

"No." Thea slowly shook her head. "Just different."

"It might even be a good thing."

"It just might be."

Maggie sensed a slight thaw in the woman across the table and tipped forward a bit more. "There is one last favor you could do for me."

"Oh?"

"There's a small part in one of the skits you'd be perfect for."

"Really." Thea's eyes sharpened on hers. "How small?"

Maggie sat back with a laugh. "Oh, this is going to be fun."

"Yes," said Thea with a slightly wider smile, "I think it will."

JODY SQUEEZED INTO her usual spot beside her best friend, Chrissy Fowler, at the sixth grade girls' lunch table. Down at the other end, one of their classmates gave her a nasty stare and made a show of whispering something to another girl.

"Don't let that stupid ol' Rachel Dotson get to you," said Chrissy. "She's just jealous. I think your new jacket is beautiful."

"I didn't pick it out, Fitz did," said Jody for the third time that day. "And I didn't want to say 'no thank you' and hurt his feelings."

She smoothed a hand over the brightly colored nylon of her expensive ski parka, secretly delighted to have something so special. Most of the time she forgot her new stepfather was a movie star and a millionaire. He was simply Fitz, the fun and affectionate guy who'd married her mom. That was one of the reasons she loved him so much—he had a way of making everyone around him feel happy and included. Not because he could buy her things like the portable video player she kept in her room or the delicate, diamond-studded chain hidden beneath her sweater.

She laid her lunch bag on its side and pulled out her ham-and-Swiss-cheese sandwich, thick with extra lettuce, drizzled with wine vinegar and sprinkled with oregano, exactly the way she liked it. Gran's fussy touches reminded her how lucky she was and helped erase the lingering unease of Rachel's whispers.

"What kind of cookies did your gran give you

today?" Chrissy leaned over the lunch table and peered into Jody's bag.

"Molasses." She spread a napkin over the table and set an apple to one side.

"The ones with the sugar glaze?" Chrissy grabbed the edge of the sack and dragged it a few inches in her direction. "Do you have any extras?"

"Enough to give you one, but that's all." Jody fingered her jacket's zipper tag and darted a glance toward the seventh grade boys' table. "I want to set a couple aside. For later."

"For Lu-cas." Chrissy tilted her head from side to side with her singsong chant. "Lu-cas Gu-thrie."

"Shh." Jody snuck a peek down the length of the table, but Rachel was busy sticking her big nose into someone else's business. "I don't want anyone else to know I like him."

"I still think if you told Tanya in the seventh grade, and then if she told Kevin Turley—"

"Then he'd know for sure I like him," said Jody, "and I'd be embarrassed if he didn't like me back."

"But he does," Chrissy whispered, leaning closer. "You know he does."

"No, I don't." Jody tried really hard not to get her hopes up, but it was too late. Her insides were tickling over Chrissy's opinion—even if she was probably just sticking up for a friend.

There was always a chance.

"He says 'hi' to you all the time," said Chrissy.

Jody shrugged. "He's just being nice."

"And Maryanne in the eighth grade said Kevin told her brother that Lucas said he thought one of the girls in the sixth grade class is real cute."

"That doesn't mean it's me."

"Maryanne thinks so."

Jody absorbed a new wave of tingly pleasure over this latest bit of news as Chrissy helped herself to one of Gran's cookies. She froze with it halfway to her mouth. "Oh, my God," she whispered. "Here he comes."

Jody pasted on a bright smile as Lucas sauntered their way. Tall and gorgeous, and the best athlete in the seventh grade, he'd already crossed the cafeteria's invisible boundaries to speak to her three times in the past ten days. Her heart pounded beneath her sweater and the blood swished in her ears like ocean waves.

"Hey, Jody," he said with a toss of his chin. "How's it going?"

"Hey, Lucas." She swiveled on the narrow bench to give him a better view of her new jacket. "Want a cookie?"

"Sure." He shifted the football he carried under one arm and held out his hand. "Thanks."

Jody sat in agony while he took a bite and nodded approval. She racked her brain for something brilliant to say, something that would start a real conversation. Something that would entice him to sit down and talk back.

Except then she'd have to keep talking, too, and she'd never be able to eat, because her stomach would be too jittery.

But she had to say something. "When's your next game?"

"Sunday." He lifted what was left of the cookie in a vague farewell and headed back to junior high territory.

"God, he is *so* cute," said Chrissy with a sigh.

"He really is, isn't he?" Jody tried not to stare as he walked away, but it was terribly hard. She picked up the apple and took a bite, but she didn't taste a thing while she chewed.

"And he likes you. I can tell."

"He likes Gran's cookies." Jody breathed deeply and tried to quiet the butterflies in her stomach, relieved the encounter had gone so well. "But I don't care. It's a start."

"Are you going to go to his game?"

"If I can get someone to take me into town."

"I bet your aunt Maggie will, if you tell her why you need to be there." Chrissy bit into her cookie and mumbled around the crumbs. "She's *so* cool."

"Yeah," Jody agreed with a smile, "she sure is."

"Are you talking about Mrs. Sinclair?" asked Rachel Dotson from the end of the table. "Not everyone thinks she's so cool, you know."

"Lots of people do," said Chrissy. "Besides, you don't know everything."

"Maybe." She shrugged it off. "But I do know what the junior high boys are saying about her. They're ticked off that she won't let Mr. Guthrie get started on the football bleachers in time for homecoming."

"She's not doing it all by herself," said Jody.

Rachel ignored the comment and continued to stare at Chrissy. "They're saying it's all the Harrisons' fault. Kevin's sister heard Lucas tell Ronnie Wolf that he thinks all the Harrisons are losers."

"Did not," said Chrissy.

"Were you there?" asked Rachel. She gave Jody a pitying glance and whispered something to the other girls, leaving Jody and Chrissy cut out of the conversation.

"Don't pay any attention," said Chrissy. "Like I said, she's just jealous. Lucas wouldn't come over here if he was mad at you."

"I should have been expecting this, I s'pose." Jody sighed and began to pack up her lunch, too upset to consider eating Gran's beautiful sandwich. "I've read in magazines about guys playing this game with girls."

"What game?"

Jody sighed again. "Sending mixed signals."

WAYNE LINGERED over the remains of his chili lunch special in a wide diner booth at the Beaverhead Bar & Grill on Monday afternoon, shaking his head over Ed Meager's latest letter to the editor of the *Tucker Tribune*. Some people simply couldn't let go of a bone, even after the dog on the other end had given up the tug-of-war and gone off to find something with a little more meat on it.

In Ed's world, the sky was always falling. And if his current diatribe was on target, the atmosphere was going to be missing a whole lot of ozone when it hit the ground.

At the moment, the sky over Tucker was shedding the kind of rain that fell in soft, fat drops and sank deep into the soil—the kind of rain that would have been appreciated back in July, before a monstrous midsummer wildfire had wiped out hundreds of acres of pasture and timber land on the west side of the range. Out on Main Street, truck tires kicked up jets of spray over the glistening street pavement and passersby hunched inside their jackets. The temperature was dropping, and snow would surely follow, drifting to lower elevations in another month or so.

Inside the Beaverhead, the overheated air filmed the window beside him and tempted him to strip off his jacket. The peppery tang of Max's chili hung in the air along with the odor of the chopped onions that had gone into it. On the kitchen radio, Clint Black wailed over the hissing grill and the chugging dishwasher. Milo Evers, in town to fetch supplies for Granite Ridge, leaned over his coffee at the counter, and across the room Susie Dotson scrubbed at a chocolate pudding smear on her youngest girl's face, murmuring stern mother's warnings in counterpoint to her daughter's fussy whine.

Cute little thing—Amanda, that was her name. Always done up in neat pigtails with tiny plastic clips and bright ribbons, and shoes that looked like something

NASA had designed for moon-walking Lilliputians. Today Amanda's shoes flashed with pink lights when she moved, the way she was moving now, kicking in frustration against the edge of the vinyl seat as she arched and slid toward the floor in a slow-motion getaway.

He wondered what it would be like to slip a glowing pink shoe onto a foot that small, or to tie a ribbon on the end of a thin, silky braid. He longed to find out.

Loretta Olmstead, the lone waitress on duty, shuffled over with a fresh pot of coffee. "Sure is quiet in here for a Monday. More Rotarians usually stick around for lunch."

"The meeting dragged on a bit longer than usual." Wayne lifted his cup for a refill. "Most of the cattle got brought down from the high country over the last week or so. Folks have their hands full getting the herds settled in for the winter."

Loretta stared out the window at the soggy street. "Still, I thought the weather might tempt them to stay inside. And Max made an extra batch of his berry cobbler."

"Maybe I should perform a kindness and have seconds," said Wayne with a smile. "Wouldn't want to see Max get his feelings hurt."

"You don't need an excuse to have a second helping of something sweet," said the waitress. "Could use a little fattening up, in my opinion."

"I'll take that as a compliment, darlin'. Even if it sounds a bit underhanded, coming as it does from someone in the food service industry." He grinned and ducked out of range as she flapped a hand at him.

"When are you going to get yourself a wife," she asked, "or someone to make your berry cobbler for you?"

"I've got Benita."

"Housekeepers don't count. Besides, Benita's got a husband of her own."

"I like the way she cooks. And the way she keeps my house. She'd be a hard act for any wife to follow."

"There's more to tending to a man than picking up after him and filling his stomach."

"You got someone in mind?" He fell into the familiar rhythm of the game he'd been playing with Loretta for years, a game that had been suspended for one short season during the months he'd spent with Alicia.

"What about that sweet Mary Wilcox, the Presbyterian Church secretary?"

"The one who plays the organ and sings like a tortured cat?" He shook his head. "She's sweet enough, I s'pose, but I don't think I could tolerate the sound of her clearing her throat at my bathroom sink in the morning."

"You're too damn picky," Loretta said with a shake of her head. "Someone with your good looks and that big spread shouldn't have this much trouble finding a replacement for the girl who ran out on you."

"If my good looks and big spread weren't good enough to keep one wife, why would they be good enough to catch another?"

"Nothing wrong with the bait, hon." Loretta patted his shoulder. "You just gotta build up your confidence. Get in some dating practice. Get out there and do a little fishing."

She pulled her pad out of her pocket and added another serving of Max's cobbler to his tab. "Speaking of fishing, what are you up to with that Maggie Sinclair? Heard you two were getting a little too close for comfort out on the dance floor Friday night."

"I don't know that I'd agree it was all that close," said Wayne, "but I will admit it was plenty comfortable."

"Well, don't go getting too cozy." Loretta tucked her pad back into her chili-stained apron. "Everyone says she's getting out of Tucker the first chance she gets."

Even though he shared her opinion, Wayne found himself wishing he wouldn't be subjected to these constant reminders of Maggie's imminent departure. "Wonder why she took that job at the high school if she didn't plan on sticking around a while?"

"Jobs don't hold people in place when they want to be someplace else."

Neither does a marriage, Wayne added silently. He took a sip of his coffee. Cooling already.

Loretta leaned over his shoulder and stared down at the paper. "Is that another of Ed's letters?"

"Yep."

"The ozone again?" She sighed when he nodded. "Gotta give the man credit for trying, I s'pose."

"That's a fine and generous thing to say." Wayne winked at her. "Care to put it in writing and send it to the editor?"

The little bell over the main diner door jounced and jingled. Trace Bardett, Frank Guthrie and Jasper Harlan

entered and crowded around Max's specials slate, ex-
amining the day's offerings while they stomped and
shook the wet off like three big dogs.

Loretta wandered behind the counter. "Hey, boys."

"Hey, Loretta." Trace leaned over the plastic pie
dome. "Is that Max's cobbler?"

"Yep."

"Think I'll have me some of that."

"Be right there."

Wayne watched the men shift and hesitate before
migrating toward his booth. He folded the paper and
shoved it aside, bracing himself for the discussion of the
donation that he knew was heading his way with them.

"Hey, Wayne."

"Hey, Trace," he answered with a nod. "Frank, Jasper."

He slid toward the window, and Trace swung in next
to him. The other men squeezed in on the opposite side
as Loretta made her way down the cafe's single aisle with
the coffeepot. She filled three coffee cups and topped off
Wayne's, took one more order for cobbler and one for
banana cream pie, and asked after Guthrie's litter of
McNab pups while neatly sidestepping Jasper's clumsy
invitation to hang around for a drink after her shift.

"What's new?" asked Guthrie with a glance at the
paper.

"Ed's at it again," said Wayne.

"The ozone?" asked Trace. "How come we never
hear anything about all the times that hole shrinks
itself up again?"

"What makes you think it does?" asked Guthrie.

"If it never shrank any," said Trace, "it'd be stretched out over most of the earth, halfway here by now, and everyone in the southern hemisphere would be screaming louder than Ed."

"It shrinks." Jasper tapped his fingertips on the table. "And then the CIA sends up a space shuttle to burn a hole in it again, to keep the Chi-Coms on their toes."

"If the CIA's behind it," said Guthrie, "why don't they burn the hole over Shanghai?"

"Don't get him started," said Wayne. "I've had my fill of conjecturing this afternoon."

Loretta returned with the orders, and Wayne's unexpected company settled down to the tasks at hand: erasing all traces of Max's desserts and Wayne's recalcitrance on the subject of Kelleran's donation.

"Interesting vote at the meeting Thursday night," said Guthrie. "I wonder how long it'll take before Kelleran gets a recommendation from the board."

"Wonder if he'll decide to stick with the recommendation when he does," said Wayne.

"Is that a possibility?"

Wayne shrugged. "Anything's possible. The board's only making a recommendation. It's his money."

"Damn." Jasper shifted in his seat. "I hadn't considered that."

"Then why would he bother with asking the board in the first place?" Guthrie frowned. "Why not just decide on his own what he wants to do?"

"Maybe he wanted some official input," said Wayne. "And maybe he's trying to ease his way along here, to find out what the people of Tucker want. To make sure he's doing the right thing."

Trace shot Wayne a dark look and leaned over his coffee cup. "Taking his time to do all that easing along doesn't guarantee he's going to end up doing things right."

"If I recall correctly, it was the board that voted to take the time, not Kelleran." Wayne fingered the handle on his coffee mug. "And I don't think a twenty-five-thousand-dollar donation to the school is something I'd categorize as incorrectly done, no matter how things end up getting decided. As to his easing along with his decision-making process, I can't find much fault with that, either."

"That doesn't come as much of a surprise," said Jasper, "seeing as how you've always been one for easing along with things yourself." He shrugged and leaned back. "Not saying that's such a bad thing in general, Wayne. Just saying maybe it's not such a good thing in this particular instance."

"It's nice to know my friends and neighbors know me so well," said Wayne with a tight, one-sided smile. "Just like it's nice to know they'll keep that in mind if they get stuck puzzling out the reasons behind my voting the way I did last Thursday night."

"An outsider like Kelleran doesn't know the people

or the situation involved," said Guthrie. "He doesn't know how things work best around here."

Wayne's smile disappeared. "Wonder how generous he'll be feeling in the future if he hears people talking that way."

"Hell, Wayne," said Trace. "You know Frank didn't mean any harm. Kelleran'll figure that out, too, if he's as sharp as some folks around here say he is."

"Yeah, I know," said Wayne with a shrug. "Just tossing out one of those rhetorical questions the way I do to keep the discussion easing along."

"I don't have time for much more discussion," said Guthrie. He shifted forward and crossed beefy forearms on the table. "I'm trying to get a ball field ready for a homecoming game."

"And I'm sure you're doing a great job of it." Wayne lifted his coffee mug in a friendly salute. "That barbecue tailgate dinner is a great idea. Hope the weather cooperates."

"I was hoping you'd cooperate," said Frank, "come the next board meeting."

CHAPTER SIX

WAYNE LOWERED his mug to the table. "Now, why do I get the feeling I'm getting boxed in here in more than one way?"

"No one's doing any boxing in," said Trace. "We just think you might have been a bit hasty asking for that delay in the vote on the donation."

"Sounds kind of funny to hear the words *hasty* and *delay* mentioned in the same breath." Wayne stretched one arm along the windowsill. "If I recall correctly, mine was one of three votes objecting to the motion."

"Everyone knew Alice and Shelby were going to back Maggie the moment she made that 'male *and* female' comment," said Jasper. "Once that point got made, all the ladies in the room got stampeded into sticking together. What I want to know is, why did you stick with 'em?"

"I didn't set out to choose one side or the other," said Wayne. "Mostly because I wasn't aware that making a decision about Kelleran's offer had boiled down to some kind of feminist issue."

"It isn't an issue," said Guthrie. "At least, it wasn't

one until a certain someone brought it up." He shoved back with a huff of disgust. "This discussion is veering off the main topic. Now that I think on it, a lot of things around here have been veering off course ever since Maggie Sinclair came back to Granite Ridge."

"Maybe you should check the ozone layer over Tucker," said Wayne. "If there's any missing, she might be the one responsible."

"You defending her?" asked Guthrie.

"Did it sound like I was?"

"Brenda Moseley said she heard you were dancing with Maggie at the Beaverhead last Friday night," said Jasper. "Said you two looked real friendly. Nice and cozy, like."

Brenda hadn't been there to see any dancing for herself, but she was one of Janie Bardett's best friends. Wayne stared at Trace and raised one eyebrow.

His friend scowled and shifted in his seat. "Hell, Jasper, it wasn't anything like what Brenda's making it out to be."

Jasper worked his jaw, obviously wanting to say more on the subject but silenced by a witness's testimony.

"Yeah, I danced with Maggie." Wayne lifted his fingers and gently pressed four ovals into the window film. "Missed out on the chance in high school and thought I'd take the opportunity to rectify the situation."

"She hasn't changed any, far as I can tell," said Jasper. "Still got her nose in the air."

"It's a nice enough nose, up close," said Wayne. Straight and delicate, he remembered, and sculptured in the cutest shape around the tip. He curled his fingers into his palm and squeezed tight. "Even if she does tend to poke it into things."

"Big city woman with a big city attitude," said Trace, and an awkward silence fell around the table.

Wayne knew they were all thinking about Alicia. Wondering if he was falling for another woman who'd get him all worked up and then desert him for a more glamorous social scene and more upscale shopping prospects. They didn't have to worry. He'd learned his lesson. Maggie may have been a good fit out on the dance floor—a surprisingly comfortable handful, with curves that seemed to match up to all his hollows as if they'd been made for that purpose—but she'd made it clear she was brushing Tucker's dirt off her high heels the moment she had someplace else to head to.

And he didn't plan on setting himself up to be brushed off along with everything else.

"Tucker doesn't need someone's idea of a big city makeover," said Guthrie.

"I don't think Maggie means any harm," said Wayne. "She just has a different perspective on things. She isn't the only person in Tucker who's ever talked about moving on and making a go of it somewhere else. Doesn't seem right to hold it against her for doing more than talking."

He shrugged. "Nothing wrong with a different

perspective or two. Tucker's got room enough for that, I think."

"You saying you agree with her ideas?" asked Guthrie.

"I'm saying I haven't had the time I need to take a good, fair look at her proposal. None of us has. She deserves just as much of a chance as you do to make her case."

"Seems she's already been making it, up close and personal."

Wayne raised his eyes to meet Guthrie's belligerent stare. "You got something a little more specific you want to say on that subject, Frank?"

"Don't go getting all riled up, now," said Trace. "Either of you. Wayne's just tossing out one of those rhetorical questions again. Playing devil's advocate. Aren't you, Wayne?"

When Wayne didn't move a muscle or shift his gaze from Guthrie's face, Trace blundered on, trying to ease the tension. "I swear, it's his favorite game."

"I don't have time to play any more games," said Guthrie. "I need to get equipment ordered and concrete poured before winter weather sets in."

"Seems to me the urgency behind that need didn't exist before Kelleran made his offer," said Wayne. "Might be better to take some time, to plan on doing the job for next year's season. Might be a little less pressure and stress on everyone involved that way."

Guthrie sat back with a shrug. "Just trying to make the most of an unexpected opportunity."

"And you've done exactly that," said Wayne. "That report you gave to the board members was a mighty impressive one."

Loretta chose that moment to make an appearance with the checks and her bottomless coffeepot. "Can I get you boys anything else?"

"Nothing for me, darlin'," said Wayne. "Time I climbed out of this booth and made my own check on the local atmosphere. Ed's right—can't leave anything to chance."

MAGGIE STEPPED from her car onto the smooth gravel drive that circled near the entrance of Wayne Hammond's sprawling ranch house late that afternoon. She gazed up at the cedar-clad angles and planes, at the expanses of sparkling glass and the smooth, sharp runs of painted trim contrasting with touches of roughhewn stone, and she imagined Frank Lloyd Wright might have come up with something like this if he'd been asked to design a rustic private retreat for a wealthy weekend rancher.

She'd heard that Wayne had pulled off a minor miracle in rebuilding his run-down inheritance, and she'd observed the respect the people in Tucker held for him. Viewing this evidence of his hard work and astute business dealings—not to mention his good taste in architecture—was enough to tempt her into a bit of hero worship herself.

Which was not what she wanted to be feeling at the moment.

She closed her car door and smoothed her hands over her fitted black suit. She'd planned to drop by for a casual, unannounced visit, to make her request in person—to catch Wayne off guard and make it harder for him to say no. Now that she was standing here, feeling a bit off balance herself, she wondered if a phone call might have been a better idea.

The front door opened and a slightly graying, somewhat thick-waisted woman in jeans and a red sweater stepped onto the porch. "Better get yourself in here before you break your neck in those shoes," she said.

"You must be Benita McGee," said Maggie as she climbed dark slate steps. "I'm Jenna Winterhawk's daughter, Maggie. Maggie Harrison Sinclair," she added.

"I know who you are," said Wayne's diminutive housekeeper. She conducted a pursed-lipped, hairstyle-to-heels appraisal of Maggie and shook her head with obvious distaste. "No one else around here would dress like an undertaker to make a social call on a ranch house."

"This isn't exactly a social call." Maggie battled back the urge to tug at her short jacket. "And I came straight from my job at the high school."

"I know where you work, too. Heard all about it." Benita flapped a hand in dismissal. "Been hearing enough about you to last me through next semester and then some. But then I bet you've heard enough about the subject, too."

Maggie donned a polite smile and prepared to change the topic. "I was hoping I'd catch Wayne at home."

"He's around here somewhere," Benita said as she moved aside and swung the door wide. "It's almost time for dinner. That ought to flush him out. Well, come on in, then."

Maggie stepped into an area of soaring walls and spilling light. The wide, raised entry area flowed down to a spacious great room. A glossy oak plank floor offset the quiet patterns of Bokhara rugs, and textured throws softened the dark leather furniture. Above a handsome mantel, a massive rock chimney rose nearly three stories to the steeply angled ceiling. Every feature, every item coordinated with the heart-stopping view beyond the windows—that lush sweep of pasture grass and the shadowy timberland climbing the craggy mountains beyond.

She couldn't resist skimming a finger along an iridescent glass salmon arching liquidly over a sofa table. The place could use a few more whimsical touches, and perhaps a splash of bolder colors here and there. An antique slot machine in the corner beside the bookcase, she thought, and agate chess pieces poised for play on the tiny table across the room. Jewel-toned pillows to mix with the casual throws on the furniture, and bright, spiky flowers in a tall, slim vase set on the oversize table snugged behind the sofa. Family photos in fanciful frames tucked here and there.

She nearly itched with the urge to experiment with the decor. "What a wonderful room."

"Yes, it is," said Benita. She rubbed at some invisible

smudge on one of the newel posts. "He's done a good job, so far."

"So far?" Maggie strolled toward the windows to gaze out over the river valley, her heels sinking sound-lessly into a plush rug. "It's beautiful exactly the way it is. It's quite a surprise, actually."

That wasn't fair, she realized. Or that much of a surprise, she thought a moment later. Wayne Hammond was a patient, thorough man. The kind of man who cared about the details, who would think a project through and take care to do it right.

"Hmph." Benita patted a fat pillow. "Would have thought a woman like you would notice the missing bits and pieces. But I suppose I should be grateful there's not much clutter to dust."

Maggie turned with a smile. "You mean the kind of clutter a woman would add."

"I wouldn't mind the extra work if there was a woman here to add it."

"You're a woman."

"I'm not his wife."

Maggie examined a print of maple leaves drifting in a pond. "What about a decorator?"

"He hired one of those. Took some advice, ignored most of it."

"Didn't his wife do any decorating?" Maggie knew she was prying, but Benita didn't seem to place much value on discretion. "While she was here, I mean."

"She didn't care enough to try," Benita said with a

sniff. "She didn't stay long enough to settle in much, anyway."

"I'm sorry to hear it."

Benita shrugged. "She was happy enough to be here, at first. Just too foolish to appreciate what she had."

"How sad, for them both."

"She's back in Las Vegas, right where she wanted to be all along." The housekeeper crossed her arms at her waist and gave Maggie a pointed look. "And he's still here, right where he needs to be."

"Sounds like a story of star-crossed lovers."

"Hmph."

Maggie slipped the strap from her shoulder and dropped her purse on a leather sofa cushion. "This is a large place for a single man."

"It'll fill up with guests soon. Hunting season is a busy time around here."

"Guests?"

"Businessmen. Cee-Eee-Ohz," said Benita, as if they were some alien life form. "Some from New York."

New York CEOs. Maggie had heard that Wayne had invested in a couple of sidelines; now she wondered if his investments were more wide-ranging than anyone in Tucker realized. "So this is also a hunting lodge?"

"It's a house. A big one, like you said." Benita climbed three shallow steps into a formal dining area overlooking the great room. "I'm going to finish making dinner. You can wait out here, or you can ask more questions in the kitchen."

Maggie smiled at the housekeeper's grudging invitation. "I don't mind a kitchen visit."

She followed Benita into another large space, this one a sleek and utilitarian mix of stainless steel and black-veined granite. Dozens of tiny recessed fixtures washed soft but substantial light over smooth, honey-toned walls and cherrywood cupboards. The exotic aroma of garlic and cumin spiced the warm air, and a tiny counter radio was tuned to a Spanish-speaking station.

"Here." Benita tugged a stool from beneath the wide island counter. "And here." She handed Maggie a tiny knife and a bright yellow pepper, and shoved a chopping board and a pretty blue-and-white salad bowl filled with greens in front of her. "Wash your hands first."

"If you knew me better," said Maggie as she headed toward a small basin sunk into the other end of the island, "you wouldn't trust me with this."

"If you don't figure it out fast, you're going to be real hungry later."

"I'm not staying for dinner."

"Hmph."

"I haven't been invited." Maggie dried her hands and draped the towel over a graceful wrought-iron rack. "Wayne wasn't expecting me."

"I want that pepper sliced nice and thin," said Benita, sidestepping the issue. "And don't get any seeds in my salad."

Maggie removed her jacket and settled back on the

stool, unfastening the tiny pearl buttons at her cuffs to fold her silk blouse up her forearms.

Benita lifted the lid from a pot on the range, and the scents of chicken and peppers and tomatoes rose with the steam. Maggie began to wish she were invited. The casserole smelled like heaven. *"Arroz con pollo?"*

"Yes," said Benita as she poked at the ingredients. "One of his favorites."

She moved to a deep double sink beneath a window and filled it with soapy water. "Why did you come all the way out here to see him?"

"I have a favor to ask."

"You couldn't use the phone?"

"If I'd called, who'd you have gotten to slice your pepper?"

"Hmph." Benita slipped a chopping board into the water and began to scrub. "I heard you had a lot of sass."

"I'll bet you did."

"You're just as bad as that sister-in-law of yours. How in the world a sweet thing like Jenna Harrison could end up with two girls like you…" Benita shook her head at the injustice of it all.

"Maybe we both turned out the way we did because of the example our mother gave us."

"Maggie," came Wayne's soft voice from behind her.

She turned to find him framed in the kitchen doorway, his hat in his hands and his thick, dark hair shoved in untidy layers where he'd raked his fingers through it. His jacket was torn near one pocket and his jeans were streaked with mud, and he looked worn and uncertain and impossibly appealing. One corner of his mouth twitched up in what appeared to be the start of a smile, and then he angled his face toward the floor and she missed the finish.

She wished he wouldn't hide himself away like that. She liked his rare, bashful smiles, the way they started at the edges of his eyes and moved across his features, gathering a quiet humor.

"Oh!" she said, suddenly remembering where she was and what she was doing. "Sorry, I—" She slid from the stool and brushed her sleeves down her arms. "I probably shouldn't have stopped by without calling first. And now here I am in your kitchen and making myself entirely too much at home."

"No need to apologize," he said.

He glanced up at her, and the expression in his eyes seemed to warm the kitchen another few degrees. She rubbed her palms down her skirt, suddenly feeling as shy and awkward as he looked. "All right, then."

At the sink, Benita splashed and muttered something in Spanish.

Maggie shifted and straightened. "I came because I have a favor to ask."

"It must be a mighty big one to drag you all the way out here."

"If I'd known your place was so beautiful," she said as she pulled on her jacket, "I might have thought up a smaller one to use as an excuse just so I could take a peek."

"Thank you." His neck and face darkened with a blush, and then he dropped his gaze toward the floor again and began to work his hat in a slow-motion circle. "You don't need an excuse to come for a visit."

"Maybe not an excuse, but I should at least have a reason. You might get suspicious if I started getting neighborly."

"Dios mio." Benita banged and slammed through a series of drawers and cabinets. "If I have to listen to much more of this," she said, "I'm going to take one of these knives to my throat instead of waiting for the conversation to do me in."

She dropped a handful of silverware on a small stack of dishes. "Ask the lady to stay for dinner. There's plenty to share." And then she swept past them, carrying the place-setting supplies out the kitchen door.

"Sorry about that." Wayne rubbed a hand over the back of his neck. "Benita makes a habit of interfering."

Maggie smiled. "I like her."

"That doesn't surprise me." He gave her a long-suffering look. "I'm sure the two of you would get along just fine."

"Because we have interfering in common?"

"No." He shook his head. "Your bad habits are all your own."

She narrowed her eyes. "At least I'm original in my faults."

"Yes, you are." He frowned. "And consistent."

She leaned back against the counter, arms folded. "This just gets better and better."

Benita swung back into the kitchen. "Have you asked her yet?"

"I think he's working up to it," said Maggie, "but I can't be sure. If insults and arguments are part of his standard method of inviting a woman to dinner, it's a wonder any of them ever take him up on it."

"At least that sounds more interesting than what I was listening to before," said Benita.

She stopped by Wayne and leaned in for a long, loud sniff. "You need a shower, and dinner's going to be ready in ten minutes."

Maggie shot him a wicked grin. "The pressure's on now, Hammond. How many more insults can you squeeze in before the timer goes off or I head out the door?"

His fingers curled around his hat brim. "I wasn't insulting you."

"Really?"

"I didn't say you interfere. You did. I said your bad habits are your own, and they are. That's a reasonable enough statement, not an insult."

She straightened and fisted her hands on her hips. "And what bad habits would those be?"

"One is that you always assume I'm thinking the worst of you." He shifted his feet. "And in that, you're consistent."

"You know something, Hammond?" She slapped one hand down on the countertop. "You're damn hard to have an argument with."

He tapped his hat against one leg. "Then why are you always trying to start one with me?"

"I don't know." She moved out of Benita's way as the housekeeper marched past to collect the salad bowl. "I guess it's just another bad habit of mine. One of those consistent ones."

A timer buzzed, and Benita extinguished the flame under the casserole pot. "There's leftover berry pie and ice cream for dessert. And now someone better finish setting the table and dish this up, because I'm leaving."

"Thank you, Benita," said Wayne as his housekeeper tugged a shearling and denim jacket from a rack of blunt wooden pegs. "G'night."

"It was nice meeting you," said Maggie.

With a parting *hmph,* Benita slammed out the back door. Maggie shivered in the chilly draft and the silence that drifted into the kitchen.

Wayne combed his fingers through his hair. "Benita's right. I need a shower before dinner."

"I should go."

"I wish you wouldn't."

She searched for something to say, some reason to say no, but she couldn't find it. The favor she wanted to ask him seemed to fade in importance as he stood there looking troubled and tousled and much, much too tempting.

"You look different tonight," he said.

"I do?"

One side of his mouth quirked up in a faint half smile. "Not a raspberry or a bouclé in sight."

"No." She smiled back. "No raspberry. Or bouclé."

"What would you call this?" He gestured vaguely toward her jacket.

"A business suit. In basic black."

"Sounds serious."

"It's a serious favor."

"You might as well stay, then," he said. "You'll have a better chance of success with that favor if you ask it after I've had my dinner. I tend to be in a more receptive mood on a full stomach."

"All right, then."

The expression that flickered across his features drew her a step closer. "Since it appears I'll have to stay, I might as well splurge and ask two favors. I'm dying to see the rest of your house, if you don't mind showing me."

He shifted and stared at the floor. "No, I don't mind."

"I have to call Jenna and let her know I won't be home anytime soon."

She started toward the door to get her cell phone from the purse she'd left in the other room.

"Maggie."

"Yes?"

"I never asked you properly, and I apologize for that. I want to do this right." He hung his hat on one of the pegs, his movements slow and measured, and then turned to face her. "Maggie Harrison Sinclair, will you please stay and have dinner with me?"

She waited for him to look away, to drop his eyes, but they stayed steady, warm and inviting on hers. Suddenly it meant a great deal to her to hold his gaze and to find out more about the man behind it. She wanted those things more than she wanted to sample Benita's chicken or to convince him to grant her favor.

"Go take your shower," she said. "I'll finish setting out the dinner things."

CHAPTER SEVEN

WAYNE SHOVED his head under the hot shower spray and hoped the water would beat some sense into his thick skull.

When he'd walked through his back door and seen Maggie Sinclair perched on one of his kitchen stools—those long legs of hers stretching toward the floor like something in a magazine picture and those slender, polish-tipped fingers wrapped around one of Benita's little paring knives—his heart had dropped clear to his knees before bouncing back up to his chest. And when she'd tossed off one of her snotty comments, that same heart had twisted sideways and started banging so hard he'd thought for sure she'd hear it over the din of the mariachi on the radio.

He would not—he could not—allow himself to have those bouncing, twisting feelings for another woman who was heading back to life in another big city.

And yet here he was, all hot and bubbly and ready to boil over with anticipation because she'd said she'd stay for dinner.

It was a big mistake. Someone would find out she'd

been here, socializing, and then that someone would tell someone else, and before he knew it, all of Tucker would know he'd entertained the woman who was set on shooting down the chance for improvements to the football field. He didn't need that kind of trouble, and he sure as hell didn't want to have a hand in stirring it up for himself.

He scrubbed shampoo along his scalp while memories of football plays and Maggie in her cheerleader outfit, of tense voices at the school board meeting and in the diner tumbled and scrambled in his brain, adding to his unease about the situation.

And in the next moment he was as giddy as any high school boy who'd ever managed to talk beautiful, popular, choosy Maggie Harrison into a date.

Maggie Harrison Sinclair. Here, in his house. Waiting for dinner and wanting a tour.

Dinner, a tour, and then she'd be gone, likely never to return. All he'd have would be this one night with her, and then she'd finish up whatever she was hoping to accomplish here in Tucker and take off again, the first chance she got. Probably for good this time.

He turned off the tap and stood in the large, tiled stall, waiting for the reality of the situation to sink in and shrivel the anticipation until it was a weak and puny thing, waited until the steam evaporated and his drying skin prickled with goose bumps.

It wasn't happening.

He couldn't wait to get downstairs, to see her in his

house, to sit with her at his dining room table, to talk with her. To know that when he glanced up, he'd see her lovely, expressive face, those clear blue eyes and that silky fringe of golden hair, those lushly curved cheeks and that generous lower lip that could spread in any number of smiles or dip in a tiny pout.

He had no business noticing, cataloguing, relishing every detail of the face of a woman who wouldn't be here this time next year. It was worse than a waste of time. It was damn foolish.

Just about as foolish as this irrational indecision over what to wear. He stalked into his room and flung open the closet door. The dress sweater and slacks he'd bought at that big department store in New York? No, too fussy for an impromptu dinner shared with a neighbor—she'd think he was trying to impress her. The shirt he'd bought for last summer's Cattlemen's Association barbecue? No, too western—he could do better than that. Maybe a compromise—a sweater over a shirt.

Wasn't that what college professors wore?

He swore under his breath and tugged a faded chamois shirt from a hanger and shoved his arms into the sleeves. And then he yanked a pair of equally soft and worn jeans over his legs. He might as well be comfortable on the outside while he was a mass of screaming nerves on the inside.

WAYNE JOGGED DOWN the stairs a few minutes later to see Maggie lighting tall tapers on the dining room table.

Her blouse stretched to outline her cover model's figure in sleek white silk, and a spurt of pure male response kicked him right between the eyes. Again.

She'd taken a bottle of Chardonnay from the kitchen rack and found two goblets to place near the water glasses, which were already dripping with condensation and spruced up with tiny slices of lemon. Benita's silly horseshoe rings circled the blue linen napkins Maggie had arranged over the tops of the plain brown plates. It made a pretty picture, a bit formal and slightly intimate all at the same time.

It looked like a date.

He halted at the edge of the dining room and stared at the clutch of mums in a vase centered on the table. Maggie turned to see him standing there, and she smoothed one hand down her skirt in what he recognized as one of her few nervous gestures. Somehow the idea that she might be as flustered as he was did little to ease his mind about what this evening might lead to. His irritation increased along with his uncertainty.

"I hope you don't mind me stealing the last of the flowers from the pots out on the front porch," she said as she fingered the blackened match. "Any woman raised by my mother is going to think a table setting isn't finished without flowers and candles."

"I don't mind." His fingers itched to curl in tight fists, so he shoved his hands into his pockets. "They're nice."

"They're beautiful. Did Benita plant them?"

His face warmed, and he glanced at the floor. "No."

She paused, but he wasn't about to admit to planting those pots himself. He didn't understand why he took the time, except it seemed like the right thing to do, one of the things he'd imagined he'd have around a place of his own. Although there'd always been a woman in the picture to take care of things like flower pots so he wouldn't have to.

"I used to buy flowers every week in Chicago," she said, twitching a napkin into a slightly different alignment beside one of the plates. "But I enjoyed helping myself to my mother's gardens this summer. It's much nicer to cut them fresh."

"I imagine it would be." He stood rooted to his spot, waiting for her to give him a hint about where she was going to settle so he could help her into her seat.

She moved to the other side of the table and fiddled with a salad fork. "And I hope you don't mind that I set out a bottle of wine."

"No, I don't mind." He stared at the shell-pink polish on her nails. "I like to drink wine with dinner."

"Good." She straightened and twisted a ring on one of her fingers. "I didn't know whether you'd want red or white."

"The white's fine."

"Well then," she said. "Dinner's ready."

"I can see that. Thank you." He stepped closer, ready to make his move.

She shifted to the side, reaching for the chair nearest

the kitchen door. He slipped behind her to take it, and between them they nearly knocked it over.

"Excuse me," he said.

"The hell I will." She slapped her hands on her hips and glared at him. "What is this, anyway?"

"What is what?"

"This…" She waved a hand in an exasperated circle. "This polite business. Pulling out my chair and getting all—all stiff and stuttery. You're making me a nervous wreck."

"I'm not stuttering." He pushed the chair under the table edge, and then remembered she needed to sit and yanked it out again.

She shoved it back. "You know what I mean."

"You mean, wrecking your nerves with my polite behavior?" He tried to ignore the way her perfume was scrambling his thoughts and narrowed his eyes at her. "Normally I'd say 'excuse me' or beg your pardon right about now, but I get the feeling that kind of talk might land me in a heap of trouble."

"That's right."

"How do you want me to act, Maggie?" He edged in and leaned toward her, making her shift back a bit. "What do you want from me?"

Her eyes widened, and he heard the tiny hitch in her breathing. And then her hand came up against his chest, and the pressure of her pink-polished fingertips was like a brand over his heart. He froze, trapped between the civilized demand to retreat and an elemental need to push back, to press his advantage, to find out if what he was seeing in her eyes was a match for what he had on his mind.

Her fingers relaxed and stroked down his shirtfront, five tiny paths of flame that made him shiver. "Maybe I should ask you that same question." One of her eyebrows arched in a challenge. "What do you want from me?"

He worked his jaw, angered and amused by the cool cover for the heat he saw in her eyes, and slowly backed off. "I want you to choose a seat and let me help you into it. My dinner's getting cold."

She shook her hair from her forehead, and it drifted back around her face in its perfectly layered style. The stylish, classy woman shifted back into place, too. "All right," she said. "I can do that."

She slid into the chair, and he managed to get her placed correctly at the table without breaking any bones. And then he took his own chair, across from hers, wondering what had just happened.

He was appalled at his behavior, the awkward stiffness and the aggressive moves. Something about Maggie Harrison Sinclair obliterated his balance and destroyed his control, driving him to extremes. He needed to try harder to maintain that balance and control when he was in her presence, because he wasn't at all sure he liked the effect she had on him.

Mostly because he liked it too much.

Maggie picked up the salad bowl and scooped some greens onto her plate. "Wayne?"

"Yes?"

"Are we going to continue to be painfully polite with each other for the rest of the evening?"

"God, no." He passed her Benita's casserole. "It would give me indigestion."

TWO HOURS LATER, Maggie couldn't decide whether it was Benita's delicious meal, the high school reminiscing or their mutual dismissal of Tucker gossip that had eased the edginess from the evening. Odds were the bottle of surprisingly excellent Chardonnay—followed by the bottle of imported Pinot Grigio that had accompanied them on their meandering tour of the house—had played a part in mellowing the mood.

And then there was her host.

She leaned a shoulder against the door of his office and watched him flip through a photo album, admiring the long, athletic shape of him, enjoying the contrast of the rugged rancher with his orderly, sophisticated space. He'd discreetly shoved aside a stack of papers when he'd entered the room, but not before she'd noticed the stockbroker's letterhead on the top sheet and a corner of *The Wall Street Journal* below.

Wayne Hammond was turning out to be a very interesting man. Not because he could easily maneuver through discussions on a wide range of topics, and not because he deftly deflected the personal topics he didn't wish to linger over. It was because he seemed genuinely interested in her, in her memories of Montana and in her experiences in Chicago. He wanted to know what she thought about those things, and why.

He was interested in her. In the way her mind worked, and in the motivations for her beliefs, and in…*her*.

It had been a long time since a man had taken the time to be that interested. A very long time—since before she'd met her husband. Alan had usually taken center stage after that.

Wayne, on the other hand, ducked out of the spotlight. Though she'd employed every conversational gambit in her arsenal, he'd remained largely closed off to her, a mystery. An intensely private man. And an increasingly fascinating one.

He had a habit of answering questions with questions—and the fact that she had the same habit often made the simple exchange of information a dance of implication and deduction that would have challenged a trial attorney. She couldn't decide whether he was being deliberately obtuse or engaging in some mysterious type of flirtation.

God, she hoped it was flirtation.

That must be the reason she sensed a simmering tension, as though they were poised on some taut, invisible tightwire above the evening's twists and turns. As they wandered through his house, sharing the remains of the second bottle of wine, she could hardly wait to see which of them tripped and fell first.

"Here it is," he said, handing her the open album.

"This was the year Tom and Will won their first team roping competition."

She passed him her glass so she could take the album. "God, he looks like he's still in his teens."

"You miss him."

"Every day. It's hard not to think of him, now that I'm back, staying in his house. And yet moments like this one seem so far away, like they're part of a different lifetime. Not connected to me, somehow."

"I guess you did your best to sever those connections."

"Yes, I did." She traced a fingertip over the face in the photo with a stab of...regret? Resignation? "And look at Will," she said. "I don't remember him ever being this scrawny."

"You might want to avoid mentioning that." He poured the last of the wine into her goblet and set the empty bottle on his desk. "Most men don't like to come up on the short end of any kind of measurement."

He returned her glass with a wicked tilt to his grin. Since this was Wayne, a man who didn't let anyone see anything he didn't choose to reveal, she realized that he was, indeed, flirting with her.

And since she'd recently become aware of other things—like the way her spine seemed to liquefy when he focused those big, brown eyes of his on hers—she decided to flirt back.

"I'm not so sure about that." She swayed into the room and reached around him to place the album back in its spot, so close she could see the smile crinkles in the corners of his eyes. "It might depend on who was doing the measuring."

"Planning on sizing me up, Maggie?"

She sipped her drink and licked its trace from her lip. "Going to give me a chance to do it?"

His gaze dropped to her mouth, and she leaned forward to see if he would take it. He angled his head toward hers, and her pulse beat through her like a hot bass drum as he paused, taunting inches away.

"Probably not," he said.

He wrapped a long-fingered hand around her arm to guide her through the office door as she struggled to catch her breath and keep pace with his long stride. Down the wide hallway he led her, past rooms she'd already seen. "Where are we going now?" she asked.

"To the wine cellar," he said. "We'll open a bottle of port and have ourselves a second dessert."

"You have a cellar?"

"That's where I keep the wine."

They moved through the cavernous main room, its corners bathed in silver moonlight and tinged with golden lampglow, to a narrow door set in a shadowy dining room niche. He shoved it open and flipped a switch, and then reached for her hand to guide her down wedge-shaped steps.

Amber light washed over wooden racks lining three roughly stuccoed walls, their diagonal patterns broken by shallow display niches featuring black-and-white photos of serene landscapes. In the center, a tall pedestal table and four high-backed bar chairs were arranged on the terra cotta tiled floor.

She pulled a bottle at random from its spot and scanned the label. A nicely aged vintage reserve from a winery in the Stag's Leap district of the Napa Valley. An expensive bottle, one Alan would have appreciated.

One of dozens.

An impressive wine collection and slightly shabby work clothes, a stock report tucked among rodeo souvenirs, classic furnishings set against wilderness views, educated conversation delivered in simple, folksy phrases. Sifting layers of contrasts, patterns that didn't make sense.

She was off balance with it all, unsure how to deal with this intriguing, secretive man who combined so many disparate aspects in his life.

"I think you'll like this tawny port," he said as he expertly uncorked a small bottle. "Goes well with Benita's cooking and house tours."

She nodded and stepped away, hoping to regain her footing, and found herself facing a museum-style matted print of a battered stone bridge arching over a reflecting pool. Light and shadow formed intricate patterns over the pockmarked architecture and mirror-like water. "Where was this taken?"

"I'm not sure."

"Where did you get it?"

"On one of my trips."

"To Butte?"

She waited for his answer, suspecting he wouldn't provide one. "It's signed and numbered."

"Does that make a difference?"

She turned to study him as she'd studied the print, wondering whether he was toying with her again in some private game where he made the rules. She knew him well enough now to understand that he knew the difference between a gallery print and something that was sold in a store bin. "Tell me why you bought it."

"Because I liked it."

"Why?"

His mouth quirked up at the corners as he tipped a half inch of the golden wine into a glass. "I hope you don't expect me to engage in any of that 'eloquent yet subtle, colorful yet understated, loud yet soft' artistic double-talk."

"Why not? You do it so well."

He handed her the drink. "I don't much like double-talk."

"Neither do I." She tasted the wine, relishing the burst of fruity sweetness on her tongue and the warm glide down her throat. "It is a kind of eloquent but subtle picture though."

His soft, rich laugh was a surprise that tickled and tumbled through her. She realized she'd never heard it before. She wanted to hear it again.

Maybe because she was a touch tipsy. Careless and a little reckless with it, wanting to scratch at him a little, to see desire and temptation in his features. She wanted to nudge him past that painfully polite point, over the edge from which they both seemed poised to fall.

She took another long, slow sip, watching his gaze flicker down to her lips before settling back on her eyes. "An eloquent and subtle print," she murmured. "Like the man who bought it."

"I'm not a work of art, Maggie."

"No, you're not." She set her glass on the table and stepped close enough to touch him. "But I'm starting to think you're a real piece of work."

He narrowed his eyes. "Somehow I get the idea you didn't mean that as a compliment."

"Is that what you're looking for?" she asked as she slid one hand along his soft shirt front. "Compliments?"

He curled her fingers inside his big, rough hand, but he didn't push her away. "I'm not looking for anything from you."

"Are you sure?"

She tipped her head back and stared at him through her lashes. Those deep brown eyes of his were intent on hers, considering, measuring, hinting at some inner struggle. For one fleeting moment she saw something dark and potent flare inside him, and a feminine thrill arced through her in response, as sweet and warm as the wine. And in the next moment she was shifting, falling, pinwheeling over the edge before him.

He lowered his face toward hers, and she lifted her chin and parted her lips in invitation, and she saw both the Wayne she'd always known and the Wayne she'd come to know tonight. And then the double image dissolved, shifted out of focus and blurred into one tall, wide form before her eyes drifted shut, and her senses hummed with an edgy anticipation and a strange, aching yearning that made no sense at all.

CHAPTER EIGHT

MAGGIE'S SCENT ROSE TO envelop Wayne, rushing
through his bloodstream like a drug. The essence of
musk and flowers and female flesh, the whisper of silk
sliding over her figure, the numbing trickle of the wine
in his system, all of it crumbled his resolve and crippled
his intentions and drew him closer to her, and closer
still, until he could sense her warmth and imagine the
fit of her body against his.

He wanted that fit, that feel. God, how he wanted her.
Helplessly, hopelessly. He needed to taste her, more
than he needed to draw his next breath.

She was both the Maggie he'd always wanted and the
Maggie he could never have, and he knew he should
turn away, should set her away from him with the same
strength he'd summoned in his office not an hour ago.
But he was weak, weakened from the effort he'd
expended this evening.

And then her hand trembled against his palm, and her
lovely face lifted toward his, and her wine-moistened
lips issued a siren's call, and he was tempted beyond re-
demption, failing, falling, grasping desperately for any

excuse, for anything—grasping her, because he couldn't stop himself, because she was so much more than he'd ever imagined she could be. And because the weak, foolish man that he was had already lost the battle, had already lost himself to her.

"Maggie," he whispered in the fragile, impossible moment before he touched his lips to hers. He combed unsteady fingers through her silky hair to cradle her head, to hold her, gently, to keep her in place as he caressed her mouth with his, and he spread his other hand across her narrow back to draw her nearer, to press her willowy length against his. "Maggie," he murmured against her cheek as he traced a moist path across her features, teasing at her earlobe, tasting the tang of her cologne where she'd dabbed it, thrilling at the tremor that ran through her as he nuzzled the tender spot behind her ear.

And then she moaned and pressed against him— Maggie Harrison, the flesh-and-blood woman of his dream—and he fought for the last, tangled shreds of his control, chaining the raging greed that threatened to take it all now, hard, fast. He dragged his mouth back to hers and plunged deep inside, tasting the wine and the woman and dark, demanding desires.

The taste of her, the feel of her. It wasn't enough. It would never be enough. Here, in the dim light of this small space, in the belly of the house he'd built as a manifestation of his ambitions and accomplishments, he'd sampled his dream and found it more than he'd expected, more than he could handle. Suddenly he was afraid to reach for more, frightened of holding her too tightly, terrified of watching everything slip through his fingers.

"Maggie," he said as he pulled away, and the hoarse sound of her name mocked him as he rested his forehead against hers. He'd done it now—he was well and truly caught on a hook of his own devising.

"Mmm." Her eyes, when she opened them, were dark with arousal, and a tiny smile curved the corners of her moist lips. "That was…interesting."

"Interesting?"

"Eloquent, but subtle."

A laugh sputtered through him, unraveling the tension. Reckless with release, he bent to kiss her throat. "With afternotes of blackberry and cream."

She ran her hands up his shirtfront and caught his lower lip between her teeth for a teasing nibble. "Flirty," she said as she slipped his top shirt button through its hole and tugged on the one below it, and the one below that. "With a hint of anticipation."

Their words skated across a slick surface, skirting the muddied emotions below. Two adults exploring a mutual passion—reality, not a dream.

"A little tart." He pressed her back against the table. "But not without promise."

She pulled his head down for another long, deep, drugging kiss. He tugged her blouse from the skirt's waistband and slowly slid his hand up her side, delighting in every inch of her soft skin, until his fingers closed around the satin and lace of her bra and the warm curve of her breast.

"Bold," she whispered against his lips, "but not without finesse."

Her fingers crept beneath his shirt, her pink nails scoring paths of fire across his chest. He dropped a hand to her knee and raised the hem of her skirt as he skimmed his fingers along her thigh. "Full-bodied," he murmured, stepping between her legs. "With a surprisingly strong finish."

He crushed her mouth beneath his, crazed with need, wild with longing, and pressed her down on the table. She took him with her, tangling her fingers in his hair to hold him closer, a feast of soft, warm, silky sensations. He dragged her shirt from one shoulder and closed his mouth over the base of her throat, reveling in the thrum of her moan against his lips.

Maggie. *Maggie.*

Not here, not like this. He didn't want this kind of reality, didn't want to rush and ruin what was happening between them.

MAGGIE WAS RIPE for the taking, and Wayne was taking her places she hadn't imagined, driving her wild with his maddening, ravishing, delicious kisses.

And then he broke the contact, and the cellar's cool air flowed between them, shattering the mood. She opened her eyes to see his, watchful and assessing, intent on hers.

He seemed to withdraw from her, shutting her out and leaving her reeling and raw with need.

He backed away, and she raised herself on one elbow and shoved a trembling hand through her hair. "I guess I've had a little too much to drink."

"I thought that might be the case." He fastened the buttons on her shirt before dealing with his. "I thought it might be a good idea to end the wine tasting before either of us had anything to regret in the morning."

Regrets. She was sure she'd have plenty, and not for the reason he'd given. Her body still hummed with desire. "I'd better wait a bit before I climb into my car and head for home."

"I'll make some coffee. Start another argument to sober you up. We could discuss my painful politeness again—that seemed to set you off."

"Yes." She narrowed her eyes at him, wondering if he was deliberately poking at her to set more distance between them. "It did. It does."

"Or," he said as he offered his hand to assist her from the table, "you could spend the night."

If this had been the old Wayne, she could have explained her reaction to his kisses on the wine or her pent-up need for this kind of contact with an adult male. But this wasn't the old Wayne. This was a new and interesting Wayne.

A dangerous Wayne, if those kisses were any measure of what he could make her feel and forget.

"A tempting invitation," she said. "But not something I should consider at the moment."

"What should you consider?" He flicked the switch and plunged them into darkness. The narrow stream of light from the open door above cast his features in a seductive mold, and his knowing smile sent shivers down her spine. "The coffee?"

"Yes." She nodded, relieved to let mundane details slap a little sense back into the situation. "Coffee sounds like a good idea. And maybe some fresh air to go with it."

He led the way up the stairs and into the kitchen, where he headed to the coffeemaker on the counter. Maggie excused herself and slipped out a door to the tiny covered porch wedged between the kitchen and the laundry.

She hugged her arms around herself and sucked in lungfuls of crisp, fir-scented night air, hoping to clear some of the wine from her head and the last traces of lust from her system.

What had happened—almost happened—in the wine cellar? One minute she was enjoying some flirting banter with an old friend and the next she was practically crawling into his lap—hard to accomplish when he was standing.

And why was she reconsidering—in a weak and shaky corner of herself—his casual offer to spend the night? Another deep breath should take care of that impulse.

And another.

God, she was pitiful.

CARRYING TWO OVERSIZE MUGS, Wayne joined Maggie on the porch. "Here," he said, handing her one. "I didn't know how you wanted it."

"Black is fine, thanks."

He watched her wrap a hand around the warm ceramic and blow across the surface of the steaming liquid, and then he dragged his gaze from her mouth to stare at the clusters of stars edging black velvet clouds. His body still ached with wanting her, but he was glad she'd turned down his clumsy invitation to bed. Neither of them was ready for that step.

"The dinner and tour portions of this evening are just about finished," he said. "There's only one thing left on the agenda."

"What's that?"

His grin was slow and satisfied. She wasn't as cool and unaffected by what had passed between them as she seemed. "I seem to remember something about a favor."

"Yes. Of course. That's why I'm here." She shoved her fingers through her hair, brushing back wispy bangs. "I want you to come to school tomorrow afternoon, during my prep period, so I can give you a tour of my own. Of the backstage area."

He frowned at his mug. "You don't have to show me. Your report was very thorough."

"My report was excellent."

"And I trust you to make the right decisions."

"I will." She took a cautious sip and winced. "But

you'll understand the situation better if you see for yourself what I want to do."

"Do you think I need a better understanding of the situation—of what you want to do—in order to make my decision?"

"I don't think it would hurt."

"Are you going to be offering Trace and Charlie private tours of their own?"

She set her mug on the railing and crossed her arms. "Would it help change their minds?"

"Probably not."

"I didn't think so."

"But you think you can change mine," he said.

"I didn't think I needed to. You assured me your mind was open."

"So I did." He leaned forward and placed his mug next to hers. "And so it is."

"So you say."

"And to prove that fact, it appears I need to come to school tomorrow for a backstage tour."

"That's as good a reason as any."

The chilled night breeze swirled around the secluded porch and lifted a few strands of pale hair back over her forehead. He stifled the urge to reach out and brush them into place.

"Come back inside," he said, "where it's warm."

"All right." She plucked her mug from the rail. "I have to get my things. It's late. I should go."

He'd known this moment was coming. All evening,

he'd been waiting for it, preparing himself for the inevitable. And dreading saying goodbye, wondering if she'd ever come again. She hadn't seen his spread, hadn't seen his stock, hadn't seen…

Hadn't seen him. Not the way he wanted her to see him.

And why should he care? It wasn't as if she was going to stick around long enough for her opinion to make a difference.

But in his final moments with her, as he followed her inside and watched her gather her things, as he agreed to meet her tomorrow after lunch and then stood on his front steps and watched her drive away, he couldn't help making a bushelful of wishes. Wishes that he could tempt her to stay, for tonight, forever.

Foolish wishes, he knew, but after those foolish kisses in the cellar, it seemed a night for them.

WAYNE STEPPED through the entrance of Tucker High School the next day and scuffed his boots across the wide welcome mat donated by the class of ninety-eight. From the open office door came the faint trill of a phone, and in the long, wide hall beyond, a student slammed a locker door and scurried away. The cherry scent of restroom sanitizer and the stale aroma of cafeteria gravy competed with the musty smells of books and old radiators.

He passed tall glass cases displaying the booty captured in countless athletic triumphs and paused to hunt for a certain photo shoved behind more recent shots. The division football championship, sixteen years ago. There he was, a stiffly posed member of a tight team line, a grimly determined set to his jaw and a hunk of hair hanging over one eye. And there was Maggie, long-legged and fresh-faced, prettily arranged with the other cheerleaders and their pom-poms on the grass in front of the players.

He wondered if she still had that sweater. She'd fill it out in a much more appealing way now.

"Hello, Wayne."

He turned to see the principal waiting at the office door and removed his hat, feeling a twinge of guilt at being caught loitering in the hall. "Afternoon, Thea," he said with a nod. "Just doing a little reminiscing."

"That's a popular spot for it." She wandered over and stooped to peer through the glass. "I forget sometimes that our school visitors might be in here somewhere. Which one is you?"

He pointed at the picture. "Back row, second from the left."

"Look how tall you were, even then." She studied the picture for another few moments. "And is that Maggie? With the other girls?"

"We were in the same class."

"My, what a lovely young woman." Thea straightened. "She must have driven all the young men a little crazy back then."

"She's still at it," he said. "Young men, old men, and most of the women, too, I expect. An equal opportunity annoyance."

Thea raised one gray eyebrow above her glasses. "I hear you have an appointment with her this afternoon."

"That's why I'm here."

"To look at the stage."

"So I've been told. Asked, I mean," he added and lowered his gaze to his muddy boot toes. "I told her I'd come and take a look around and listen to what she has to say."

"It's good of you, Wayne."

"Just part of the school board job."

"It's more than that Maggie, I'm sure."

He glanced up, but he couldn't see any hint in her expression that she'd meant the comment in the personal way he'd taken it. Not that he had any reason to take a comment like that in a personal way, he reminded himself, since he wasn't here for personal reasons.

"We met yesterday afternoon," said Thea, "and discussed her plans for a theatrical revue."

"A revue?"

"That's right. Something fun, to get the community interested and involved in the theater here." Thea's pale eyes glittered behind her lenses. "Her ideas are very clever."

"I'll bet they are. Clever is what Maggie does best."

"She's more than clever. She's taking on a project that will require a great deal of her spare time. And all for a school at which she's employed on a temporary basis."

Wayne didn't want to appear ungrateful for Maggie's efforts on the school's behalf—not at the same time he was considering a dozen ulterior motives for her sudden generosity. "She's an alum," he said.

"As are most of the people in Tucker."

"Maggie's not like most people."

"No, she's not." Thea's lips thinned in one of her slight smiles. "She has such wonderful...flair, don't you think?"

Wayne shifted his shoulders in something that passed for agreement.

"And a real gift for teaching. Which isn't surprising, since she's a savvy woman who has channeled her talents into her chosen profession. But not many people can bring her level of energy and creativity to the classroom."

Thea crossed her arms over a narrow chest. "She's doing a terrific job so far, even though this isn't the type of school or students she's accustomed to. Several parents have commented on how motivating her assignments are, and the students seem to enjoy her lessons. She's turning out to be a real asset to Tucker."

"That's good to hear."

"Yes, it is. And that's why it's going to be so hard to lose her."

Lose her. Thea's words hit his midsection like a sucker punch, knocking back into place some of the cold, tough reality that the kisses of the night before had jogged loose. Maggie wasn't staying, and he needed to remember that fact. And it would be a good idea to avoid any more of the tempting physical contact they'd enjoyed in the wine cellar.

"I doubt she'll stay until the end of the semester," Thea said.

"I thought she'd agreed to fill in for the year." He frowned and circled his hat brim through his hands. "Even though some folks have been saying she won't stay through the winter."

"I don't think weather has anything to do with it." Thea tapped her fingers on her arms. "I wish we could keep her. I'd offer her a contract for next year in a heartbeat, if I thought it would help change her mind. But she's already asked for a letter of recommendation. She told me she's applying for a position at a school in San Francisco."

San Francisco. So far away.

"She's looking for a placement in a larger city. It makes sense, really. It's where she says she feels most comfortable." Thea dropped her arms with a sigh. "I have to admit, Tucker isn't the best fit for someone with her professional background and experience."

"No. I don't suppose it is." Nothing about Tucker would ever measure up to Maggie's standards. Including him.

"Still, if there were any way…"

Thea looked at him expectantly, as if she thought he might be able to do something about the situation. And why would she think that? Why did she think he had any solution to the situation—or any influence over Maggie? What had she been hearing around town—

about the dance at the Beaverhead or the nighttime visit to his ranch? "Any way to do what, exactly?"

"To make her stay." She lifted her chin. "To offer her a reason to do so."

"No one can stop Maggie from doing anything she's got her mind set on doing." He shook his head at the futility of the notion. "If she wants to go to San Francisco, she'll go to San Francisco. New teaching job or not."

"She strikes me as the kind of person who enjoys a challenge."

"Yeah." He narrowed his eyes. "You could say that."

"She might enjoy the challenge of rebuilding the theater, if she thought she had a chance to do it."

So, Thea was throwing her weight behind Maggie's proposal—and for reasons Wayne hadn't anticipated. He wondered if she'd already spoken to Shelby and Alice. And he wondered how Trace and Charlie would deal with the kind of pressure this wiry, wily lady could exert.

"That's why I'm taking the time to look into the possibility," he said.

"I appreciate that, Wayne." Thea reached out and gripped his arm with her bony fingers. "Not all the board members would be so obliging. And I know you'll keep an open mind."

"I can't keep it open forever." He gave a silent farewell to the kisses he had already resolved to do without. The kisses he was already missing. "All the common sense might leak right out."

CHAPTER NINE

"Maggie."

She turned at the sound of Wayne's soft voice to see him standing near the stage apron, his worn work boots planted on the auditorium floor and his hat spinning a slow circle in his hands. He looked as solid and substantial as ever, but there was a cautious, shuttered quality to his expression—no trace of the intensity she'd seen in his features the night before.

"Glad you could make it," she said. "Come on up."

His jaw set with resignation, he walked to the steps and slowly climbed to the edge of the stage, stopping near one of the footlight boxes. He seemed oddly reluctant to join her at stage center.

"All right," she said, "we might as well start over there." She crossed the open space to join him, holding up a hand in a restraining gesture. "Don't move."

She pulled a Phillips-head screwdriver from her pocket and knelt to insert it into one of several coin-shaped slots. Part of the floor dropped away with a clank and a whoosh, swiveling to reveal a section of the footlights hidden beneath the stage. She pulled the curved metal hood into place to direct the oversize colored bulbs toward the backdrop and locked it in place with the tool.

"These were installed when the stage was built," she said, "when lighting of this kind was considered essential. Times and styles have changed, and most theaters don't use footlights now."

He scuffed one of his boots over another box outlined in the hardwood. "Are there more of those lights under here?"

"Yes. And not all the catches are stable. Some are difficult to open, others are difficult to close. I worry about one of them failing when someone steps on top of the box." She glanced up. "A broken leg would be the least of your worries, considering the potential for electrocution."

He came down on one knee for a closer look. "If you don't need these lights, I s'pose these boxes could be fixed shut. Permanently."

"They could, yes." She pushed the light box back into place and locked the catch. "But then we'd lose most of the lighting we do have."

She stood and brushed at her slacks, and then pointed to a row of similar bulbs directly above the footlights boxes. "See those lights up there?"

His gaze lifted to the spot she indicated. "The ones strung along that bar?"

"Those make up the second part of the lighting system."

She moved past him to the electrical panel set in the wall near one end of the front curtain and lifted several switches. Brilliant red, yellow and blue bulbs lit up in a random, gap-toothed pattern. "As you can see," she said, "several of the bulbs need to be replaced."

"That seems simple enough." He squinted up at the lights. "Why are they different colors?"

"To create different moods." She manipulated the switches to demonstrate different combinations. "Here, the light is warm and intense. And now," she said, switching off all but the blue bulbs, "it's evening."

"Interesting."

"It is, actually. The technical and backstage aspects of a production appeal to many students who wouldn't be comfortable playing a role. It's a science, and an art, in itself."

He gave her a bemused look. "Something for everyone."

"That's right," she said with a smile. "There's one big problem with replacing these, though."

"What's that?"

"Look where they're casting their light."

He tipped his head back again and stared up at the bar. "Well, I'll be damned. They're shining straight into that little curtain up there."

"The curtains hanging above us are called teasers. As you can see, the front teaser—the proscenium valance—is trapping most of the light. Only a fraction makes it to the stage. And that valance is responsible for the shadow along the backdrop." She pointed behind them, to a rippled pattern darkening two-thirds of the sagging canvas. "Only the footlights can offset that shadow, and we've just established that they aren't necessary—and probably aren't safe."

He glanced at her before tilting his head to study the proscenium lighting. "Do you plan to replace those bulbs on that bar up there with some of those Fresnel and ellipsoidal spotlights you mentioned in your proposal?"

So, he'd studied her paperwork well enough to familiarize himself with the terminology. Not many people would have bothered, and she was impressed with his effort. "That's one option."

"Can't you lower that bar of lights so they don't shine on the curtain—the teaser?"

"If we do, they'll be visible, a distraction for the audience. And you'll lose the attractive appearance the teasers create when the stage isn't in use."

"So, what do you want to do?"

"Get rid of the footlights, like we agreed. Move the overhead lights section to that spot, there," she said, gesturing to a place further upstage, "and redirect the lights at a different angle. But most importantly, purchase some of those spotlights you mentioned. We could light more effectively from the side, as needed, with portable trees."

She pulled a sketch of a light tree from her pocket and handed it to him. "This same illustration is in the packet of material I've already given you."

"I recognize it." He glanced at her. "It makes a whole lot more sense now."

"That's the reason for this tour," she said with a smile. "I hope you can see now that nothing I've suggested is unnecessary."

"I said I trust you."

"That's because you don't know enough to be able to do anything else." She folded her arms and gave him a challenging look. "Don't you think it's better to make a decision when you understand what's at stake?"

He gave her a neutral smile. "What else do you have to show me?"

She walked past him and slipped behind the front curtain to grab the frayed pull. "Most of the pulley system needs to be replaced. The tackle is still in good shape, but these ropes are an accident waiting to happen."

He'd ducked behind her to watch as she opened the curtain, and she was acutely aware of his large, solid form at her back. The odor of his work clung to him, that candy-sweet scent of grass hay and the metallic wash of mountain air. She glanced over her shoulder to see him staring at her, his features silhouetted in the brilliant lights overhead. They touched his wavy hair with blue and red and outlined his sharp cheekbones with gold.

"It's warm back here," he said.

"Hmm?" A sensory memory of those long, deep kisses they'd shared a few hours ago passed through her, and an unexpected wave of lust caught her by surprise and swept her thoughts out to sea in an undertow.

She had to agree. Things were definitely warming up back here.

"The lights," he said. "They heat things up a bit."

She cleared her throat. "Yes, they do."

He continued to stare at her with that bland expression, and a prickle of annoyance worked its way up her spine. Was she the only one who remembered what had passed between them last night—and wanted more of the same?

His mouth curved in a lazy smile, and she realized he was waiting for her to continue her lecture.

Too bad she'd temporarily forgotten the point she wanted to make.

"If you're finished talking about the lighting and the curtains," he said. "Maybe you could give me the rest of the tour."

She led him deeper into the backstage area, where he dutifully noted the racks of dusty, ragged flats and the motley collection of props tossed into messy bins. But when she marched across the stage, describing her plans for the new sound system, he didn't follow.

"Wayne?"

"Hmm?"

"I'd like you to see the dressing area."

He hesitated behind one of the tormentors dividing the stage from the wings, glancing around the edge of the curtain at the auditorium. Two sophomores who should have been focused on the texts open on the table before them were watching the tour instead. One of them whispered to the other, and they both laughed.

"Wayne?"

He stared at the floor and ran his hat brim through

his hands. He glanced at the girls again, and then at Maggie, and she thought she saw something like panic flicker in his eyes.

His throat worked and his head tipped down, and then he stepped out on the stage. By the time he reached her side, his features were strained.

"Have you ever been in a play?" she asked.

"No." His gaze remained fixed on the stage floor instead of aimed at her.

"But you must have been on stages. To make campaign speeches or run programs."

"I don't make speeches." He made an awkward, shruglike motion and twisted his hat again. "I say what needs saying, and then I sit down."

Terrific. She was already facing an uphill battle to secure the funds to improve the high school theater area, and now this. Wayne Hammond—possibly the one person she most depended on to make her proposal a reality—had stage fright.

"HELLO. IS ANYONE HERE?"

Maggie dropped the ancient cardboard box she'd been about to flatten two days after Wayne's tour and turned to see Janie Bardett shove aside one of the dusty tormentors. "Hey, Janie."

"Boy, what a mess." Janie wrinkled her nose as she lifted a soiled shirt from the pile of costumes on the floor. "Aren't you afraid of contracting some horrible disease handling this stuff?"

"You mean something besides a case of terminal disgust?" Maggie swiped her hands on the old work jeans she'd brought to change into after school hours.

Janie tossed the shirt into a box of trash with a shudder. "Looks like it would be fatal, all right."

"Guess I can write you off as a volunteer."

"Actually, that's what I came to talk to you about." Janie picked up a broken candlestick holder shaped like a dolphin and dropped it on top of the shirt. "My girls have been full of talk about your revue. Sounds like a lot of fun."

Maggie shoved hair out of her eyes and waved a hand at the backstage chaos with a sigh. "Does it look like fun?"

"Not right now, no." Janie opened a box of cap pistols and rubber knives. "These look like keepers."

"You can set them over there." Maggie pointed to a crooked bookcase doing duty as prop storage. "I'll sort through them and label them later. For all the good it'll do me."

"I heard you didn't get a very big turnout at the organizational meeting last night."

"Bad news travels fast." Maggie sighed and picked up the box again, eager to vent her frustrations on the cardboard. "Too many conflicts with fall sports and too many parents concerned about after-school commitments means too few students available for what I had in mind. Looks like I've only got a handful of potential actors interested in coming to the auditions next week, and all of them are going to have to pitch in as back-stage hands. I wonder how many will back out when rehearsals begin and the going gets a little tough."

"Actually, that's what I wanted to talk to you about." Janie placed the box on a top shelf and wiped her hands on her pants. "I was wondering if you might have any parts my girls could play. Anything at all."

"Aren't your girls in junior high?"

"Lizzie is, in the seventh grade. Holly's only in the fifth grade, but she's tall for her age," Janie said. "And she's even more excited about this than Lizzie. She's our drama queen—always has had stars in her eyes. You'd be doing us a favor, letting her get some of it out of her system away from home."

Janie gingerly plucked another ruined item from the pile of old costumes and tossed it on the trash heap. "But I'm sure she'd be happy just being a part of it. Maybe she could be one of those backstage hands you mentioned."

"Hmm." Maggie narrowed her eyes in consideration. "I hadn't thought of working with younger students."

"Maybe you should. They're going to be high school students in a few years, and they'd benefit from this, too."

Another community angle. Another group of people to get involved in the project, to get invested in the proposal. More parents to buy tickets and put some pressure on the school board.

"You know, it's not such a bad idea, now that you

mention it." Maggie stepped into the box to punch out its bottom. "I'll have to run it by the junior high staff to see if they'd have any objections."

"I don't see why they would. You wouldn't be taking their students out of class, would you?"

"No, but I wouldn't want to ruffle any feathers, either. Speaking of ruffling feathers…" Maggie folded the cardboard scraps and aimed a level gaze at her friend. "What does Trace think about this?"

"He doesn't know I'm here."

"I don't want to get caught in the crossfire when he does."

"There won't be any," said Janie. "It's three against one. He's outgunned from the get-go."

"Poor Trace." Maggie grinned and shook her head. "I actually feel sorry for him."

"Don't be." Janie flapped a hand. "He's used to it. And I'm careful to keep the henpecking at home, where it belongs. In public, he's still the cock of the walk."

Maggie picked up a piece of ragged purple velvet that might at one time have been some kind of cape and discarded it. "Whatever works for you."

"I want you to know I'd never put any pressure on him. About his vote on the school board," added Janie. "We agreed that subject is off-limits at our house. This is a completely separate issue."

"I don't see how you can make the distinction." Maggie picked up her bottle of filtered water and took a sip. "I'm hoping this revue will influence the board's recommendation. If your girls are involved, that's got to have some effect on Trace's vote."

"Not necessarily," said Janie with a smile. "But no matter how the board votes, no matter what gets decided, this revue of yours is happening. It's going to be quite the event, from what I'm hearing, and I want to know if my girls can be a part of it."

Maggie replaced the bottle cap. "Are you willing to be a part of it, too?"

"Is there going to be a chance of coming into un-expected contact with small rodents?" asked Janie. "Because as much as I love my girls, there are limits to what I'm willing to do."

"No small rodents. I haven't seen any since I set out the traps."

Janie glanced toward a dim corner. "You've removed all those, right?"

"What I have in mind won't involve much backstage work." Maggie cocked her head. "Unless you want backstage work?"

"I'll pass, thanks." Janie gave her a curious glance. "What did you have in mind?"

"Remember how good you always were in art class?"

"Art." Janie smiled. "My favorite subject."

"Want to relive the glory days?" Maggie tugged her briefcase from beneath a jumbled stack of old posters on the stage apron. "I'll show you what I've got in mind, although my sketches aren't half as good as what you could come up with."

"You want me to draw?"

"And paint." Maggie produced a thin stack of papers. "I'm thinking minimal set designs, mere suggestions of scenery with a few pieces of furniture and some props. Maybe some new flats, if I can get the materials donated. What I'd like you to do is create some free-standing pieces, like these."

Janie looked through Maggie's drawings and notes, nodding her head. "Sure, I could do this. It would be fun."

"Thanks, Janie." Maggie gave her a quick one-armed hug. "I appreciate it."

"Tell you what." Janie folded the sketches into her purse. "I'll agree to do this if you give my girls parts in the production."

"It's not a trade. I'm sure they'll pass the auditions based on their natural talent." Maggie snapped shut her briefcase. "Believe me, everyone and anyone who auditions next week will discover they have loads of talent."

CHAPTER TEN

MAGGIE TOSSED her briefcase on the front room sofa as she entered her cozy cabin late Friday afternoon and headed down the short hall to her bedroom. She planned to slip into her silk kimono, slide a Doobie Brothers CD into the player and open the bottle of Cabernet Sauvignon she'd purchased to toast the day's successes.

Kicking off her heels and shimmying out of her work suit, she reveled in the kinetic energy that several jolts of good news had sent surging through her. The prospects for her revue were on an upswing. The junior high teaching staff was delighted to have their students included in the project, the high school art instructor had agreed to loan the services of one of her classes for a unit on set decoration, and Thea was delighted with the intracampus cooperation. Janie had rounded up some parent volunteers, and a local women's service club had offered refreshments during intermission.

Maggie wriggled into her tightest jeans and stepped into new sandals with amber beads and bronze spangles stitched over the toes. She didn't want to count auditioning chickens before they hatched, but it looked like she might have enough student and faculty participation to allow her some latitude in assigning roles.

She smiled as she reached for the bohemian-chic top shot through with gold threads, and then stopped with her hand on the hanger when she realized what she was doing. She wasn't dressing in a comfy wrap for an evening at home. She was dressing up for an evening on the town.

An evening at the Beaverhead.

And why not? she asked herself as she leaned toward the dresser mirror to dash some color over her lips. Why celebrate alone at home on a Friday night when she was riding this wave of positive energy? She'd bottled herself up at Granite Ridge for too many weeks, feeling like a failure and hiding the proof, worrying whether she'd ever regain control over her future.

During the past week she'd taken some major steps toward solving her problems, setting in motion plans that would benefit Tucker and pad the résumé she'd already faxed to San Francisco.

And she'd shared some steamy kisses with an attractive, interesting man.

She outlined her eyes with more color than usual, enjoying the smoky effect and the way it coordinated with the casual, offbeat outfit. She looked as vibrant and alive, as hyped-up and hot as she felt.

"Look out, Tucker," she said as she shook back her hair. "This bottled-up babe is ready to pop her cork tonight."

FROM HIS STATION behind the burled expanse of the Beaverhead bar, Gil Canham stared at the door late Friday night and pursed his lips in a low whistle. "Whoo-ee. Will you look at that?"

Wayne glanced over his shoulder to see Maggie sauntering his way, her long legs outlined in skin-tight jeans and her slender torso hugged by some kind of filmy wrap that dipped low over her breasts and skimmed the top of her waistband and didn't leave much to the imagination in between. Sparkly drops swung at her ears and spiky heels peeked from beneath the pant hems. Her toenails were painted a come-and-get-it red.

He stared at those toes, and all his good intentions and wise resolutions melted in a white-hot blast of lust to leak through the pointy toes of his boots where they hung over the rungs on his stool.

"Hey, Gil," she said as she slipped her purse strap from her shoulder and placed the glittery bag on the bar. "How's it going?"

"Can't complain," he said. "Want the usual?"

"'The usual.'" She laughed and ran a hand through her hair. "I like the sound of that. Makes it sound like I'm a regular around here."

Gil slung his dish towel over his shoulder and leaned an elbow on the bar. "Nothing much regular about you, darlin'."

"I like the sound of that, too," she said. "You've got yourself quite a way with words, Gil."

"Got myself quite a way with women, too."

"Is that so?"

Their flirting exchange gave Wayne the time he needed to gather up a few shreds of his sanity and self-control. He frowned into his beer glass with the effort.

"How about you, Wayne?" Gil asked. "Ready for a refill?"

"No. Thanks."

"Hey, Wayne." Maggie slid her curvy rear end onto the neighboring stool, one long leg swinging close to one of his.

God help him.

"Hey, Maggie," he answered.

She thanked Gil for the glass of wine he set at her elbow. "So," she said as her fingers played along the stem of her glass, "what brings you here tonight?"

"The usual."

"Hmm." She raised one eyebrow in amused specu-lation. "Business? Pleasure? Or habit?"

"Since Gil here probably thinks I came in for his company, I s'pose I'd better say it's pleasure." Wayne emptied his glass and shoved it aside. "How about you? Why are you here tonight?"

"Well, I didn't think I had a habit connected with this place," she said, raising her wineglass, "but it appears the evidence is stacked against me."

"Not for business or pleasure, then."

"That depends." She sampled her drink. "What kind of business could I do in a setting like this, do you think?"

He narrowed his eyes. "That depends on the kind of business you had in mind."

She set her glass on the bar and edged toward him. The thin gold chain around her throat slipped and slid and rearranged itself in a tantalizing shape over her breasts.

"I thought you might like to take the opportunity to discuss a little school board-related business," she said. "Out on the dance floor."

"I can take that opportunity right here, I think." He tugged his gaze from her cleavage and wondered if he should change his mind about that refill. He seemed better able to deal with Maggie when he had a buzz on— she seemed less irritating that way. On the other hand, he seemed less able to deal with some of her other qualities.

He gave up trying to rationalize the situation and signaled for another beer. "What is it you want to discuss?"

"I thought I'd give you an update on my plans for the theater revue."

She took another sip of wine, and he tortured himself waiting for her tongue to sneak out and lick the moisture from her upper lip. There it was, pink and perfect. That second beer couldn't come fast enough.

He shifted on his stool. "You don't need to make reports to the board members."

"I know that." She stroked a red-tipped finger along the rim of her glass. "Maybe I'm just trying to be neighborly again. Or maybe," she said, leaning a fraction of an inch closer, "I'm working on that weak link."

He thanked Gil for the beer and took a fortifying gulp. "Make up your mind, Maggie. Either you're working one angle or the other."

She leveled a long, knowing look at him, and then she straightened on her stool. "Business, then."

She shoved her wineglass to one side. "I've decided on a program of short pieces —skits, scenes from plays, an original spoof one of my English classes is writing— in order to involve the greatest number of people. I figure at least two audience members will come to watch each member of the cast, so I can increase the size of the audience by increasing the size of the cast. Not to mention increasing the amount of community involvement and potential investment."

He'd figured she could be creative; he'd forgotten she could be inclusive, especially if it served her purposes. School parents, local businesses, community interests—she'd figure a way to tap into just about everyone's concerns and resources.

It was obvious, even this early in the game, that if she managed to pull it off, her theatrical evening might be a genuine success.

"Of course," she continued with an exasperated sigh, "that means squeezing more people into that dreadful backstage area. On the other hand, the actors are the people most likely to want to help me clean it up. Then again…"

Wayne settled back and let her words tumble over him, caught in her spell much as he'd been when she stood at the front of one of their high school classes to make a presentation, much as he'd been when she spoke at the school board meeting the week before. The old, familiar ache settled over him and wrapped around him, slowly squeezing him in its bittersweet trap. That same helpless sensation of inevitability, of being swept along wherever she wanted to take him, of wanting to go along for the ride even though he knew she'd leave him to crash and burn at the end of the road.

"The biggest expenses will be the materials for the set decorations and the costumes," she continued, her fingers ticking off the items. "I'm going to drive into Butte this weekend and scout around the secondhand shops, see what I can find. I can base my designs on the shopping results, and then for the rest…"

In spite of his inclination to throw his support behind the athletic proposal, he found himself caught up in her enthusiasm for her project. Maggie Harrison Sinclair was a born salesman. He wondered how Guthrie was going to deal with the situation when she started turning that charm of hers on the local business folks and hitting them up for donations. Guthrie might view her efforts as a threat, carving servings from a pie of finite size.

She laid her hand on his arm. "Do you have an air compressor out at your ranch you'd be willing to loan us?"

"I s'pose I might."

"That's so good of you—thank you."

She gave his arm a little squeeze and sat back. His noncommittal answer hadn't been a definite yes, but she'd just made it damn hard to squabble over the fine points. And when she smiled up at him and blithely sailed on to another topic, he knew Guthrie was up against a whole lot of trouble.

"So, what do you think?" she asked at last.

"Sounds like a lot of work."

"That's what Thea said." She gave him a brilliantly confident smile. "I'm not afraid of hard work."

"I never thought you were." He drained his beer and set the glass on the bar. "It also sounds like you're going to need the assistance of a lot of people to make it happen."

"It's going to be a lot of hard work for everyone involved."

"Why do you think people will do it?"

"Why do you think people put the kind of effort they do into sporting events?"

"I have no idea," he said.

She laughed, obviously delighted with his answer, and the sound of it got his pulse jumping for too many reasons to count or examine. He knew he'd pay a painful and expensive penalty later for the foolishness he had in mind right now, but he lifted the glass from her hand and pulled her from her stool. "Dance with me, Maggie."

"Is the business phase of this discussion over?" she asked.

"I don't know," he said, letting her fingers slip through his in a teasing friction. "Are you finished discussing it?"

"That depends on what happens out on the dance floor."

He rested his hand along the back of her narrow waist and guided her toward the tiny space near the pool tables. Beneath her gauzy top he could feel the curve of her spine and the flare of her hips, and the slip and slide of the fabric over the silky, lacy thing she wore underneath made his mouth go dry.

She turned to face him when they reached the center of the room and glanced up with a combination of anticipation and challenge in her eyes. From the jukebox, Faith Hill reminded him to just breathe as he pulled her close and curled her hand in his.

"This is one Friday-night habit I don't mind falling into," she said as she slid her free hand around the back of his neck. "You've got some smooth moves, Hammond."

"Flattery will get you once around the dance floor."

She teased her fingers through the hair that brushed the edge of his collar and skimmed one of those bright red nails along his nape, and he caught his breath at the tickling sensation.

"And after that?" she asked.

He guided them in a slow-motion circle. "Just where do you want to take this?"

"As far as it will go."

His fingers tightened around hers. "You don't believe in doing things halfway, do you?"

"What's the point in that?" She snugged up against him and gave him a witchy smile. "It won't get me any place but stuck in the middle of nowhere."

"Like you're stuck here in Tucker," he said, reminding them both why he shouldn't take her up on the invitation he saw in her eyes.

The corners of her pretty mouth turned down in a pout. "I don't think of Tucker that way."

"You don't seem to think of it as a destination, either."

"It's my family's home."

"What about your home, while you're here?" The song was winding down, and their steps slowed to a stop. "You can't quite bring yourself to say the words, can you?"

"Why is that so important to you?"

"Believe me," he said, putting another inch between them. "I don't want it to be important at all."

"What *do* you want?" She edged in close again, those polished toes nearly touching the tips of his boots. "Come on, Hammond. You asked me that same question not so very long ago. Now it's your turn. What do you want?"

Something inside him sizzled and snapped. *"This."*

He brought his mouth down on hers in an impatient and none-too subtle answer, a greedy gulp of a kiss.

Nothing else mattered at the moment, not the witnesses in the Beaverhead, or his position on the school board, or his reputation for slow and sober consideration of the consequences of every action—actions like a public display of some mighty headed affection with another woman who'd leave him the first chance she got. Nothing else meant anything at all to him, nothing but the thrill of her hot and eager response.

He raised his head and noted with bone-deep satisfaction that her eyes were clouded with desire. "Does that answer your question?"

SATURDAY MORNING Maggie tossed a saddle on Noodle, a gelding who'd be patient with an out-of-practice rider, and headed out into the pastureland along Whistle Creek to find her sister-in-law. Ellie had left at dawn to pound fence posts and stretch wire—her favorite activities when Fitz was away tending to his movie-making business.

Maggie had wondered, at first, whether it might be difficult to manage a marriage when one of the partners was absent so often, sometimes for weeks at a time. Ellie had never been separated from Tom, from the day of their marriage until the day of his death, but she and Fitz seemed to be coping with his crazy schedule well enough.

In fact, the arrangement seemed to keep them in a state of perpetual honeymooning during his visits to Granite Ridge.

With a sigh, Maggie nudged Noodle into a lope. Her own marriage, like Ellie's first, had been one of constant togetherness. Shared professions, shared social circles, shared recreations and interests. Alan had been insistent that she be a part of every aspect of his world, and she'd been happy to soak up all he had to teach her about it.

She understood now that he'd wanted her to witness and admire his mastery of the finer points of upper crust culture, to view him with the same degree of awe that others accorded him. But she proved to be too clever a student, and his pleasure in her accomplishments began to dim when those accomplishments began to outpace his own.

It was *her* catered parties that their friends raved about, *her* witticisms that delighted their guests, *her* ideas that received the most enthusiastic responses, *her* style that others noticed. And her career achievements and advancements at the college-preparatory academy where she taught came more frequently than did his at the university.

She'd been surprised, at first, when he'd agreed to seek the help of a fertility expert. Now she wondered if his agreement to proceed with the tests and treatments was one last form of subtle competition, one last contest between them he thought he might win. There was an excellent chance their childless state would be revealed as the result of the physical problems that had always plagued her. And to make sure there was no doubt in the matter, Alan proved his own fertility by impregnating his latest admiring grad student.

"Bastard," she said, but there wasn't much heat behind the word, and the wind carried the sound away along with the moment of pain. She focused instead on the rocking power of the horse beneath her and the shadowy beauty of the mountains on a cloudy autumn day and promised she wouldn't let memories spoil the moment.

And she gathered up the lingering pain of knowing

she'd never carry a child inside her and buried it deep
again, deep inside the empty part of herself, the part she
covered over with hard work and endless plans.

Like today's plan to expend some of her energy on
a horseback ride and find some privacy to have a little
chat with Ellie. She slowed Noodle to a jog and rehearsed what she'd say when she found her sister-in-
law. "Hello, Ellie. Nice day. Except I'm freezing my
butt off out here and it looks like rain's coming on."

She sighed. "And then she'll probably say, 'thanks
for riding all the way out here to tell me something I
could have figured out for myself, except for that fascinating bit of information about your butt.'"

Shivering, she tugged her jacket tab up to her chin
and wondered if she could play on sentiment. "Hey, sis.
Remember how we used to gossip about boys? Want to
do it again?"

God, this was going to be awkward, and she hated
to be at a disadvantage. Maybe she should head back,
to wait for another opportunity or another time when the
words would be easier to grasp.

Coward.

Yep, that just about summed it up.

But it was too late now, because there was Ellie,
topping the next rise, slowing her ATV and waving her
hat in the air in greeting.

CHAPTER ELEVEN

MAGGIE WAVED BACK with a smile as she rode the last few yards separating them. "Hey there."

Ellie turned off the puttering engine and squinted at her with suspicion. "What brought you clear out here?"

"Sheer boredom."

"Must have been a pretty impressive attack to get you to risk your manicure on saddling a horse."

"Don't worry. I wore gloves."

"Oh, God," said Ellie. "Tell me no one saw you."

"The groom took the day off, and I was desperate."

"Bored and desperate, and now you're here to share it with me." Ellie craned her neck, looking at the saddlebags. "Bring anything to eat?"

Maggie pulled two of Jenna's sugar cookies out of a roomy jacket pocket and made a great show of unwrapping them. "Yep."

"Hand one over."

"Say *please*."

"I'm not going to beg." Ellie twisted the key in the ATV's ignition and wrapped her fingers around the throttle. "I'll go get my own."

"These are the last of them." Maggie bit into one. "Mmm-mmm."

"I don't believe you."

"Mom made them for the Quota Club bake sale. I stole these off the tray when she went upstairs to dress for town."

Ellie switched off the engine again with a frown. "All right. What do you want?"

"Besides torturing you?" Maggie extended the wrapper with the one remaining cookie. "To talk."

Ellie swiped the cookie out of her hand. "So talk."

"It's awkward."

"Oh, for cryin' out loud." Ellie bit into the cookie and then held up a hand. "Wait a minute. Let me get this down and semidigested before you spoil my appetite."

Maggie watched her sister-in-law lick sugary crumbs from her lips and wondered for the hundredth time what it was about the little brat that had first attracted one of *People's* Sexiest Men Alive. She wasn't particularly beautiful, not by any objective standard, although she did have an arresting foxy cast to her features. And the moment she opened that sassy mouth, she was likely to drive most men away, although she could be a lot of fun when she decided to cut loose. Maybe it was the devilry in her dark hazel eyes and the no-holds-barred delivery of her barbs that had made Fitz take a second look and see the woman behind the attitude.

She had to give her glamorous brother-in-law credit

for finding the diamond under that rough exterior and for hanging in through all the grief Ellie had put him through before she'd agreed to marry him. Maggie would never, not in a million years, admit she admired Fitz Kelleran, but she could allow herself to appreciate him for loving his wife the way he so obviously did.

"Okay." Ellie brushed her hands over her jeans. "Talk."

"It's about Wayne."

"Yeah?" She frowned. "What about him?"

"He…he and I…Wayne and I—"

"Oh, my God." Ellie closed her eyes and groaned. "I knew you'd make me sick."

"Wait a minute." Maggie nudged Noodle closer. "It's not what you think."

"How do you know what I think?" Ellie covered her face with her hands. "I don't even want to think what I'm thinking."

"Then don't. Stop." Maggie readjusted her grip on the reins. "Nothing happened."

"Nothing?" Ellie peeked through a gap in her fingers. "Nothing happened?"

"Well…"

"I don't want to hear about it."

"All right."

Ellie dropped her hands and reached for the ignition. "If we're finished with this talk you wanted to have, you can just take Noodle and head on out to—"

"Wait a minute." Maggie crossed her hands over the saddle horn and leaned forward. "You didn't automatically assume this had anything to do with the situation with the school board."

"Why would I think that?"

"Isn't that what most people around here would think?" Ellie paused. "Yeah. Probably."

"So why didn't you come to that conclusion?"

"Because I saw the way Wayne was avoiding looking at you at the school board meeting last week."

"What?"

"You know—the bashful routine. He turned red a couple of times, too."

"He did?"

Ellie groaned. "God. We sound like we're in high school."

"I knew it was going to be like this." Maggie fingered the reins. "I almost didn't come out here."

"So why did you?"

"To make sure this…this whatever-it-is is going to be okay with you."

"Maggie." Ellie heaved a huge sigh. "I'm married. Of course it's okay with me if a man I'm not married to makes big brown cow eyes at my recently divorced sister-in-law."

"It doesn't bother you that he was, you know, making cow eyes at you just a few months ago?"

"He never made cow eyes at me. I was strictly a business venture."

"He's not that cold."

"No, he's not. But he's that desperate."

Maggie narrowed her eyes. "You mean desperate enough to be looking in my direction?"

"Any male who doesn't look in your direction is either blind or still in diapers." Ellie rubbed at her cold-reddened nose. "What I meant, is, it must have been desperation that drove him to come sniffing around me last summer. He must have known I wasn't interested and wasn't going to be, but he gave it a shot, anyway."

Ellie paused, her expression troubled. "He wants a family. He wants to make a home, a real home out of that big, empty place of his. He wants it bad enough he's looking real hard for any woman who seems a likely candidate for a wife. And he's needy enough to be looking at some that aren't so likely."

She aimed a pointy finger at Maggie. "And if you hurt him, I'll kick that skinny butt of yours all the way back to Chicago myself."

"I'm not going to hurt him."

"Then why did you ride out here looking for permission to make cow eyes back at him?"

Maggie shifted in the saddle and cast about for some clever retort, but there was nothing to do but accept the fact that Ellie had hit the mark. Again. "I hate it when you do that."

"Yeah. I know."

Thunder rumbled in the distance, and a cold gust of wind tossed Maggie's hair into her eyes. "Rain's coming. Better head back."

"Yeah." Ellie fiddled with the ignition key. "So…anything else you want to talk to me about?"

"Like what?"

"Oh, I don't know." She shrugged. "Now that I've heard this much, I might as well hear the rest."

"What else could there be?"

"Did he kiss you?"

"Oh, yeah." Liquid heat pooled in Maggie's center at the memory of Wayne's hands tangling in her hair and that big, solid body rubbing against hers. She closed her eyes with a satisfied sigh. "Did he ever."

Her eyes opened again and she stared at her sister-in-law. "Did he ever kiss you?"

"Once." Ellie dismissed the experience with a matter-of-fact shrug. "It wasn't even lukewarm."

"All right, then," Maggie said with relief.

"Did you get what you wanted when you came looking for me?" Ellie asked. "You got things squared away now?"

"Yeah. Thanks."

Yeah, right. Things weren't any more squared away at that moment than they'd been the moment before.

JODY MOTORED ACROSS the creek bridge on one of the ranch ATVs on Sunday afternoon, headed toward the log cabin where she'd lived until her father's death. It seemed odd, sometimes, to knock on the door and wait for an invitation to enter, but the strange feelings were fading. For several months now—since Fitz had bought the ranch in July—the little cabin with the sloping porch roof and the river rock chimney had been Aunt Maggie's place.

She crossed her fingers on the four-wheeler's handlebars and wished extra hard that Aunt Maggie would stay forever. And right after that, she made a wish for a baby brother or sister.

Tess Owen in the fifth grade had a new baby brother, and he'd been so tiny and wiggly and smelled so sweet when Jody had taken a turn holding him. She'd been hinting to Fitz and her mom that she wouldn't mind taking care of a little brother or sister, but neither of them wanted to discuss babysitting opportunities.

The ATV squelched through a patch of soggy road, and Jody swerved to avoid a low-swooping cottonwood branch as she sped along the creekside path. Soon she spied Aunt Maggie's freshly washed car. Maybe it was a waste of time and effort to fight the mud, like Will said, but Aunt Maggie's stubbornness about certain things was one of the qualities that made her special.

Like the way she drove all the way into Butte, twice a month, just to get her hair trimmed and her nails polished. Or the way she stopped at the florist shop to buy fresh flowers on the way home from the grocery store. Gran said Aunt Maggie was extravagant, but Jody admired the way she could make things seem nicer than they usually were.

She pulled to a stop near the old chicken coop and

shouldered her backpack before trudging up plank steps to the tiny front porch. She knocked once and opened the front door a crack. "Hey, Aunt Maggie."

"Hey, Jody." Aunt Maggie swept into the front room, wearing some Asian kind of robe, all slinky and silky and colored with big parrotlike birds. "I hope you've got some of your gran's snickerdoodles. She told me she made a batch this morning."

"Yep." Jody dropped the pack on the little dining table tucked beneath the wide window in one corner of the room. "I brought some sandwiches, too. I made them myself."

"Roast beef?"

"With horseradish sauce."

"Excellent." Aunt Maggie reached into the pack and fished out the cookies. "All we need now is a flash flood to wash away the bridge and cut us off from civilization—or what passes for civilization around here, anyway—for a week or so."

"I didn't bring enough sandwiches and cookies for a week."

"We don't need them. I've been cooking."

Jody pasted on a wide, fake smile. One thing Aunt Maggie needed to be less extravagant with was her cooking. "Oh, boy."

"Knock it off." Aunt Maggie sashayed back into the kitchen. "I'll admit last weekend's *salade Niçoise* wasn't the best choice for a get-together, so I came up with an easier theme for this one. Mexican."

"Chili?" Jody sniffed, hoping to catch a whiff of pepper. "Nachos?"

"Quesadillas and tomatillo sauce." Her aunt lifted the top of a heavy pot and stirred.

"Is that the sauce?" Jody wrinkled her nose. "It's green."

"It's good."

"That's what you said about that Japanese stuff."

"Sushi." Aunt Maggie clanged the spoon against the side of the pot and set it on a small plate. "I didn't hear any complaints."

"That's 'cause I'm a good sport."

"And that's why I put up with your lip."

Jody grinned. "What are we doing today?"

"Pedicures." Aunt Maggie looked down at her toes and wiggled them. "I'm in the mood for something pink and frosty."

Jody pulled out a chair and plopped down at the table to watch her aunt grate a block of orange cheese—the perfect opportunity to casually introduce the topic that was on her mind most of the time these days. "Aunt Maggie?"

"Hmm?"

"When did you first start liking boys?"

"Boys?" Aunt Maggie glanced over her shoulder. "What do you mean 'liking,' exactly?"

"I mean, you know, *liking* them. Like you want to hang out with them and stuff."

"Let me think." Aunt Maggie spread the grated

cheese over tortillas. "I guess I had my first serious crush on a guy, oh, when I was in the fifth grade. Rollie Stromstad."

"Mr. Stromstad?" Jody made a gagging sound. "You can't be serious. He's fat and bald."

"He wasn't bald in the fifth grade." Aunt Maggie turned and wiggled her eyebrows up and down. "And he let me ride his new barrel racing pony."

"But what about like on a date?" Jody asked.

"Ahh. *That* kind of liking." Aunt Maggie moved to the sink to wash her hands. "It sort of snuck up on me, I guess. One moment I thought I'd die if a boy actually tried to kiss me, and the next moment I thought I'd die if a boy didn't."

This was exactly the kind of stuff Jody had been wanting to hear from another girl. None of her friends had any real experience. None that she could trust, anyway.

It wasn't that she couldn't talk to her mom about these things. It was just that her mom tended to turn all red and give really short answers, shoving things into place as if everything had a quick solution. Sometimes Jody wanted to drift along on these new feelings, afraid they might settle too quickly and lose all their mystery.

And other times she wanted to take the mystery out of the whole process before the butterflies in her stomach made her feel like she'd explode from the tickling. It was all so confusing.

"So," said Jody, "did you start wanting to go out on dates when you started liking boys?"

"Oh, I liked boys long before I got asked out the first time."

"That's because boys aren't as mature as girls." Jody had read that in her magazines often enough to accept the theory as fact.

"What's the reason for the dating questions? Or should I say who?" Aunt Maggie lifted a bottle of pink lotion from a wire-handled shopping bag and set it on the table. "Is there a boy you like?"

"Lucas Guthrie."

His name came out in a big, hot rush of air that seemed to set the butterflies free. Saying his name out loud was like uttering a charm or casting a spell. Suddenly she was free to talk about everything, free to open up and let her feelings escape and drift along on the outside for a change. "I think he's so cute. Don't you?"

"You do realize I'm not exactly attracted to guys in the seventh grade."

"I know." Jody rolled her eyes and leaned forward, wanting someone else to wallow with her in all of Lucas's finer qualities. "But he's *so* cute, don't you think?"

"What's important is that you think he's cute." Aunt Maggie opened the bottle and sniffed. "It doesn't matter what anyone else thinks."

Jody groaned and rested her forehead on her arms. "But he's cute, right?"

"Is this the Lucas Guthrie who's the tallest boy in the seventh grade?"

"Yes."

"The Lucas Guthrie who's got big blue eyes and a dimple in one cheek when he smiles?"

"Yes." Jody groaned again. She loved his dimple.

"Well, then."

She lifted her chin and stared at her aunt.

"If I were a girl in the seventh grade—or the sixth grade," Aunt Maggie added, "I'd think Lucas Guthrie was absolutely gorgeous."

"He is, isn't he?"

Aunt Maggie turned to check her ugly green sauce. "You know, Lucas's dad probably isn't too happy with me right now."

"I know." Jody stared down at her hands. "Rachel Dotson said something about it."

"What I'm doing…the revue. It isn't going to cause any problems for you, is it?"

"I don't know." The butterflies in Jody's stomach began to whirl and buzz. "I don't think so."

"I hope not." Aunt Maggie slid the tortillas into the microwave. "Because I'm counting on your help with it."

"My help?" Jody swallowed. "I can't act."

"You did a great job as an extra last summer, walking around on the film set."

She hadn't forgotten that Fitz had arranged a tiny part for her in his film. But Aunt Maggie was suggesting something completely different.

And Lucas would be watching this time.

Jody clasped her hands together and squeezed. "I

don't know if I could go out on the stage in front of all those people."

Aunt Maggie sighed and leaned against the counter. "Oh, well. I suppose one actor in the family is enough. And in Fitz's case, it's definitely more than enough."

Fitz had been so proud of her that day on the film set. He'd probably be really disappointed if she didn't give acting another try.

"I want to help." Jody smiled bravely. "I'll do it."

She hoped Lucas would understand about her family connections and expectations. But she had a feeling he wasn't going to be happy with the situation, no matter what she did.

The butterflies fluttered away, and a cold, hard knot took their place.

CHAPTER TWELVE

"EXCUSE ME, Thea," said Maggie from the principal's office doorway on Wednesday morning. "Have you got a minute?"

"Yes, Maggie. Please, come in." Thea removed her glasses and rubbed the bridge of her nose. "I could use a break. Too much time staring at the monitor makes me a little bleary."

Maggie handed her a thin booklet. "The script for the airplane skit. You're playing 'Passenger Number Two.'"

"How many lines do I have?" Thea flipped through the pages. "Enough to steal the scene, if I want to?"

"That's up to you." Maggie smiled and settled into the visitor's chair facing Thea's big oak desk. "You know, your fellow actors are very excited about working with you."

"And I'm looking forward to spending some unofficial time with them." The creases at the corners of her pale eyes deepened with amusement. "The auditions last night were a lot of fun. I never imagined Sam Ingersoll could be such a ham."

"If you had him in class it wouldn't come as such

a surprise. He definitely enjoys being the center of attention."

"Then this revue should give him a good dose of it."

"Yes, it will." Maggie crossed one leg over the other and smoothed her herringbone tweed skirt. "I'm thinking of giving him a special part, one with lots of lines. One that will keep him so busy he'll stay out of trouble."

"That should make his mother happy."

"The fact that Shelby Ingersoll is a school board member has nothing to do with my decision." Maggie aligned the edges of the scripts in her lap. "He was great last night."

"Yes, he was." Thea removed her glasses and wiped the lenses with a handkerchief. "I thought everyone did well."

"They're a wonderful group of students." Maggie smiled again. "I'm going to enjoy working with them."

This revue had come to mean so much more than a way to spotlight her proposal or strengthen her résumé. She truly enjoyed working with the students at Tucker High. They were unaffected and enthusiastic. They didn't hesitate to express genuine emotions or appreciation, and they supported each other and their school with a fierce loyalty.

She'd miss them, all of them.

Thea opened a drawer and slid the script inside. "This is an unusual idea of yours, mixing students with staff."

"We tried it at Lakeland Academy, back in Chicago. It was great fun." Maggie's smile widened over the memories. "I'm betting that seeing their teachers onstage may be an even bigger draw for the students than watching their peers."

"Ah, yes. A bigger audience. More ticket sales."

"And more backstage management." Maggie tapped the stack of scripts against her leg. "It's going to be crowded backstage the night of the performance. Having more than one adult in the immediate vicinity will help keep the chaos to a minimum."

Thea tilted back in her swivel chair. "As I said before, you've certainly thought things through."

"There's a lot to think about with a project this complicated. Extra sets, costumes, props. A staggered rehearsal schedule. The start of hunting season. But I'm enjoying the challenge. It's keeping me out of trouble, too," she added with another smile.

Thea shifted in her seat. "You've planned a very tight schedule. A performance in less than four weeks. Why the rush?"

"To keep everyone focused and fresh. These short scenes can be prepared and rehearsed quickly. And I want to keep the pressure on the school board, to keep my proposal in the members' minds."

Maggie hesitated. She needed to be open with Thea about everything. "And there's one more reason—my second reason for coming to see you this afternoon. I got a call from the school in San Francisco. They'd like me to come out for an interview."

"When?"

"By the end of next week, if possible."

Maggie gazed out the window at the Tobacco Root Mountains towering over Tucker's rooftops, comparing the view to one of soaring buildings and sparkling bay water. Considering the pleasures of city living in a milder climate, weighing the delights of shopping, and theater-going, and museum-visiting, of working with more sophisticated peers in a more challenging academic setting.

Missing her family already, more than she thought she might. Missing her laid-back friends in Tucker, more than she imagined she would.

"I'm thinking Friday might work," she said, "if you could find a substitute teacher."

"Of course. I'll arrange for whatever you need." Thea leaned forward and clasped her hands tightly. "I don't suppose there's any chance I can convince you to stay."

"There's always a chance." Maggie rose from her chair. "Break a leg, Thea."

WAYNE DROVE HIS TRUCK down one of the narrow ranch roads late Thursday afternoon, grateful to be closer to a hot shower, a warm dinner and an early dive into his soft bed. He faced another early day tomorrow, with less than a week to see to business matters with his foreman before the first round of hunt guests arrived.

Tightening his grip on the steering wheel, he reviewed his plans for opening weekend. Benita's husband, Roy McGee, would prove he was the best guide in southwest Montana, helping the visiting executives get their kills and ship home quality venison. Benita would serve up satisfying fare with plenty of sass. And the visiting telecommunications specialist and the commercial banker would once again ask Wayne to reserve their spots for next September when he delivered them to the airport in Butte.

Last year the businessmen had discussed a couple of promising business ventures while sampling the wine in the cellar. Wayne had reserved a few bottles in hopes of another enlightening evening.

If the weather held, if the hunt trips went well, if he pleased his guests and his side business continued to grow by word of mouth, he could ease back on his worries about paying off the loan he'd taken to expand and improve his house. There were a lot of ifs on that list—and he wasn't the kind of man who was comfortable with the risks they represented—but his other investments were doing well enough lately to tide him over in a pinch.

He'd likely never feel completely secure about his financial situation, not after the rough days following his father's death, when he'd stretched payments and fended off creditors. He swore he'd never have to live like that again.

He turned his truck up the smooth stretch of gravel leading to his garage and spied Maggie's shiny SUV parked near his front door.

"What the hell does she want now?" he muttered

with a martyred sigh. But his system geared up for action and his blood pulsed hot and heavy by the time he stomped through his mudroom door.

He stalked through his house, moving from the kitchen, thick with the cinnamon-sweet scent of hot apple pie, through the dining room, where the table sported Sunday-best linens, and into the great room, where the remains of the morning's fire glowed behind the massive wrought-iron screen. "Benita!"

"Hold your horses," came her scolding reply from the direction of the guest wing. "We heard you come in. What do you want, a brass band to welcome you back?"

We heard you come in. He paused in the wide hallway. "Is Maggie here?"

"She's here." Benita stepped out to scowl at him from a guest room doorway. "She's busy."

Wayne stuck his hands in his pockets and rocked back on his heels. "I'll just be in my office, then."

"Suit yourself." The guest room door slammed shut behind her.

He slowly climbed the stairs to the second floor, thinking of the paperwork he should squeeze in before dinner. But as he fell into the deep leather seat at his desk and punched absentmindedly at the keyboard, the knowledge that Maggie was somewhere in his house—and the flood of sweet, hot memories that thought unleashed—proved a powerful distraction.

"Hey, Wayne." The woman on his mind sauntered into his office and dropped into the oversize chair in the corner.

"Hey, Maggie."

"How's it going?" she asked.

"Well enough."

"Glad to hear it." She crossed one long, jeans-clad leg over the other. Stylish suede boots covered her long, narrow feet. He wondered if her toenails were still painted red.

"By the way," she said, "I'm not staying for dinner, so you can—"

"I didn't invite you."

She tilted her head and gave him a bemused look. "No, you didn't."

"And I don't s'pose I could change your mind, even if I tried."

"Well, now." Her lips turned up in a wicked smile. "That might depend on how hard you worked at it."

"I'm mighty tired tonight," he said with an apologetic smile. "I might not be up to the effort."

"Or up for anything else, either."

His face warmed, and he dropped his eyes to the floor. He decided to let that last remark pass by. "What were you and Benita working on?"

"Costumes. For the revue." Her suspended foot swayed like a lazy pendulum. "I hope you don't mind us working here. It's easier for Benita this way, and since she's doing me a favor…"

"No, I don't mind."

She straightened, shifting to business mode. "I know you don't want or need reports on my proposal's progress, but I'd like to fill you in."

He tipped back in his chair and listened to her news, enjoying the expressions that flitted across her features and the way her slender hands waved to emphasize a point. Her energy filled the room, filled him, reviving his spirits with a dreamy pleasure.

How's it going?

Well enough.

How was your day, dear? And yours?

What's for dinner? What do you want to do after dinner?

And after that?

"What do you think?" she asked, jarring him from his meandering daydream.

"About the progress on your revue? I think it doesn't matter what I think."

"Technically? No." She smiled and stood. "But that won't stop me from fishing for compliments."

He walked with her to the door. "You don't have to fish, Maggie. You're doing a good job with this. With everything. More than anyone here expected."

"And why is that?" She crossed her arms and leaned against the jamb. "Doesn't anyone around here think I'm capable?"

"No one in Tucker doubts your abilities." He gave in to the temptation to touch her and brushed her bangs from her eyes. "It's the reasons behind the extras that have me concerned."

She frowned. "Don't you trust me?"

"To do a good job?" He dropped his hand into his pocket. "Absolutely."

"And the thing you don't trust me with?"

"Sticking around to see it through to the end."

He tried to read what was behind her wide blue eyes. Maybe it was her own confusion about the matter that was making what he saw in her features so difficult to translate.

Maybe he'd better stop projecting his own wishful thinking into the situation.

And maybe it was time to stop all the second-guessing and self-lecturing and accept what was. He enjoyed her company, and he wanted more of it. He wanted *her.* And if all he was meant to have with her was a few short weeks, it was past time to quit all the guesswork and make the most of whatever she chose to share.

He'd dealt with a woman leaving him before. He could do it again.

"I'd better go," she said. "I promised Jody I'd take her to town tonight, treat her and a couple of her friends to burgers at Walt's."

"I'll see you to your car."

They walked in companionable silence through the upstairs hall, down the long, open staircase to the airy great room, out to the front porch and her car. Her presence seemed to fill the empty spaces of his house.

He waited beside her while she scrounged in her purse for her keys. "I don't suppose you'd care to eat Walt's burgers twice in one week?"

Her head snapped up and her eyes met his. "Are you asking me out on a date, Hammond?"

"Yes, I believe I am."

"Hmm." Her boots shifted on the gravel and her brow wrinkled. "Well."

"If it's that hard to make up your mind, maybe I should withdraw the offer."

"Oh, my mind's made up," she said with one of her sly smiles. "I'm trying to figure how to work a date into this weekend's schedule. I need to squeeze in some stage cleanup sessions between all the rehearsals."

"And then there's the football game tomorrow night," he said.

"Yes." Her smile faded a bit around the edges. "The game."

"How about a horseback ride on Sunday morning? Bright and early?"

"What time does 'bright and early' start around here?" she asked suspiciously.

He laughed and wrapped his arms around her, hauling her up against him. He wouldn't think about the funding proposals or the revue. Or San Francisco. "I'm going to kiss you now, Maggie."

She slid one hand around the back of his neck. "I was hoping you would."

He lowered his mouth to her throat first, enjoying the

way she tipped back her head to give him better access and the buzz her soft moan made beneath his lips. "Were you?"

"Yes." She nipped at his earlobe. "I was wondering if you'd pick up on the signals I was sending."

He brushed a series of featherlight kisses along her jaw. "What signals were those?"

She tangled her fingers in the hair at his nape. "I can't tell you. It's against girl rules."

"Then you'll have to show me," he whispered against her lips.

He brushed his mouth over hers once, twice, and then the casual mood dissolved into something pounding and molten, dark and devastating.

She arched against him, and he shoved her against the car door, pressing his length along her front, punishing them both with deep, stroking, liquid kisses. She dropped her purse and twined a leg around one of his, and he ground his hips against hers, and her fingers speared through his hair to pull him closer, faster, and his arms tightened around her to drag her nearer, harder.

A gust of wind swirled bits of grass hay and fir needles around them, and a red-tailed hawk screamed in annoyance above. On and on the insanity surged, spiraling out of control, sucking him down into a place where all he was aware of was her ragged breath in his ears and the echoing rush in his blood and the feel of her against his lips, his hands, his hips. More, more—he wanted more of her. It wasn't enough.

It would never be enough.

He rested his forehead against hers and closed his eyes with the effort of keeping his voice from quaking like the rest of him. "What's your answer, Maggie? Will you go riding with me?"

"Yes," she whispered. She ran a hand along his face in a gentle caress, and he noticed she was trembling, too. "My answer was always *yes*."

THE LIGHTS STREAMING down on the Tucker High football field Friday night seemed to carve up the frosty air as if it were imported crystal. Wes Dunaway's amiable drawl rumbled from the speakers, announcing fund-raising baked goods at the snack stand and a special deal on snow tires at Simm's Garage. The tang of tobacco coasting on tiny gray clouds and the aroma of coffee curling from foam cups, the flashes of smiles on wind-chapped faces and the glint of silver on high-brimmed Stetsons, the muffled scritch of popcorn in red-striped paper sacks and the crunch of peanut shells underfoot, the shifting mass of down jackets and dark denim huddled in the bleachers—up in the stands, every Tucker football game seemed to feature the same old players and the same old plays.

Wayne leaned against the low chain-link divider separating the worn wooden bleachers and the home team's benches, eavesdropping on the chat between the referees while he scanned the crowd in the tiers above, looking for Maggie.

"Hey, Wayne." Trace Bardett eased in beside him, taking one last drag before flipping aside a cigarette butt.

"Hey, Trace."

"Fine night for a game."

"Fine night for just about anything."

"Good hunting weather."

"Yep." Wayne glanced at the dusting of stars and thought of his guests flying into Butte next weekend. "Hope it holds."

"Hey, Hammond. Bardett." Frank Guthrie joined them and studied the field. "Looks like our boys have a good shot at beating Madison tonight."

"Looks like it, all right," said Trace.

Over the speakers, Wes's voice kicked up a notch in enthusiasm as he announced the appearance of Tucker High's cheerleaders. A half dozen girls in bulky sweaters and short, boxy skirts jogged out onto the field, and the crowd in the stands applauded and whistled.

"Got the ball in the air too much, though," said Guthrie. "Too many chances for interception. Wonder when Coach Buchanan is going to pull his head out of his ass and start using his line to gain some yardage. It's what they're there for."

"Don't be so hard on him, Frank," said Trace. "It's not like he's got a lot of depth on the bench to turn to if he loses one of his stars to an injury."

Above them, a familiar tune blared through the

speakers, and the girls on the field began their dance routine.

"I'm not saying anything anyone else hasn't been saying for weeks," said Frank. "It's like I told—

"What the hell?" Trace whipped around to stare at the field. "What the hell is going on around here?"

"What?" asked Guthrie, squinting at the dance squad. "What is it?"

Wayne turned to take a look for himself. Out on the trampled grass, the girls were swinging their hips and waving their arms about in the usual combination of in- comprehensible moves and gestures. But tonight their dance steps seemed a bit jazzier, matching the music they moved to: "There's No Business Like Show Business."

"Nice routine." Maggie squeezed in among the men and wrapped her fingers around the chain-link triangles on the top of the barrier. Her eyes laughed up at Wayne. "Don't you think so?"

"I think you're asking for trouble," he said.

"Is this your doing?" Trace glared at Maggie. Before she could answer he stomped off toward the stairs leading to the announcer's hut, with Guthrie dogging his heels.

Wayne imagined half of the folks in the bleachers behind him were beginning another debate on the proposal issue, and the other half were wondering what he was doing cozying up to the one person standing between them and new bleachers to sit in.

"It's called subliminal advertising," said Maggie.

"I know what it is," he said, "and there's nothing subliminal about it."

"The next number is 'That's Entertainment,'" said Maggie. "It's a personal favorite of mine these days."

"How did you pull this off?" He was tempted to throttle her—after he kissed her senseless. "You *are* responsible for this, aren't you?"

"You're not the only one with community connections, Hammond. I'm using the ones I've got, and working hard on making plenty more."

"You don't fight fair, do you, Maggie?"

"I fight with everything I've got."

His gaze dipped to her mouth and back up to her eyes. "That's what I meant."

"Why, Mr. Hammond." She tilted her head and gave him a smug smile. "I do believe you just paid me a compliment. Or two."

"That's some mighty creative accounting, Ms. Sinclair." He tugged at the brim of his hat in a farewell salute. "But cooking the books might land you in some mighty hot water."

CHAPTER THIRTEEN

MAGGIE SURPRISED HERSELF on Sunday morning by climbing from bed before her alarm started its irritating chirping. A fast shower, a faster breakfast, and a speedy session in front of her dresser mirror helped her arrive in Wayne's front drive at nine o'clock.

He ambled out on his porch, all long legs and wide shoulders and soulful brown eyes. She told herself her heart was racing only because he was carrying two of his oversize mugs, but she wasn't buying it. The man seemed to get more tempting every time she laid eyes on him.

"I hope one of those is for me," she said as she jogged up the slate steps.

"I figured if I saw you before noon you'd be needing it." He handed her a coffee with a shy smile. "Welcome, Maggie."

She took the mug and went up on her toes to give him a quick thank-you peck on the cheek. He caught her around the waist and lowered his mouth to hers for one of his breath-robbing kisses.

Oh, my. If her heart started pumping and thumping

any harder than it was at that moment, she'd have to skip
the caffeine.

"Mmm," she said when he set her loose. "Coffee
and kisses. Twice the jolt."

He took her hand and led her around the side of the
house toward a tall white barn. Their boots crunched on
the chipped gravel, sending mourning cloak butterflies
flitting among the fading asters that listed beside the
fence posts. The late September sun warmed her back.
"Nice day for a ride," she said.

"Nice day for a lot of things," he answered, and then
he briefly squeezed her hand before releasing it and
stepping into the barn's dark interior.

She hesitated at the entry to let her eyes adjust to the
sudden change in light, and then she followed him to a
center support post where two saddled horses were tied
with leads.

"This is Dixie," he said, running a hand down a roan
mare's pretty face. "She'll take good care of you."

"Hey, Dixie." Maggie let her have a getting-to-know-
you snuffle before untying the lead. "You be nice to me,
you hear? I'm a little out of practice."

Wayne ducked into a tack room and emerged with
two bridles. He tightened the saddle girths and gave
Maggie a leg up, and then they headed out of the barn
and turned east, moving in an easy jog past neat
paddocks, toward the mountains.

The horses swished through an open hay meadow
dotted with silvery yarrow and blushing mountain hol-

lyhocks. In the distance, a red willow hedgerow marked a trout stream, and above them a pair of buzzards coasted in a lazy spiral, crooked black gashes against powder-puff clouds and a blue-grey sky.

"How're you and Dixie getting along?"

"Just fine." Maggie patted the mare's warm neck and smiled. "She's a sweetheart."

"Feeling up to a race?"

"Where to?"

"See that snag up—"

She touched her heels to Dixie's sides and shot ahead. A moment later she heard thunder behind her, gaining fast.

They galloped through the tall grass, the horses' hoofs drumming a wild bass rhythm against the hard ground and their manes whipping in the wind. Maggie's heart raced as if it were a separate part of the competition, leaping and thrilling to the speed and the freedom. Laughter bubbled up, a wild and carefree tickle she couldn't hold back, even when he edged past her and they reined to a stop near the snag.

He slid from his saddle and strode to her side, his arms upstretched. "Come down from there."

She reached for his shoulders and slipped into his embrace, and she laughed again as he made a show of staggering beneath the burden and collapsing on the ground, rolling under her as they fell.

He turned again and trapped her beneath him, tossing one of his long legs over hers, his big body settling

with a pleasing weight on top of her, and then he carefully brushed her hair from her eyes as one of his
bashful smiles softened his features. "You sure are
pretty, Maggie."

"Thank you." She relaxed in the sweet-smelling
grass and waited for him to kiss her. She was beginning
to crave his kisses.

"But your racing start needs some work," he said.

She shoved him away and raised herself on one
elbow. "Guess I'm out of practice with that, too."

"We're both out of practice with a lot of things." He
shifted to his side, stretching out on the grass with his
arm crooked to rest his chin on his hand. "I haven't been
with a woman like this since Alicia left. My dating
conversation's kind of rusty."

"You're doing just fine." She plucked aimlessly at the
grass and let it drift from her fingers. "That was the first
time you've mentioned your ex-wife. Most newly
divorced people tend to talk about nothing but their
exes."

"You've never mentioned yours."

She frowned. "That's because he's not worth mentioning."

"He must have had some special quality to make
you fall in love with him."

"It was purely physical," she said with a disgusted
sigh. "He is one of the handsomest men I've ever met."

"He is handsome." Wayne nodded in agreement. "He
was walking down the street one day when I was having

lunch at the Beaverhead. I pointed out the window and said, 'who is that handsome man,' and Loretta told me who he was."

"You didn't do any such thing." She tossed a handful of grass his way. "But I'd love to know what else Loretta had to say."

"It's not worth mentioning."

This relaxed and friendly Wayne was a revelation. They hadn't needed an argument to get things going, and they hadn't soaked their inhibitions in wine. She was beginning to appreciate his understated humor and to read his quiet expressions.

She was beginning to like him a great deal more than she had.

"I was attracted to Alan at first because of his looks," she continued. "And because he was charming, and intellectual and engaging, and popular with his students. He was my instructor in a grad-level university class."

"He was your teacher?"

She shrugged at Wayne's disapproving frown. "It wasn't exactly ethical, but we were consenting adults. And then I thought I might be pregnant, and he asked me to marry him."

He waited for more, studying her with those deep, dark eyes full of quiet patience and understanding, and she knew she could tell him everything.

"I wasn't pregnant. I was—" She took a deep breath and shook her head. "I'll never be pregnant. I...I can't."

He squeezed his eyes shut and grew very still.

Several long, silent moments opened up between them, and then he fell on his back and gazed up at the sky. "I'm sorry for that, Maggie. Truly sorry."

She worked her jaw, but the sincere regret in his voice made it too difficult to force words through the feelings.

"So," he said after another long, empty minute had passed, "handsome, charming Alan married you because he thought you were pregnant?"

"No." She straightened and drew up her legs to cross her arms over her knees. "We knew by then that I wasn't. But we started talking about what ifs, and taking ourselves—our relationship—more seriously. And one thing led to another, and we got married."

"You stayed married a long time."

"Nearly eight years. Not so very long."

"Longer than I was married."

Now it was her turn to wait, prepared to listen to whatever he wanted her to know.

"A lot of people think Alicia was wrong to leave me the way she did," he said at last. "But it was the right thing to do. She was unhappy here, and there was nothing I could do to make it right."

"Why did you marry her?"

"She made me laugh."

He smiled at some secret memory, and it hurt her heart to see how lonely and lost that smile made him seem.

"She knew me in a different way than everyone else around here knows me," he said. "She didn't have any preconceived notions about who I am or what I'm supposed to do."

Maggie remembered the boy he'd been in high school, the shame he'd lived with and the struggle he'd faced to overcome it. "Those kinds of notions can be a terrible burden," she said.

He turned his head to look at her. "I s'pose you understand the burdens and notions a little better than most people."

"I think everyone in a town like Tucker feels a little trapped every now and then." She smiled. "The trick is to find a way out."

"By leaving?"

"Or by reinventing yourself so thoroughly that no one remembers who you were before."

He frowned and turned his face away from her, staring again at the sky. "You can never leave that person behind."

"You can try." She brushed her fingers along his shoulder. "Maybe the effort is all that matters, in the long run. It's who you are inside that counts."

He reached up and caught her hand in his. "Wise words, Maggie. I wonder if you'd agree that they're true for everyone."

She pulled her hand away and stood, brushing bits of grass and leaves from her clothes. "I suppose you think I should test my theory on myself," she said, "before I start applying it to others."

He got to his feet and headed toward the horses. "Today I don't want to think about anything more strenuous than racing you back to the house to see what Benita left in the refrigerator."

She watched him gather up the reins and run his big hands over his stock in his quiet, steady way, and she tried not to think about how easy it would be to slip from liking him into loving him.

MAGGIE MARCHED into the Harrison mudroom that afternoon, grumbling to herself about the sophomore class essays waiting to be graded and the freshmen class lesson plans needing to be written. Designing sets, trolling for donations, shopping for props, arranging for scenery and directing rehearsals didn't leave much time for her regular job. And what in the world was so important that her niece had phoned and insisted she rush right over? "Jody!"

"In the parlor."

Cursing under her breath, Maggie made her way toward the front of the house. As she moved through the dining room, the rich perfume of dozens of roses assaulted her. "Here we go again."

In the second parlor, Jenna arranged pink long-stemmed roses in an old earthenware pitcher. "I think Fitz sent more this time than when he was courting," she said. "I've run out of vases."

"At least we won't have to buy any flowers for his funeral," said Maggie. "Whatever he did this time, he must think Ellie's going to kill him." She leaned forward to inhale the heavenly scent of a perfect pink bud. "Although he's sure got a nice way of making up."

"He's not in trouble." Jody clipped another stem before handing it to her grandmother. "He's celebrating."

"What's the deal? It's about ten months too early for their anniversary."

"Ellie's in her room," said Jenna. "Go ask her."

Maggie stared at Jody and her mother, curious about this mystery that only Ellie could reveal. She made it halfway up the wide front stairway before she figured it out, and then she let out a whoop and dashed down the hall to the door of the room her former sister-in-law shared with Fitz. "You're pregnant."

Ellie hauled herself higher against the bed pillows stacked behind her back. "They told you."

"I guessed. It wasn't hard." She settled carefully on the bed but couldn't resist throwing her arms around Ellie for a quick, tight hug. "Two people who can't keep their hands off each other for five minutes in a row, a man who's crazy about your family and obviously wants one of his own, a house full of flowers…"

She gave Ellie's shoulders one last squeeze before edging back. "I'd have to be blind and deaf, and incapable of smelling the roses not to figure out the results."

Ellie plucked at the old chenille spread. "Fitz is pretty pleased with himself."

"I expect we'll see the news on all the major networks tonight." Maggie closed her hand over Ellie's. "How are you feeling?"

"Sick as a dog, just like I was with Jody." Her smile was beatific. "And pretty pleased with myself, too."

"I'm so happy," said Maggie as she laced her fingers more tightly through Ellie's. "For both of you."

"You'll have this someday, too."

Maggie pulled her hand away. "Four out of five fertility specialists disagree."

"Alan wasn't the right man to be the father of your children. When you meet the right one, then things will work out the way they're supposed to."

"It's biology, not magic." Maggie rolled her eyes. "And why am I explaining this to a rancher?"

"It's biology, sure. Part of it." Ellie rubbed her hand across her flat belly. "But part of it's still magic."

Maggie watched her sister-in-law's hand move over the place where her tiny niece or nephew slept, and another wave of happiness surged through her. "You're right. It is magic."

She scooted closer. "What do you want, a boy or a girl? What does Fitz think? What did he say when you told him?"

"I know what I want." Jody came into the room and climbed up next to her mother. "Twins. A boy and a girl."

"Shut your mouth," said Ellie, looking a little green. "And hold still. You're making me seasick."

"Better clear a path to the bathroom door." Jody motioned Maggie away from the bed. "We've had some close calls the last couple of days."

Maggie stood and gazed at Ellie with sympathy. "Is there anything I can do?"

"No, thanks." Ellie leaned her head back against the pillows and closed her eyes with a sigh. "I'll be okay in a couple of months."

"And this is what you're hoping I come down with." Maggie backed out of the room, certain that Jody would pester and pamper Ellie enough for them all.

She wandered slowly down the hallway, pausing to admire the same pictures that had been hanging in the same places for as long as she could remember. Great-grandma's painting of the mountain range beyond the pastures, her mother's first engagement portrait, Tom as a toddler. And there was a five-year-old Maggie astride her first pony, smiling at the camera with a dark gap in the middle of her grin. The family changed and shifted, but in this lavender-scented hallway, people and places were caught and suspended in time.

She gazed at the pieces of her childhood and felt suspended, too, trapped again in this time and this place, snagged in the same starting place while around her the rest of her family moved on, expanded, grew.

She wouldn't be able to have the child Ellie wished for her, but she could have the man—the right man, in the right time and the right place.

Wayne Hammond wasn't that man. He was too much a part of this place she'd always longed to escape.

The last thing he needed was to get involved with a woman like her, another woman like Alicia, who would leave him for the city. And she wouldn't let herself settle again for a man and a situation that weren't exactly what she wanted.

A case of lust had clouded her better judgment all those years ago in Chicago, had set in motion events that had brought her back here to square one. This time she wouldn't let herself fall for the trap of a physical attraction, for a pair of deep, dark eyes and kisses that curled her toes. She wanted more, she needed more.

She needed to get her life back.

CHAPTER FOURTEEN

A JAGGED WHITE SHARD of lightning split the inky sky above Wayne's office Monday evening. Brutal wind battered his window and howled through the trees it threatened to topple. The rain was holding off, but he doubted they'd make it through the night without a soaking.

He checked another online weather report, receiving another reassurance that the weather would clear in time for the weekend's hunting trip. He only hoped the snow wouldn't stray too far below the forecast elevations.

Another crack of thunder nearly disguised the pounding at his front door. He hurried through his darkened house, flicking on lights as he approached the entry.

The wind sucked at the door as he opened it. *"Maggie."*

She moved past him into the great room, toward the fire, and dropped a craft store bag on a nearby sofa. Her thin cloth jacket and matching short skirt weren't much protection against the rapidly falling temperatures.

"Let me get you a drink," he said. "Some brandy to warm you up."

She shot him a brief smile. "Trust you to have a wine for every occasion."

"I can make some hot cocoa, if you like," he said.

"Tempting. But no, thanks." She gestured at the bag on the sofa. "I came to drop this off for Benita."

"She's not here."

"I didn't figure she would be." She combed reddened fingers through her hair. "I'm sorry to disturb you. I know this isn't a good time, but rehearsals ran late, and I—"

"Sit down," he said. "Put your feet up for a bit. You must be chilled clear through, out on a night like this. I'll build up the fire, bring you a blanket."

"No." She shook her head. "I've got to get going. I've got papers to correct and lesson notes to organize for tomorrow."

"You're dead on your feet."

"And I s'pose I look like it, too." She sent him another weak smile and climbed the steps toward the door. "I doubt I'd be good company with all I've got on my mind."

He took her arm. "Maggie—"

"Not tonight, Wayne." She stilled, waiting until he dropped his hand. "Please make sure that Benita gets her package."

He opened the door, and a cold gust swirled inside and around them. She hesitated at the threshhold, and then she went up on her toes to give him a light, impersonal kiss on the cheek before heading out into the night.

He braced himself in the doorway, holding steady

against the wind while his thoughts chased each other in their endless circles, about his position on the school board and her project that made things so damn difficult. About his loneliness and her leaving, about what he needed and what she wanted.

About his desire for family and her inability to have one.

He closed his eyes against a fresh wave of pain. The situation between them was as tangled as cottonwood branches whipping about in the storm.

THE THREATENING RAIN HIT as Maggie headed down Wayne's ranch road, streaming from the blackness to pelt the windshield, obscuring everything but the darting silver droplets caught in the headlights. The tires jounced and slid over unseen bumps and thickening mud, and she shifted to four-wheel drive and tightened her grip on the steering wheel as the wicked night shoved her stormy mood back to envelop her.

The car's twin beams caught the pale endposts of an intersection with a narrow service road, and in the next moment they bounced across a black, rain-streaked form and flashed in rolling, white-rimmed eyes. Maggie slammed both feet on the brake, and the tires spun over slick mud and gravel, sending the car into a wild fishtail and then a tilting, sickening spin. She wondered, as her fingers were torn from the wheel, whether that jarring thump was her rear end smashing into the white face that had wandered into the road. And then she was thrown against the seat belt as the car jerked to a stop.

She reached for the ignition, but her fingers were shaking too hard to close around the key. The cheerful voice on the radio announced another tune by Wynonna as Maggie's heart ricocheted around her ribs. She wasn't sure which way she was facing, whether the front end of her car was angled toward the ranch exit or Wayne's house, whether her tires were inches from the ditch on the south side of the road or her fender was caught in a wire fence. The wipers beat their own chant: *stupid, stupid, stupid.*

No, not stupid. Out of luck, out of control. Everything—this day, her job, her personal life—out of control. She'd run aground in bitterly familiar territory. Lowering her head to the steering wheel, she dragged in deep, trembling gulps of air, fighting the tears that threatened to suck her into a bottomless well of rage and grief and fear.

Damn her husband for betraying her, and damn her body for betraying her, and damn her own notions of what was best for herself—and best for everyone else, too. Damn, damn, *damn.*

Propelled by a wave of despair, she wrestled her way out of her safety belt and clawed at the door handle. Slicing rain plastered her hair to her forehead and soaked the front of her suit, and mud oozed around her heels as she stepped from the car. The wind did its best to beat her back, pummeling her as she staggered toward the front of the car. In the headlights she could see a road stretching ahead. No ditch, no fencing, no black carcass.

No indication of her direction.

Shivering, she climbed back into the driver's seat, forcing herself to focus on her options. She could continue in the direction she was pointed and take a chance on reaching the main road or Wayne's house. But if she headed down the service road by mistake, she might lose her way in the night or miss a chance to turn back. No matter what she decided, she had to contact Wayne about his wandering—and possibly dead or injured—livestock.

"I'm not going to cry. *I'm not going to cry,*" she said, grinding her teeth to keep them from chattering. She pawed through her purse with shock-clumsy hands and pulled out her cell phone, and then the first hot tear plopped on her lap as her fingers refused to cooperate and hit the right numbers. Her vision blurred, and she squeezed the phone against her chest with a choking moan.

"I want to go ba-ack. I w-want to go home. I want to have a home to go to." She rocked against the back of her seat. "I want a child. I want—oh, God, I want what Ellie has. What my mother has. I want a life. I want…someone. I want someone to love me. I want my life back, the way it used to be."

No, no, she didn't want that, not really. She didn't want a cheating, overbearing husband and a high-pressure job and meaningless climbs up ever-lengthening social and professional ladders.

She didn't know what she wanted. And she didn't want to worry about it, to make a decision about what her life would be. What it *should* be. Not now, not when she was cold and wet and needy and miserable and oh, so very tired. She slumped back against the seat. "I'm so tired. So tired."

Eventually her sobs eased, and her eyes cleared, and the cold creeping in around her brought her to her senses. She picked up the phone again and pressed the keys. *"Wayne."*

"Maggie? Is that you?"

"Yes. I—I'm out on your road. Somewhere. I'm not sure where, exactly. There was a white face—"

"Are you in your car?" His deep voice was steady and comforting, and the sound of it made her weepy again.

"Ye-es," she said with a huge sniff.

"Stay right there. I'll come find you."

She disconnected and let the phone slip from her fingers. The rain beat against the windshield, and gusts of wind rocked the car, and she wondered again if she'd killed the cow in the road. If it was lying out there in the dark, wounded and helpless and suffering, and another tear slipped down her cheek as she imagined the pain she might have caused.

Blinding light filled the tilted rearview mirror and swung past her, and then another wave of cold and wet swept over her as Wayne yanked open her door. His long, strong arms slid around her and hauled her against him. Rain stung her face before she buried it against his shoulder, and then he bent and caught her up behind her knees and carried her to his truck.

"Is the cow dead?" she asked, her voice muffled against the coarse denim of his jacket.

"I don't know." He swung her into the warm truck cab and settled her on the bench seat. "My foreman's going to check it out."

"Where's my car? Is it ruined?"

He shut her door and trudged around the front of his truck, hunched against the wind and the rain, and then pulled his door open to slide in behind the wheel. "Don't you worry about any of it right now. I'll take care of everything."

"Are you taking me home?"

"Yes."

She didn't ask which home he had in mind. It didn't matter, anyway. She didn't have a home here, not really. Her head fell against the stiff back of the seat, and she closed her eyes. The cab smelled of wet wool and sweet grass hay, and the heater blasted currents of hot, stuffy air at her throat and ankles.

He handed her a flask. "You're going to drink some of that brandy after all."

She tipped the tiny opening toward her lips, and the fiery liquid slid down her throat, making her cough to clear it. "I'm sorry I bothered you."

"I'm not too sure about that anymore." He shifted to her side and pulled her into his lap, cradling her against his chest as he tugged a scratchy blanket around her shoulders. "You seem to be making a habit of it."

"I would have checked things out back there for myself, but—"

"But you forgot to wear those boots I told you to get."

She started to laugh, but it came out on something like a sob, and he pulled her against him and let her shiver and settle and find some peace in the folds of his damp jacket.

It was so pleasant to burrow deep, to soak up the heat of his big body while his arms tightened around her and his wide hand rubbed slow circles over her shoulder, to let go and let someone else take charge for a while. Someone bigger, and more substantial, and steady, so steady.

So patient with her. "I'm sorry, Wayne."

"For what, specifically?"

"For coming back here and messing things up."

His fingers scraped along her scalp, pushing her damp hair from her face in a tender, practical gesture. "Sorry, Maggie, but that's one apology I can't accept."

She breathed in the scorched air and the arid tang of the brandy. Wayne stroked her hair in a soothing, hypnotic rhythm while the shock waves ebbed and the adrenaline rush subsided, leaving her fogged and drowsy. Her puffy, aching eyelids drifted closed.

"Maggie."

"Hmm?"

"I'd better call Granite Ridge and let someone know where you are."

"You don't need to do that." She sighed against him. "I don't check in with them, and they don't expect me to."

"Knowing Will Winterhawk like I do, I'll bet he's all too aware of your comings and goings up and down every inch of those ranch roads."

She frowned against his chest. "Sometimes I hate all this nosiness about my business."

"And sometimes it's good to know folks care enough to watch out for you."

She tipped her head back against his arm and gave him a sleepy look through her lashes. "Is that what you're doing? Watching out for me?"

"Sweetheart, when you're around, I'm aware of every move you make." His lips closed over hers in a warm, tender caress.

"You're right," she said on a sigh. "That's good to know."

And it was. Very good. Comforting and reassuring, nothing that fired up her warning systems or pricked at her privacy, nothing that smothered her independence or crowded her boundaries. Nothing that added another item to her load of responsibilities or another layer to her pile of guilt.

He shifted against the bench seat and tugged the blanket more tightly around them both. She knew, in some dim corner of her mind, that her pleasure in his embrace wasn't right, that she shouldn't seek more of this kind of comfort from him, but her spirit seemed aimless, weightless, lost in sensation. At this moment, nothing made as much sense as the firm support of his body and the splay of his fingers across her back, the gentleness of his touch and the tenderness in his kisses that swept through her and made her feel so very cherished.

She drifted, floating on the dry, spicy wine and the steamy atmosphere in the truck and the solid frame of the man beneath her, she struggling to keep her promises of the day before—all those cold and harsh things she'd told herself outside Ellie's room. But as his warmth and steadiness seeped into her, her memories and visions clouded with confusion, and her decisions and judgment seemed storm damaged and off kilter.

What was one more mistake in the final equation?

Without waiting for her own answer, she surrendered to the inevitable and sank below the surface of reason and into a murky, rippling pool of need. And as she lifted a hand and wrapped it around Wayne's neck as if he were a life-preserver, the last traces of her shakiness disappeared.

She pulled his face closer to hers. *"Wayne,"* she whispered against his lips.

"Maggie," he answered in that way he had of speaking her name, and the sound of it was the best thing she'd ever heard. She pressed her mouth against his, seeking more of his steadiness. He responded, giving her more of his strength.

She waited for his kiss to deepen, demanded it with the rasp of her teeth across his lips, and he gave her that, too. She tasted his desire and met it with impatience. He dragged her higher and ravished her mouth.

"I want to feel you against me," she said, slipping the first of his shirt buttons through its hole. "I want you to warm me up, all the way through."

He stilled, and her breath caught through what seemed an eternity of heartbeats, and then the blanket fell to the floor as he twisted the jacket from her shoulders. His teeth sank into the skin at the base of her throat, and her neck arched back as she fought for air, while his rough, warm hands raced over her, frenzied and punishing, yanking her jacket over her wrists and cupping her breasts, teasing and thrilling.

He heaved them both into a new position and she toppled against him. His chest rose and fell with each labored breath, lifting her up and dropping her in a giddy ride. Lust pumped through her system, making her wild and reckless. She popped the next few buttons and dragged his sleeves down his arms, imprisoning them at his sides. He struggled and managed to slide his hand along her hip, raising the edge of her skirt.

She pried at his belt, tugging the leather through the buckle.

"What are you doing?" he asked.

"You'll figure it out."

He strained and grabbed for her busy fingers as she undid the first button on his jeans. "Not so fast."

She smiled against his lips and continued to work her way down his front. "You want to slow this down?"

"I want to stop and discuss a few things before we get in over our heads here."

"I'm already in over my head." She caught his lower lip between her teeth. "Come on in, Wayne. The water's fine."

He groaned when she touched her tongue to his, and shuddered when her fingers found him, and plunged up into her when she took him inside, and then she was warm, so warm, all the way through. Falling, and floundering, and out of control, riding the raging, pounding beat of their rhythm, lost in the pulsing thrill of their passion.

And she knew, when that passion was spent, that he'd help her find her way back—and because of that, she knew she'd want him again, and soon.

WHILE WAYNE FOLLOWED Maggie's car to the parking spot in front of her cabin he had plenty of time to do plenty of swearing, and only some of it involved making serious vows.

Why hadn't he stopped and called Will the moment he'd thought to do it? Why hadn't he sent Maggie away from him the moment their kisses got a little too hot to handle? Why hadn't he fought her a little harder when she—

Yeah, right. Like that was going to happen. There was only so much a weak and sorry specimen such as himself could put a stop to, and Maggie Harrison Sinclair bent on seduction wasn't one of the items on the list.

But that didn't mean he couldn't make an effort to do things right—or at least do them better—the next time.

God, he hoped there was going to be a next time.

He climbed from his truck to walk her to her door. "This can't happen again."

"What can't happen?" She let them inside and flipped on the front room light. "Making love?"

"I mean, I want—I want to make love with you again, but it can't happen like that."

"Like what, exactly?"

"Without protection."

She set her briefcase on a table. "I haven't been with anyone in nearly a year. And from what you've told me, neither have you."

"That's not the only thing to worry about."

"Yes. It is." She ran her hand through her hair. "I told you, I won't get pregnant. I can't."

He caught her hand and brought it to his lips to kiss her palm. "I'm sorry, Maggie. I didn't mean to make you feel low."

"You didn't. You don't. You make me feel good. Amazingly *good*." She stepped in close to him and ran her hand down his jacket front. "Of course, I may have played a small part in the mutual satisfaction department."

He nodded. "You might have at that."

"And now I'm wishing we had some of that protection you set such store by," she said, "so I could give you a proper thank-you and good-night."

He took her by the shoulders and kept his distance when he kissed her. "That's proper enough for us both."

Turning his back on the invitation in her eyes and walking out of her cabin was one of the hardest things he'd ever done.

CHAPTER FIFTEEN

WAYNE SHOULDERED HIS way through the entrance to Pollard's drug store the next morning, wishing he could spare the time for a shopping expedition to Butte. There were moments such as these in which Tucker's small-town charm wore a bit thin.

"Morning, Wayne." Janie Bardett waved from the periodical stand.

"Morning, Janie." He ambled over, knowing he'd have to wait until Janie left the store. In fact, he'd prefer to be the only customer on the premises when he was ready to make his move toward the personal care aisle. "What's new?"

"Not much." She flipped through the last few pages of a shiny tabloid and then set it back in its slot on the shelf. "I was thinking there might be something in here about Fitz and Ellie's baby. But now that he's turned respectable, no one seems to care anymore what he does."

"It's probably too soon for something to show up in print." He picked up a hunting magazine and studied the cover. "And maybe they're trying to keep it quiet."

"You know that's just about impossible around here."

He stifled a sigh and tucked the magazine under his arm. It would make a handy piece of camouflage. "I s'pose so."

The bell over the door signaled another customer, and he peered around a display and smothered a groan. Brenda Moseley, Janie's good friend and Tucker's best source of local gossip, stomped in and folded her umbrella into a limp and soggy bundle. Now the two women would likely start chatting and trap him in here indefinitely.

Maybe he should cross the street to the Beaverhead. He could get a window booth and a cup of coffee, and watch for his chance to make his purchase in private.

And maybe he should stop wasting his time, get what he came in here to get and step up to the counter like a man. He moved down one of the aisles closest to his final destination and let his eyes drift over a selection of denture adhesives, antifungal ointments, cold remedies and dietary supplements.

"Hey, Wayne," said Inez Pollard from her station behind the cash register. She tore open an envelope and glanced at its contents before tossing the entire mess aside and picking up the next piece of mail.

"Hey, Inez." He rubbed a hand over his chin and reached for a tube of toothpaste. He didn't need any, but the extra tube wouldn't go to waste.

"Nasty weather out there last night," said Inez. "I heard the snow line's dropped another thousand feet."

"Yep. Heard that, too." Might as well pick up an

extra toothbrush while he was at it. Maybe a couple, for unexpected overnight company.

Or the expected kind. He hadn't had to consider details like this for quite a while. Not that he minded. He caught himself grinning like a kid with his fingers latched on to something sweet in the cookie jar and coughed into his hand.

"Coming down with something?" asked Inez. "We got some new cough drops on aisle five." She named a brand he'd never heard of and continued to sort her mail.

Aisle five—right where he wanted to be. "Thanks, Inez. I don't feel too poorly, but cough drops might help with this tickle."

He ducked around the corner and made a couple of quick passes by the boxes of condoms stacked right below eye level. So many brands and features. Why the hell did people need so many choices?

He snatched a likely looking product off the shelf and rolled it in the hunting magazine along with the toothpaste. And then he turned and nearly ran down Brenda, who'd been standing behind him. "Excuse me," he muttered.

"No harm done." She gave him a knowing smile and stepped out of his way.

The store's main door swung open, knocking the little bell into a tinkling dance. "Morning, Inez," called the new customer.

"Morning, Jenna."

Damnation.

MAGGIE TUCKED HER hands into the deep pockets of her comfortable corduroy slacks and strolled into the faculty room during Tuesday's lunch break. Russ Gamble and Maxine Hahn, the math and art teachers, sat across from each other, rehearsing their lines for the toga skit.

"Fabulous, dah-lings," Maggie said with a grin. "You'll be the hit of the show."

"Wait'll you get a load of the costume Thea's putting together for her bit part," said Russ. "She'll have the audience rolling in the aisles before she says her first line."

"Sounds fun."

Maggie slid into the chair across from Harland Moss, the health and physical education instructor. "Hey, Harland."

"Hey." He picked up his soda and glared at her over the rim.

"I need to borrow the track pistol."

"What for?"

"For the revue."

"It's a track pistol."

"I know, Harland," said Maggie with as much patience as she could muster. "It's the school's track pistol. And it's a school revue."

"It belongs to the physical education department."

"I'm certain it does." Maggie gave him her sweetest smile. "And I'm certain an allowance can be made in this case, seeing as it's not exactly track season."

"I'm not sure about that," said Harland, shaking his head. "Wouldn't want it to get misplaced or broken."

"I wouldn't want that to happen, either." Maggie folded her hands on the table and leaned forward. "That's why I want you to bring it backstage and fire it yourself the night of the performance."

Harland blinked. "You want me backstage?"

"I need a sound effects engineer, Harland. Someone who can stay focused, who won't lose his cool. Someone I can trust to do things with absolute precision. That gun has to go off at exactly the right moment, or a pivotal scene will be ruined."

"Track pistols are reliable more than ninety-nine percent of the time," he said.

"Is that so?" Maggie widened her smile. "I knew I'd come to the right person. So, you'll do it, Harland? You'll save the burglary scene from possible disaster?"

"I'll think about it," he said, and then he took a sip of his soda.

But he wasn't glaring at her anymore.

JODY'S HEART BANGED against her ribs as Lucas and Kevin Turley walked toward her lunch table. He hadn't come near her for days. She didn't want to think he'd been avoiding her, but she expected the worst.

"Hey, Lucas," she said with her brightest smile.

He paused, and for one excruciating moment she thought he was going to walk right by without saying anything. "Hey, Jody," he mumbled.

Kevin punched him in the arm. "Come on, Guthrie. We gotta go."

"Jenna packed oatmeal-raisin cookies this morning," said Jody. She winced at the pitiful, begging sound of her voice.

"Huh," he said with a furtive glance at the brown bag behind her on the table.

Kevin walked off, and Lucas frowned. "Gotta go," he said, and then he jogged after his friend.

Chrissy muttered something loyal and sympathetic, but all Jody heard was Rachel Dotson's nasty laugh. She forced herself to take another bite of her sandwich, to chew and swallow and nod at whatever Chrissy was saying, but inside she was imagining crawling into her bed at home and pulling her pillow over her head, and already counting the moments until she could do exactly that.

WAYNE GRABBED a fast burger lunch at Walt's before heading out to the edge of town to make his last stop of the day. He pulled into a parking spot in the lumberyard attached to Pete Cooley's hardware store and climbed out of his truck.

He found Pete in the back, sticking price tags on gallon cans of paint with a little plastic gizmo. "Afternoon, Pete."

"Hey, Wayne." Pete straightened and stretched with a groan. "What brings you in today?"

"Need a couple of pounds of short grabbers." He followed the elderly proprietor through the store and propped himself up with one elbow on the counter while

Pete dropped a scoop of screws into a hanging scale. "Things been busy this week?"

"Not so much." Pete pulled a carpenter's pencil from behind one ear and noted the price on a paper sack. "Been meaning to talk to you."

"Oh? What about?"

"That girlfriend of yours has been in to see me a couple of times."

"She's not my girlfriend."

Pete leveled a disbelieving look at him.

Wayne bit back a sigh. "And what does Maggie coming in here to talk to you have to do with me?"

Pete slid the nails into the bag. "She wanted me to cut up some scrap lumber for the stage. Some one-by-fours."

"For the stage, huh?" Wayne straightened. "She say what she was going to do with it?"

"Build some flats." He handed the bag to Wayne. "Whatever the hell those are."

Wayne folded the end of the bag over in a neat line. "So? You got what she wants?"

"I don't have a whole lot of one-bys on hand. I could probably come close by ripping some two-bys." Pete shook his head. "The problem is, what she has in mind isn't exactly scrap. More like seconds. And then there's the added labor."

"I suppose she could find someone else to cut them up for her, if you're too busy."

"I'm not too busy." Pete cleared his throat. "The problem isn't the labor."

"Is it the lumber? Don't you have anything she can use?"

"You know I could probably find something. But that's not the point."

"What is the point?" asked Wayne.

"She wants it for that theatrical production of hers."

"I see."

Wayne made another fold in his bag. "You've earned yourself quite a reputation for always being real generous with donations for local causes, Pete. It's no surprise she'd have made this her first stop."

The storekeeper shrugged. "I do what I can."

"I know that, and I appreciate it." Wayne smiled pleasantly. "People like you make my job on the school board a whole lot easier, believe me. And if you choose not to make this particular donation at this particular time, well, I certainly wouldn't hold something like that against you. Wouldn't change the way I think of you one bit, you can be sure of that."

Pete nodded and shoved his hands into his work apron pockets.

"And don't you go getting yourself a guilty conscience over turning Maggie down, either." Wayne pressed the crease of his bag. "I'm sure you've got your reasons, and they're no one's business but your own."

"That's right."

"Times are tough," Wayne said with a sigh. "They always are, but people feel the pinch a bit more sometimes than they do at others. And if you can't afford to spare some seconds for a school fund-raiser, well, like I said, that's no one's business but yours, and no one's going to think less of you for it."

Pete hitched one shoulder in a tight shrug. "Things aren't so bad."

"I'm relieved to hear it. Real happy, considering how worried I was getting there for a moment." Wayne leaned on the counter again. "Of course, Frank won't be too happy to hear you're not going to be able to donate the lumber for the bleacher forms, seeing as how you don't have any scraps or seconds available."

Pete narrowed his eyes at him.

"I saw a copy of Frank's estimate," said Wayne, "and I know he was counting on some of that famous generosity of yours. But don't you worry," he added with a smile, "I'm sure we'll all be able to figure something out."

Pete was silent for a few moments. "You know something, Hammond?"

"What's that?"

"I think you missed your calling when you decided to stick around and make a go of your daddy's ranch." He managed a weak smile. "I think you could have been one hell of a lawyer."

"You think so?"

"Yep." Pete nodded. "And it looks like I'll be discussing the possibility of donating some scrap lumber for those flats with that girlfriend of yours real soon."

"She's not my girlfriend."

Pete's cackling laughter followed Wayne out the hardware store door.

AFTER HER FINAL CLASS that afternoon, Maggie dropped an unusually quiet and subdued Jody at Chrissy Fowler's house and then headed to the hardware store in one last attempt to get old man Cooley to cough up some lumber for the flats. After a quick, successful chat with Cooley—and a lengthier, illuminating chat with Reva Dickerson, Cooley's chatty customer who just happened to mention hearing about a certain purchase in Pollard's drug store that very morning—Maggie decided to make an unscheduled detour to Wayne's ranch.

She climbed out of her car and jogged up the steps to his wide front door. "Hammond!" she called as she lifted the big iron knocker and let it fall. "I know you're in there."

He opened the door and stared down at her. "You're right. I am."

"Is Benita in there, too?"

"It's her day off."

Maggie placed a hand square on his chest and pushed him inside. And then she jumped into his arms and wrapped her legs around his waist and covered his face with quick, breathless kisses.

"You annoying—" she kissed his cheek "—interfering—" and his nose "—indiscreet—" and then she settled on his lips for one heavenly second. "Wonderful man."

"Mmm." He spread his fingers across the back of her head and trapped her against his mouth for a longer, deeper kiss. "Tell me what I did, and I'll do it again."

"You talked Pete Cooley into donating the lumber for the flats."

He shook his head and pried her legs from his waist. "If Pete decided to do such a generous thing, he decided it all on his own."

"Uh-uh. You can't weasel out of this one. There were witnesses. You were brilliant, I heard. A real politician." She pressed her lips to his again with a loud smack and wriggled to the floor.

And then she gave him a good, hard shove. "And I ought to slap you silly for barging in like that on my behalf, as if I couldn't manage things on my own. I won't tolerate it, do you hear me?"

"Yes, I hear you." He winced and rubbed his chest. "The thing is, Maggie, this donation is good for the school."

"I know it is," she said, swatting the hair out of her eyes. She'd missed her last beauty trip to Butte, and she was beginning to look a little ragged around the edges. "That's why I'm doing it."

"And what's good for the school deserves the support of the school board."

"Don't you play this game with me, Hammond." She pointed a finger at him. "I've been watching your moves, and I know what you're trying to pull here."

"What is that?"

"You're going to mosey on along in that oh, so pleasant but slightly confused and bemused tone of voice," she said, "circling around me, cutting off all my escape routes and arguments until I reach the conclusion you wanted me to reach all along. Aren't you?"

He gave her a confused and bemused—and not entirely innocent—half grin. "How could I pull off a stunt like that with such a clever woman?"

"You won't, 'cause I'm not giving you the chance."

She moved into his great room to stare out the window at the mountains. The snow line was dropping; winter would be here soon. "I want you to stay out of this, Wayne. You're in trouble enough with some people because of the perception that you're siding with me on my proposal for Kelleran's donation."

"I'm not siding with anyone."

"We'll see about that," she said, tossing a challenging glance over her shoulder. "But I said the *perception* is that you're taking my side in this. I don't want to cause problems for you."

"I can handle my own problems."

She turned to face him, her hands on her hips. "And so can I."

He scratched at the back of his neck. "You know, you're not so bad at circling around things yourself."

"By the way, that's not all I found out." She wiggled her eyebrows and started across the room toward him. "You were a busy boy, from what I heard."

"Oh?" His brow furrowed with confusion, and then his face turned positively crimson before he dropped his gaze to the floor. "*Oh.*"

"I think you're about to get even busier." She began to unbutton his shirt. "Very, very busy."

He grabbed her hands before she could undo the next button. "Maggie."

"Yes?"

"We...we need to talk about this."

"About what?"

"About what I bought at the drugstore this afternoon. About what it means."

She moved her hands, still trapped in his, behind his back and stepped up against him. "I know what it means when a man buys a supply of condoms, Wayne."

"It wasn't exactly a supply."

She smothered a smile and kissed the base of his throat. "I'm sorry. It must be embarrassing having everyone in town know what you're doing and who you're doing it with."

His throat worked beneath her lips. "Everyone?"

"You know," she said as she pulled her hands from his loosened grip, "I have to be back to school for evening rehearsals in about two hours." She started work on the next button. "If you want to do a little consumer research on today's purchase, I could probably, you know, squeeze you in."

He narrowed his eyes at her. "You've got a fresh mouth on you sometimes, you know that?"

"My mother used to scrub it clean on a regular basis." She pushed his shirt off his shoulders. "Oh, my, I do love a man with muscles."

He sucked in his breath when she closed her teeth over his nipple. *"Maggie."*

"Yes?"

"I think we'd better go open that box."

"I think that's a very good idea."

"I just wish we had more time." He lowered his face to hers for a scorching kiss. "I don't like to be rushed into things."

Two hours later, Maggie had a deeper understanding of what a solid and steady man—a patient and thorough man, the kind of man who cared about details, who thought a project through and took care to do it right—could do to a woman when he finally got her into his bed.

CHAPTER SIXTEEN

MAGGIE GLANCED AT Jody's somber profile on the drive home from school on Thursday. "Anything new?"

"No."

"Anything you want to talk about?"

"No."

"Nothing?"

"Nothing to say," said Jody with a jerky shrug. "Guess I'm just tired."

Maggie bit back a sigh and tried not to worry too much about her niece's listless behavior the past couple of days. It was probably just some minor teen trouble. Still, she'd make a point to talk to Ellie about it and offer to help if she could.

"For cryin' out loud." Maggie squeezed her SUV into the one spot left on the gravel drive near the main ranch house's back door. "It's getting to look like Grand Central Station around here."

"That's Fitz's truck!" Jody threw open her door before Maggie had a chance to turn off the ignition. "He's back early!"

"Oh, joy," said Maggie under her breath. But she was

relieved that whatever problem Jody had, her stepfather seemed to be the cure.

Inside the mudroom, she added her coat to the growing assortment of outerwear hanging from the old brass hooks and finger-combed her hair. The aroma of baking bread mingled with faintly floral fabric softener and the earthy smell of manure-streaked boots. "Home sweet home."

"Maggie? Is that you?" Her mother walked around the corner and secured Jody's jacket before it fell from its hook. "I hope you can stay for dinner?"

"I'd like that, thanks." No time like the present to make a personal report on theater project progress to the man who'd be funding it. "Need any help?"

"No, thank you. Fitz and I have everything under control."

"Fitz is cooking?" The man had plenty of faults, but he made up for most of them in the kitchen. "What's he making?"

"A salad. And a fancy dessert. He brought me a little blowtorch. For making crème brûlée."

"My, my. Aren't we getting fancy around here?"

"Behave," said her mother with a stern look, "or I'll cancel the dinner invitation."

Fitz peeked around the corner. "Don't let her make you resort to idle threats, Jenna. Go ahead, cancel it."

Jenna rolled her eyes. "If this is a sample of what I can expect at the table tonight, I'll have to separate you two. One of you will be eating in the kitchen. Alone."

"One of us lives here," said Fitz.

"And one of us is an invited guest," said Maggie.

"You're family, not a guest," said Jenna. "Besides, we have a real guest. Fitz brought Nora with him."

Nora Daniels had been Fitz's leading lady in the film shot at Granite Ridge the summer before. She'd struck up a friendship with Jenna, soaking up her mothering during the early stages of her pregnancy.

"How's she doing?" asked Maggie.

"She's a little tired from the trip, poor dear," said Jenna. "She's upstairs, resting. I'm glad she's here, where I can fuss over her a bit. She deserves a little pampering, what with her divorce and all, don't you think?"

"I'm sure your pampering is the main reason she came all this way," said Maggie. "How long is she staying?"

"As long as she wants to," said Jenna. "I'll enjoy the company." She headed back into the kitchen, and Maggie listened to her scold Jody about getting into the after-school cookies before she took her things upstairs to her room, followed by the sound of Jody's feet pounding on the treads.

Nora Daniels, here on an extended visit. She might get bored with life on the ranch and accept an invitation to help with the revue.

Which would probably increase the level of community participation.

"I can almost hear the gears turning in that devious mind of yours." Fitz leaned a shoulder against the doorjamb and slanted across the opening, barring Maggie's path to the kitchen. "What are you plotting?"

"Besides your imminent demise?" She raised an eyebrow. "I'm wondering what you're going to do for a follow-up to the crème brûlée."

"Want to play with the blowtorch?" One side of his mouth kicked up in a teasing grin. "How about if I toss in a can of gasoline?"

"So sweet of you to offer."

He looked tired, the laugh lines at the corners of those famous cornflower-blue eyes more pronounced than usual. He and Nora must have begun their trip before dawn in order to arrive in time for dinner, and Maggie knew from experience that Jenna's fussing was nothing compared to the way Fitz could worry and hover over and care for his long-time friend.

Now that he'd delivered her, safe and sound, into Jenna's care, he'd have a few more hours to spend with his wife and stepdaughter. It was obvious that extra time with family and friends was more precious to him than his own comfort.

She tilted her head with a smile. "By the way, congratulations. *Daddy*."

His features softened with amazement. "How about that?"

"I think it's wonderful." She brushed a brief kiss across his cheek. "I missed you, Kelleran. Welcome back."

"Fawning will get you nowhere." He swiped at her lipstick smudge. "I didn't bring you a present."

Fitz's habit of bringing gifts from every trip to Los Angeles irritated Ellie, and he'd been cutting back.

"I don't need a bribe," said Maggie.

"'Bribe' is too delicate a term. I think of it more as protection."

"You don't need that, either."

"Why not?" He gave her a suspicious look. "What's your angle?"

"Dinner." She stepped over his feet and grabbed a chocolate-chunk cookie from the plate on the kitchen table. "What are we having, anyway?"

"Stew," said Jenna from the sink. "And Fitz's salad."

"Chopped broccoli and walnuts with cranberries and coleslaw dressing," he said.

"Sounds good," said Maggie.

Fitz narrowed his eyes at her. "It does?"

"You're making it." She smiled sweetly. "Don't you think so?"

Jody thumped back down the stairs and launched herself at Fitz. "Thank you, thank you, thank you!"

He caught her up and hugged her close. "You're welcome. But whatever it is you're thanking me for, I didn't buy it for you. Nora did."

Jody pulled back and grinned at him. "Liar."

"It wasn't me. I swear."

"Chicken."

"That's right, and I've got the yellow feathers to prove it," he said. "Didn't you read the card? It said, 'To Jody, from Nora.'"

"It was in your handwriting."

"Are you sure about that?" He gave her one more squeeze and let her go. "Maybe you'd better go get it. We can use it for blowtorch practice."

"Look!" She wriggled away and held up a hand to display an oversize gemstone on her finger. "It's so cool!"

"A bling ring." Maggie snagged her niece's hand for a closer look. "*Very* cool. Aquamarine?"

"Topaz," said Fitz. "Not that I would know anything about it, since it's from Nora."

"What's a bling ring?" Jenna tapped a stirring spoon on the edge of the stew pot as Jody danced over to show her. "Oh, my goodness, look at that. It's so…so big."

Jody fluttered her fingers. "Look how it sparkles."

"Anyone within a quarter mile could see that thing shine," said Jenna with a shake of her head. "Fitz, I wouldn't want to be in your shoes when Ellie sees this."

"It's from Nora," he insisted.

"You should see Nora's stomach," Jody told Maggie. "It's getting *huge*."

"I doubt it's all that big," said Maggie. "She's only about five or six months along."

"I can hardly wait until Mom's stomach starts sticking out," said Jody. She lifted her arm toward the fixture over the sink, twisting her hand to catch the light and crowding Jenna at the cooktop.

"Better take that ring upstairs and put it away," Jenna said, "before you blind us all."

Maggie was curious about the other glittery items Fitz might have picked up at the jewelers. "What did Ellie get?"

"Besides me?" he asked with a wicked grin.

"Forget I asked."

Jenna pulled a loaf of bread from the oven. "Set the table, would you, Maggie?"

"Sure." She headed toward the dining room, where Jenna kept the linens for the big table.

"For eight," Jenna added.

"Eight?" Maggie paused at the door. "Who else is coming?"

"Wayne."

Wayne Hammond. Sitting down to dinner with Fitz. And Ellie. And her mother.

"I ran into him at the post office this morning," said Jenna. "He told me Benita went to Bozeman for her niece's *quinceañera* this weekend. He's all alone over there, and we've always got room for one more here. Besides," she added with a meaningful look, "I didn't think you'd mind, under the circumstances."

"I don't," said Maggie.

"What circumstances?" asked Fitz.

"Nothing that needs to be discussed here, at the moment." Jenna's cheeks were turning a warm pink. "Especially since it's being discussed all over town."

The drugstore. *Protection.* Maggie suspected her cheeks were getting every bit as pink as her mother's.

"Use the good china," said Jenna. "I know we're

having plain old stew, but it's starting to feel like a party tonight."

"Sounds like fun." Fitz's grin was wicked.

Maggie stifled a groan. "Whoop-dee-do."

MAGGIE SPREAD an ivory linen cloth over her great-great-grandmother's wide table and trimmed the stems on some of Ellie's roses to make a fat bouquet for the centerpiece. She chose Hannah Harrison's pink Spode and embroidered napkins to match, and added the Sunday-best silverware and crystal.

As she leaned across the table to straighten ivory tapers in silver candlestick holders, the muffled *thunk* of the front door's horseshoe knocker signaled Wayne's arrival.

"I'll get it," she called out. She practically skidded around the corner before slowing to a more decorous pace through the twin parlors. Pausing at the mirrored antique hat rack, she fluffed her hair and took a steadying breath. And then she opened the massive entry door.

"Hey, Maggie." Wayne stepped across the threshold, dashingly handsome in grey flannel slacks and a shawl-collared navy sweater. He handed her two bottles of wine and bent to kiss her cheek.

She twisted her neck, straining to keep him from hitting his target. "Don't do that."

He froze. "Don't do what?"

"Kiss me."

"Why not?"

She glanced behind her toward the stairway landing. "You don't want people to think we're sleeping together, do you?"

"We *are* sleeping together."

He slipped an arm around her waist and caught her before she could duck out of range, the crinkles at the corners of his eyes deepening like silent laughter. His solid body pressed against hers, and the crisp scent of his aftershave smelled more enticing than the aromas in Jenna's kitchen.

"Aren't we?" he asked.

"Well, yes, but—" She made a token, feeble attempt to escape. "Do you want everyone to know it?"

"I don't know." His mouth tipped up at one corner. "Do I?"

"The correct answer to the question is *no*."

His smile spread, slow and teasing, across his face. "I had a feeling that was it."

"So why did you ask?"

"I just wanted to make sure."

He skimmed his lips along the edge of her jaw, pausing at the sensitive spot near her throat. "There's something else I want to be sure about," he said.

"What?" she managed to whisper.

His breath flowed over her ear, hot and moist, making her shiver as he nipped at the flesh beside her earring. "Can I stretch my arm behind your chair during dinner and let my hand accidentally land on your shoulder?"

"No."

His tongue traced the shell of her ear. "How about your breast?"

She exhaled on something between a strangled moan and an exasperated laugh. "Are you enjoying this?"

"Yes."

"Why?"

He gently combed his fingers through her hair. "Because you always get to be the annoying one, and I never get a turn."

"This turn is making up for all the others."

Her eyes fluttered closed as he brushed a kiss, light as a feather, over her lips. "Mmm," she said. "This tastes like something different tonight."

"It does?"

"This is…fun. It tastes like fun."

His hands dropped to her waist to bring her hips in closer contact with his. "We could have ourselves another taste of some fun right now."

"No." She sighed as he bent to press another kiss to the other side of her neck. "Maybe." His lips toyed with her earring. *"Wayne."* She squeezed the wine bottles as her toes curled. "Can't you keep your sense of fun in check tonight?"

"Where's the fun in that?"

She groaned and rolled her eyes. "What is it with you tonight?"

"I'm feeling inspired." His gaze roamed over her face, hot and hungry. "And I want to feel other things, too. Later."

She tried without success to wriggle free. "Stop tempting me."

"I'm tempting you?"

"God, yes."

"Tempting could be a substitute for fun."

"It is," she said as he took one of the wine bottles from her and pressed a warm kiss into her palm. "Oh, it is."

"Maggie," he said as he folded her fingers over the moist spot on her palm.

"Hmm?"

"Jenna's calling."

"Behave." She snatched her hand from his and pointed a stiff finger at his chest. "No kissing. No hand grabbing. No sudden inspiration, of any kind. And no tempting."

A smile spread, slow and seductive, across his features. "How about later?"

She groaned and turned her back on him, heading toward the dining room and likely disaster.

AFTER JENNA HAD accepted Wayne's gift of the dinner wine and Will had admired the label, and after Nora had made her entrance in her larger-than-life style, and after Wayne had been introduced to the lush, exotic actress and cast his usual bashful glances at the floor, the extended Harrison clan sat down and served up autumn salad, beef stew and Jenna's homemade cracked wheat bread along with a steady stream of conversation about the ranch's preparations for winter.

Maggie waited for Ellie to make some remark about Jody's ring, but when she noticed the flash of new diamond drops at Ellie's ears, she figured the subject wouldn't come up anytime soon. So she decided to introduce another topic to steer the conversation away from livestock management. "Jody's doing a wonderful job in rehearsals," she told Fitz. "I hope you'll be able to make it some night to watch."

Jody shot Maggie a panicked glance across the table. "He doesn't want to spoil the surprise before the performance. Do you, Fitz?"

"I'm not going to spoil anything." He lifted his wineglass and sipped. "I'm real proud of you, Jody."

"Thank you," she said with a stiff smile, twisting the ring on her hand.

"Everything is going very well," said Maggie, although she wondered again what was worrying her niece. "Better than I expected it would."

She gave a glowing review of the actors' enthusiasm and the community's support, in addition to explaining for Nora the terms of Fitz's donation. "It's a shame we won't have the new lighting and sound equipment in time for the revue," she added, "so that everyone in the audience could see and hear more easily."

"Yep," said Fitz. "It's a shame, all right. Maybe the board will make a decision in your favor in enough time for you to put a rush order on what you need to make it work."

"And maybe we wouldn't have to wait for the board's decision, if you decided to fund both proposals right now."

"Maggie," said Wayne in a low, warning tone.

"He can afford it."

"That's not the point."

"Yes, it is," said Fitz. "One of the points, anyway."

He took his time, slowly dabbing at one corner of his mouth with his napkin, playing the moment for the maximum dramatic effect. "Maggie's right. I could just as easily donate twice the amount I originally offered."

"Show-off," muttered Ellie. She shot a dark look at her husband and Maggie and poked her spoon into her stew.

Fitz sighed and shook his head, the image of a henpecked husband. "You can see how much trouble I'd land in if I did."

"You wouldn't land in any more trouble than you find yourself in on a daily basis." Maggie shifted forward, pressing her case. "You have to admit, both proposals have merit. It would be better for the school—and even better for your reputation here in town—to fund them both."

"I probably will end up funding them both," said Fitz. "Eventually. With another donation next year."

"Why wait?" asked Maggie.

"Why, indeed?" One of Fitz's devilish grins spread across his features. "What reason could I possibly have for wanting to make things any more difficult for two of my most favorite people in all of Montana?"

"Oh, for cryin' out loud." Ellie snatched up her glass of milk. "Don't tell me you're still holding a grudge against Wayne because of what happened last summer."

CHAPTER SEVENTEEN

"WHAT HAPPENED LAST summer?" Nora paused with a spoonful of stew halfway to her mouth. "What did Wayne do?"

"He asked me to marry him," said Ellie.

"No, I didn't," said Wayne, pausing in his chewing like some placid old cow waiting for another chunk of cud to come up. "You just assumed that's where I was heading."

"Weren't you?" asked Ellie, her eyes narrowed in challenge.

"No way of knowing now." Wayne slathered butter over a thick slice of bread. "Obviously, I didn't make much progress."

"How far did you get?" Nora dropped her spoon in her bowl, looking too fascinated to think about eating.

Wayne shot a glance at Fitz, who was frowning at his meal. "Not all that far."

"Far enough," said Maggie, seizing her chance to give the actor a sample of the grief he'd been giving her all night. "You kissed her."

"You did?" Jody turned to stare at her mother. "He did?"

"He did?" Fitz narrowed his eyes at Ellie. "You never mentioned that part."

"Because it wasn't any big deal." Ellie shrugged a quick apology in Wayne's direction. "It wasn't anything like the way he's been kissing Maggie."

"He has?" Jody's jaw dropped as she shifted her gaze to Maggie. "He's kissed you, too?"

"I think we should change the subject," said Jenna, her face blooming a shade of pink that competed with the roses in the centerpiece. "I don't want to hear a replay of town gossip at my dinner table. Especially in front of little ears."

Jody's eyes widened as she looked at Wayne.

Maggie stifled a groan and concentrated on rearranging the leftover bits of broccoli on her salad plate.

"It sounds like you've been a busy boy, Wayne." Nora dug back into her stew. "I'm feeling a little overlooked."

Fitz's attention was still focused on Ellie. "Why didn't you mention this before?"

"Because," she said with a frown, "it wasn't worth mentioning."

"I happen to think it's worth mentioning when a man kisses you and asks you to marry him—"

"I didn't ask her," Wayne repeated.

"—and I have to wonder why it is that you don't think it's a big enough deal to mention it."

"Well, I didn't at the time." Ellie hunched her shoulders and shot a helpless glance across the table. "Sorry, Wayne."

He shrugged. "No need to apologize."

"More wine, anyone?" Nora picked up the bottle with a brilliant smile. "Wayne? Fitz?"

"I think we've all had enough," Jenna said in an overly bright hostess voice. "Coffee, anyone?"

"I'm not so sure I've had enough," said Will. He handed his glass to Nora. "I'd like some more of that Cabernet, thank you."

Nora dribbled some wine into his goblet. "You know, Fitz, I can see where you might have some objections to Wayne's proposal—"

"I didn't propose," said Wayne.

"—to the *sports* proposal," Nora clarified.

"I didn't make that one, either." Wayne scraped up another bite of stew. "It's Frank Guthrie's idea."

"But if you've already agreed to follow the board's recommendation," Nora persisted, "and if the athletic field gets the board's support, why would you put off fixing up the stage?"

"Yes, Fitz," said Maggie. "Why would you?"

Fitz shifted his scowl from his wife to his sister-in-law. "Because you've been on my case since the moment you met me."

"Not true."

"All right, I take it back. Since *before* you met me."

Jenna sighed. "If you two can't be civil at the table—"

"What's for dessert?" Will interrupted. "I heard there's something special tonight."

"Crème brûlée." Jody broke off a chunk of bread. "You make it with a blowtorch."

"Imagine that," said Will.

"So," said Nora, ignoring the effort to sidetrack the conversation. "If you doubled your donation to the school—"

"I'd be funding athletic field improvements for the best friend of the man who kissed my wife," said Fitz, "and fixing up the stage for the woman who hates my guts."

"I don't hate your guts," said Maggie.

Fitz lifted an eyebrow at Wayne, who continued to chew in guilty silence.

"And if you don't?" Nora persisted.

Fitz's dark expression lightened considerably. "I get to sit back and watch the two of them fight it out between 'em."

"Sounds like fun," said Nora.

"This isn't a game," said Maggie. "This isn't some fight you're refereeing."

"He didn't say it was," Wayne pointed out.

"Ellie." Maggie turned to her sister-in-law. "Tell him it isn't a game."

"It isn't a game, Fitz," Ellie said in a deadpan tone as she extended a hand toward Jenna. "Pass the bread, please."

"It sounds like a game." Jody glanced around the table expectantly.

"It isn't a game." Wayne lowered his spoon to his empty bowl and picked up his glass of wine. "It's a very generous donation, doubled or not. One for which the citizens of Tucker ought to be grateful. One that shouldn't cause such a ruckus getting sorted out."

"This isn't much of a ruckus," said Jody, sounding disappointed.

"I wasn't talking about the dinner conversation," said Wayne. "I was talking about what's been happening around town."

Maggie glared at him. "Are you insinuating that my preparations for this theatrical revue are causing a ruckus?"

Wayne shook his head. "No."

"Good."

"I'm coming right out and saying that your methods are causing some problems."

"Need a little help clearing the table, Jenna?" Will rose from his chair so quickly the china rattled.

"Coward," said Jenna and Ellie in unison.

"That's right." He winked at Jenna as he collected his dishes and disappeared through the kitchen door.

"Which of my methods are you referring to, specifically?" asked Maggie.

Wayne shook his head. "I don't think this is the time or place to get too specific."

"Please," said Fitz, settling back comfortably in his chair with an evil grin. "Go ahead. Be specific."

WAYNE FOLLOWED Maggie's car down the winding ranch road and across the narrow creek bridge to her little log cabin after dinner. He knew he might not be welcome tonight, but he had to take the chance.

He was amazed by all the chances he'd been taking lately. He was even more amazed he wasn't suffering vertigo from all the teetering he was doing on the edge of a cliff with a black and bottomless chasm below.

"I suppose you want to come in for a while," she said as she slammed her car door shut.

"There's a favor I want to ask of you."

"Your timing leaves a lot to be desired." She led the way up the porch steps and into the dark cabin. "I'm fresh out of port."

He smiled at the reminder of their first night together, the first time he'd kissed her.

The first chance he took.

"I can probably find some other way to get you liquored up," she said as she switched on a lamp and flooded the small front room with mellow light.

She turned and flowed into his arms. "Why don't you ask me your favor first, so you don't have to interrupt that liquored-up part later on?"

She went up on her toes to take his lower lip in a soft, gentle nip.

He spread one hand along the back of her waist and the other through her hair to hold her close. "You can be an extremely agreeable woman when you set your mind to it, Maggie Sinclair."

"I can be a great many things you haven't begun to discover." She smiled and slid her hands beneath the hem of his sweater and began to drag it up his torso. A tremor shimmered through him at the scrape of her polished nails along his sides.

"Looks like I'd better hurry and ask that favor," he murmured, and then he lowered his mouth to the side of her throat. Soft. Warm. Woman. *Delicious.*

"Yes," she said with a sigh. The backs of her knuckles teased across his chest. "Hurry."

He smiled as he trailed his lips to her jaw. "Have dinner with me tomorrow night."

She stilled, her fingers clutching his bunched sweater hem. "Tomorrow night?"

"Some hunt guests are coming for the weekend. I thought you might enjoy visiting with some big city folks for a change."

"Normally I'd love to meet your guests, but I'm not going to be here."

"You're not?"

She dropped his sweater hem. "I'm leaving for San Francisco in the morning."

Now it was his turn to freeze in place. "The job interview."

"Thea must have told you." She smoothed the sweater across his chest. "I'll be back in time for revue rehearsals on Saturday afternoon."

"Right. The revue." He wondered what this production was adding to her résumé, and the thought turned him cold. "You wouldn't want to miss any practices."

"Not with the performance coming up so fast. Just two weeks from tomorrow. It'll be here before I know it."

Two weeks. Two weeks, and then she'd be finished here. No matter how the board voted, she'd have accomplished her goal. She'd prove the need for the funds, whether she secured them this year or not. There would be nothing holding her here.

Nothing.

"I'm sorry, Wayne," she said and pressed her lips to his cheek. "I'll have to take a rain check."

Her light, dismissive kiss sent something dark and desperate swirling through him. He fisted his hand in her hair. "No rain check on this," he said as he dragged her against him. "Not on this."

He was still poised at the edge of that cliff, staring into that black, bottomless chasm, and the fear he'd fall made him frantic to take her and hold her like a lifeline, to keep her with him, to make her his. He pulled her into her room and down to her bed, stripped her clothes and took her to the first peak with intense efficiency.

But it wasn't enough. His throat ached and his eyes stung with frustration as he tried, with every stroke of his fingers, to give her more than pleasure. He sought some way, any way to explain, as he gathered her close, what he couldn't express with words. *Do you know how much I cherish you?* he asked as he framed her face in his hands. *I yearn for you every moment you're not with me,* he said as he moved over her, *and*

I treasure every moment we're together, he said as he slipped inside her.

She arched against him on a wave of passion that swept him up and carried him along with her.

Over and over he thrust into her, exulting in the feel of her nails scoring his back and her legs twining with his as she strained closer, her delirious moans filling the dark room.

With each powerful surge of his body, he told her what he wanted her to hear. Needed her to hear. *Don't leave me. Don't leave me. Love me. Love me.*

I love you.

"Wayne, I—"

"Stay with me," he said with a growl. "Stay with me, Maggie."

He held her tight, so tight, and loved her hard, so hard, and took her with him, over the edge.

MAGGIE CLIMBED INTO her SUV on Sunday afternoon and headed to the main ranch house. Images of steep, crowded, noisy city streets seemed to flicker among the naked cottonwoods, and she sighed over her confusion about the job offer.

It was everything she'd told herself she wanted. But lately she wasn't listening to her own lectures.

She probably had too much on her mind—lesson plans, correcting exams, collecting the last of the props, checking on the scenery and costumes. And she continued to worry about Jody's behavior. Her niece seemed tense and withdrawn, apprehensive about her performance and reluctant to discuss the revue. Maggie would try again to get Jody to confide in her.

And then there was her relationship with Wayne. She was getting in over her head, and the fact that she was the least bit tempted to pass up the excellent opportunity in San Francisco and extend her stay in Tucker was setting off warning bells. The lovemaking was incredible—addictive—but she'd already made the mistake of letting a strong physical attraction for a man blind her to a situation that wasn't right for her. She didn't intend to repeat the error.

Besides, what did she really know about Wayne Hammond? A good neighbor, a successful businessman, a respected member of the community. Gentle, kind, patient—all the boy scout qualities neatly in place. But he had too many secrets, too many shadows, and he was too good at tucking them—and himself—away from her.

She'd misjudged Alan, who'd turned out to be nothing more than what was displayed on the surface. How much worse were her chances with a man who had hidden depths buried beneath all the layers?

With a noisy sigh, she walked through the mudroom and into the kitchen, helping herself to the comfort of a butterscotch brownie from the old-fashioned honey-bear cookie jar. In the second parlor she found her mother tucked beside Nora on the bay window settee, their heads bent together over some complicated knitting technique.

"Hey, Nora," Maggie said between mouthfuls of brownie. "Don't you look domestic."

"She's doing so well." Jenna patted her protégée on the knee. "Cables already."

"I've been practicing." Nora smiled and held up a fuzzy, lemony square that was probably the start of a baby's sweater. "There wasn't much to do after the sound work on the film wrapped up."

"Plenty to do around here," said Maggie. She plopped herself down on a pressed-back rocking chair. "I don't suppose you'd like to help out?"

"Me?" Nora lowered the bundle to her lap. "What could I do?"

"Paint sets, direct rehearsals, that sort of thing. You don't sew, by any chance, do you?"

"No." Nora ran a hand over the yarn. "Knitting's the only domestic thing I know how to do."

"Why don't you come into town with me tomorrow night, after dinner?" Maggie stood and started to brush crumbs from her jeans, until she caught her mother's scolding look. "I could use some professional assistance with the blocking for the burglary scene. And I'm sure there must be a better way to stage the airplane scene than what I've been able to figure out."

"It sounds like fun."

"It is fun."

And she was counting on the excitement of rehearsing with a Hollywood star to keep the Tucker actors and crew members actively engaged during the last stressful days leading up to the performance.

JODY KNELT on the high school stage floor on Monday afternoon, brushing a mixture of old paint, water and glue over the flimsy muslin draped across a wooden frame. Behind her, the *whumps* of the staple gun attached to Mr. Hammond's air compressor competed with a portable CD player blasting number fourteen on the weekly country countdown.

"Hey, Jody." Lucas knelt beside her, his backpack sliding off his shoulder. "What are you doing?"

"Making flats." She didn't look up. She wouldn't allow herself to dwell on Lucas's dimple or anything else about him. She wouldn't let him hurt her, not anymore. "What are you doing?" she asked.

"Waitin' for a ride. My dad's out watching my brother's practice."

Whump, whump.

"Why are you painting the cloth?" he asked.

"So it will tighten up and stretch over the frame when it dries."

"Huh." He edged closer. "Interesting."

"I think so."

"So do I."

She looked up then, to see him staring at her. "Really?"

"Yeah." He settled on the floor, crossing his long legs and shoving his backpack to one side. "I think it's all interesting. Especially the acting." He smiled. "Although I think you have to be kind of brave or something to walk out on a stage like that."

She swallowed. "Or something."

"Yeah. Well." He shrugged. "I would have liked to try it."

She set the brush down in the tray and wiped her hands on her messy jeans. "Why didn't you?"

"Lucas."

Jody turned her head to see Mr. Guthrie standing at the entrance to the auditorium, glaring at his son.

Lucas stood and slung his backpack over his shoulder. "Guess I wasn't brave enough," he said.

He stared at her for a long moment before he turned away. The butterflies woke up and fluttered a bit, but the sensation was pleasant and sweet.

Unlike the next feeling that swamped her—the feeling she got every time she imagined standing in front of an audience. She hoped she'd be brave enough to do the right thing before it was too late.

CHAPTER EIGHTEEN

MAGGIE STARED at her reflection in the old cheval mirror in one of Wayne's guest rooms Monday evening. Benita's clever alterations of a standard sewing pattern had produced a lovely Victorian gown from inexpensive broadcloth and scraps of lace. It would add a dash of period feel to the minimal set she'd designed for the proposal scene from *The Importance of Being Earnest*.

Wayne suddenly appeared in a corner of the reflection. She hadn't seen him since he'd ducked out of her cabin early Friday morning, a few hours before he'd begun another hunt trip and she'd left for San Francisco.

His eyes were smudged with fatigue, and beard stubble darkened his jaw. But when she turned to face him, a warm smile brightened his weary features, and her heart lifted in a bittersweet response.

"Don't you make a picture," he said, moving into the room. "Pretty as one, too." His hungry eyes took her in, from her slightly disheveled hair to the drifting train of the dress, and he ran a finger down the gown's puffed sleeve. "Is this a costume for your revue?"

"Yes." She unfastened a pin, and the sleeve opened at her wrist. "Benita's a wonder."

"So she's told me, often enough for it to sink in." He smiled and pulled at a loose thread. "I don't suppose you can stay for dinner."

"No, thank you. I'm picking up Nora, and then we're heading back into town for a quick burger at Walt's before rehearsals."

She removed another pin and pushed it into Benita's tomato pincushion. "I don't want you to feel as though you have to offer me a meal every time I show up at dinnertime. It's already a little awkward, working on the revue in your house like this. I feel as though I'm putting you in a difficult situation."

"I put myself in my own situations. And if they get difficult, I deal with them."

She added another pin to the cushion. "Still, my presence here might be viewed as aiding and abetting the enemy."

"Are we at war?"

"I don't know." She glanced up at him. "Have you chosen a side yet?"

"What if I had? Would it matter?"

"Have you chosen a side?"

He sighed and stabbed a hand through his hair. "Why do you answer so many of my questions with another question?"

"That's a case of the pot calling the kettle black." She gingerly plucked at a pin at her nape.

"Here," he said, gently turning her back to him. "Let me help you with that."

"This is getting to be a bad habit," she said as the costume gaped across her back, exposing the silk-and-lace camisole she'd worn to school beneath an old fisherman's knit sweater.

"What is?"

"Undressing me."

"Is it a bad habit, or just a habit?"

"There you go," she said, "asking questions again."

"Maybe we keep asking questions so neither of us has to come up with any answers."

"What answer do you want?"

He turned her to face him. "I want you to tell me why you went to San Francisco."

"Why do you think I went there?"

He tightened his grip on her. "Is that your version of an answer?"

She twisted away and brushed the costume down her arms. "You already know why."

"I may have a theory, but I'd like to hear your reason. I'm curious to see how well they match up."

"In your capacity as a member of the school board?"

He waited, stubbornly, for her answer, and she huffed out a frustrated breath. "It's the kind of job I'm used to doing," she said.

"Teaching."

"No, not just teaching." She freed her wrist from the

other sleeve, wincing as a forgotten pin poked her. "Teaching at a college-prep school."

"Teaching college-prep students."

"That's right."

"And there aren't enough students of that type at Tucker High to satisfy you."

"I didn't say that."

"No, you didn't."

He walked to the window and placed his hands on the sill, gazing at the mountains. His bleak profile tugged at her heart, opening a gap to let something hugely painful— something she didn't want to face—rush through her.

"You didn't say much of anything at all," he said.

"What do you want me to say?"

"I want to hear why you think you have to leave."

"Maybe because I never meant to stay."

He lowered his head with a sigh. "That's a mighty sorry reason."

"I happen to think it's an excellent one." Her chin came up, but she was mortified to feel it tremble. "It's honest, and it's consistent. It's the same reason I've had for most of my life."

"Glad to hear you're keeping an open mind on the matter."

"It's not that I haven't been happy here. It's just that I—"

She struggled for the words, and then she realized she didn't have any more reasons. Nothing that she could imagine saying made any sense when he was standing there with his back to her, solid and steady and in pain because of what she was going to do.

Her hands were shaking. She had to escape, to get out of this house and away from the solemn man at the window. The spreading darkness outside seemed to press in on her, robbing her of breath and will. If she stayed another minute she'd crumple and collapse and never rebuild herself again. "I've got to go."

"Yes. I figured you would."

He turned and gestured at the costume drooping along her hips. "Do you need any more help with that?"

"No." She shoved it down to pool at her ankles and quickly stepped out of it. Benita would have a fit about the wrinkles—she'd deal with that tomorrow. "I'll finish dressing in the bathroom, and then I'll head on out."

"All right." He stared at her for a long, agonizing moment, and then he lowered his gaze to the floor. He walked out of the room, heading toward a solitary dinner in his big, empty dining room.

She dashed into the bathroom and shut the door, shivering and fighting back tears. Damn, damn, *damn.*

She'd fallen in love with him.

THE ACTORS HELPED Maggie and Nora rearrange tables and chairs to form a temporary stage area Thursday night. While the school board met in the auditorium, those involved in the revue's second act would rehearse their lines in the library.

Outside, a mountain thunderstorm blazed and roared

in an impressive tantrum. Maggie hoped the weather would calm and clear for the hunting guests meeting Wayne in Butte tomorrow afternoon.

"I thought you were grounded," Lizzie Bardette said as she helped Tanya Wolf drag a table toward a wall.

"Nope." Tanya shoved the table against another. "I used to get grounded, but my parents decided it was too much of a punishment for them to have me around the house. Now they send me over to ol' lady Gamble's house and make me read the bible to her."

Nora grinned at Thea.

"My parents are driving me nuts," said Sam Ingersoll. "They used to send me to my room. But then they realized I had a computer and a TV with a DVD player, and I'd rather be in there, anyway. So now they make me sit in the family room and watch some educational channel and talk to them."

"Oh. My. God," said Tanya. "That's *evil*."

"Maybe we should get a cable hookup for after-school detention," said Cade Montgomery, the science teacher who was Maggie's partner in the proposal scene.

"Good idea," said Thea. "I like to watch educational channels, too."

Maggie smiled as she arranged chairs in rows for the airplane skit. She treasured the camaraderie of these late night sessions. She'd only been at Tucker High for a few weeks, but they'd been happy ones. She'd felt as though she were a real and necessary part of things, as though she were coming home again, on so many levels.

"Burger delivery." One of the young fry cooks at Walt's stood in the library doorway. He shook water from his jacket as he handed two fat white bags to Sam.

"Who ordered burgers?" asked Maggie.

"I did." Nora pulled a stack of bills from her purse and handed them to the cook.

"You didn't have to do that," said Maggie.

"Yes, I did." Nora took one of the paper-wrapped burgers from Sam. "You're a slave driver. You'd sooner see a pregnant woman starve than stop for a break."

"We haven't even started yet."

"See what I mean?" Nora beckoned to a group of junior high school students. "Come on, people," she said, "you can chew and practice your lines at the same time."

Maggie watched Jody refuse a burger. Jody never refused one of Walt's burgers.

Time to get to the bottom of the problem. She crooked a finger at her niece. "Come help me out here, kiddo."

Jody crossed the room and added another chair to one of Maggie's rows.

"How's it going?" Maggie asked.

"Okay."

"Just okay, huh?"

Jody's eyes filled with tears. Horrified and panicked, Maggie took her arm and dragged her around a book-stack, out of sight.

"What is it, sweetie?" She ran a hand down the side of her niece's face. "Are you sick?"

"No." Jody rubbed her stomach as if she were. "It's just that I—I don't want to do this anymore."

"The rehearsal?"

"The play." Jody stared past Maggie's shoulder. "But I don't want to m-mess things up for you, and—" A tear tickled down her cheek. "And I d-don't want Fitz to be disappointed in me."

"Oh, Jody, he won't." Maggie pulled her close and hugged her, hard. "He would never be disappointed in you."

She rocked her back and forth, soothing them both. "Is this why you've been so quiet lately?"

Jody nodded and sniffed. "I didn't want to hurt anyone's feelings."

"Of course you didn't. And you haven't." Maggie stroked a hand across her shoulders. "Do you want me to call Gran and have her come get you?"

"No." Jody pulled away and wiped a hand under her nose. "I'd like to stay and have a burger and hang out with everyone."

"They're fun to hang out with."

"Yeah." Jody took a deep breath and managed a smile. "I'm okay now, if you want to go back out there. I'll just stay here for a while."

"All right." Maggie gave her a quick, tight squeeze and walked out of the stacks.

She headed toward the actors, numb and drained of purpose. How many of the joking, teasing group had made unknown sacrifices, paid too high a price for this project? Yet she'd forged ahead, focused on her goals and ambitions.

Sick and shaky, she turned down one of Walt's burgers, too.

WAYNE PRESSED at the ache behind his forehead as he scanned the school board agenda for the next item of business. Beside him, Charlie droned on just to hear himself talk. And seated in the front row across from him, Frank Guthrie waited with obvious impatience to make a few comments of his own.

A gust of wind howled through the entry, and one of the big front doors slammed shut with a rattle. Boot Rawlins jogged into the auditorium, his clothes dripping rain on the floor and his wet hair hanging in his face. "Lightning strike out on the field," he said when he caught his breath.

"The football field?" Guthrie jumped from his chair and grabbed his jacket. "The bleachers?"

"The scoreboard," said Boot. "It's a goner."

WAYNE CHECKED HIS WATCH early the next morning and settled back against his booth in the Beaverhead Bar & Grill. In the kitchen, Max crooned a quiet, off-key duet with Tim McGraw's latest radio number while he cracked eggs and pooled pancake batter on the sizzling grill. Across the room, Loretta flirted with a couple of ranch hands who'd come down from the Holmesby spread to replace the spare tire on the ranch truck.

Wayne listened in on their talk about recent elk sight-ings and tuned out their news about a brawl at the bar in Patch Creek.

Stretching his arm along the booth windowsill, he glanced with relief at the clear sky and then curled his fingers in a tight fist, wishing he could think of a way to avoid the awkward situation he'd set up for himself. Maggie wouldn't be happy to hear about this meeting, and he didn't have time to discuss it with her before he left to collect his next hunt guests in Butte.

In the street outside, Fitz Kelleran climbed from his pickup, lifting a hand in an answering wave to Howie Miller as he coasted by in the sheriff's department cruiser. He paused to exchange a friendly greeting with a housewife exiting North Town Market and stooped to examine the cast on her son's arm.

Hollywood millionaire movie star playing a support-ing role in the small-town scene.

Wayne knew it wasn't fair to keep thinking of Kelleran in those terms, but it was a hard habit to break. Especially when the man took every chance to remind Wayne of their tangled circumstances.

The little bell over the Beaverhead's main door jingled as the actor made his entrance. He nodded to the ranch hands and planted a neighborly peck on Loretta's cheek before checking out the list of daily specials. Then he shoved his hands into his pockets and ambled down the narrow aisle toward Wayne's booth. "Morning, Hammond."

"Morning, Kelleran." Wayne nodded a greeting as Kelleran slid into the space across from him. "How are things out at Granite Ridge?"

"Can't complain." Kelleran bestowed one of his trademark smiles on Loretta as she filled his coffee mug. "Will finds plenty for me to do. Keeps me out of trouble, makes me feel useful. And yourself?"

"Got a hunting trip lined up. Heading into the foothills early tomorrow."

"I'd like to make one of those trips myself one of these days. Find out what all the excitement's about." Kelleran picked up his coffee and winced a bit over his first steaming sip. "Guess I'd better learn to shoot first."

"Might come in handy."

"Might at that." Kelleran aimed a wry smile over the edge of his mug. "And it might make some folks around here more than a touch uncomfortable to see me with a rifle in my hands."

Wayne relaxed at the actor's self-deprecating comment. He couldn't help liking the man, in spite of their rough start. "I appreciate you coming into town like this to meet with me," he said. "I imagine you try to set aside as much of your time as possible to spend with your family."

"And there's a whole lot of family to spend it with," said Kelleran as Loretta placed a chunk of Max's cranberry coffee cake in front of him. "I don't mind a chance to get out on my own every once in a while."

"How's Ellie?"

"Sick as a dog and more ornery than usual."

"Then I guess you didn't mind coming into town for this meeting."

"Not all that much, no." Kelleran picked up his fork and dug into his pastry. "Take your time."

Wayne filled him in on the scoreboard disaster. "The news came last night right before the board meeting adjourned, and we've agreed to recommend that your donation be used to get a new scoreboard in place as soon as it can be arranged. Might as well get the bleachers set up while we're at it."

"Are Shelby and Alice in on this, too?"

Wayne nodded. "They understand the difference between an urgent need and something that would be real nice to have some day."

Kelleran chased a piece of cake around his plate with his fork. "Sounds like a genuine emergency."

"It is." Wayne straightened in preparation for the unpleasant part of the meeting. "You probably weren't expecting to transfer the funds for a while yet."

"That's not a problem." Kelleran waved the issue away. "My accountant will probably weep with joy at the prospect of another tax deduction this year."

Wayne twisted his mug in a tight circle on the table. "I don't suppose you'd like to make your accountant even happier."

"You mean by doubling my donation?"

Wayne set the mug aside and leaned forward. "She's worked hard for this."

"Yes, she has." Kelleran slouched back against the booth in a seemingly casual pose. "This revue of hers is going to make quite an impression on a lot of folks around here."

"Maybe enough to change a few minds about the necessity of fixing up the school stage."

"Maybe so."

Wayne waited for more of a response, and the actor continued to let him. The two men stared at each other across the stained and nicked booth table.

"You're going to make me beg, aren't you?" Wayne asked at last.

"No." Kelleran shook his head. "No, that would just embarrass us both. But you might as well go ahead and make your pitch. It's the real reason you dragged me down here, isn't it?"

"You said at dinner the other night that you wouldn't double your donation."

"That's right."

"I don't s'pose you'd consider changing your mind in light of this new development?"

Kelleran toyed with his fork. "Why does it matter whether I fund the improvements to the stage this year or next? I doubt anything could be in place in time for the revue, anyway."

Wayne looked down at his hands. He pulled apart his tightly laced fingers and rested one hand over the other. "Maggie might not be here next year to oversee the project."

"Why do you need her? You've got her proposal," said Kelleran. "All neatly itemized and prioritized and tied up in a big pink bow."

Wayne acknowledged the fact with a nod.

"So, what else do you need?" asked Kelleran.

I need her.

Loretta shuffled up to their table and topped off their coffees. "Can I get you boys anything else?"

"Nothing for me, thanks," said Wayne. "Kelleran?"

"No, thanks," he said, and then looked up at Loretta. "You tell Max for me that his coffee cake is better than anything I can get in Beverly Hills, okay, doll?"

"You bet, hon. I'll do that."

Kelleran reached for the check, but Loretta handed it to Wayne. "I'm getting this," he said. "I'm the one who asked you to come in."

"Fair enough," said the actor, settling back into his nonchalant slouch to wait again.

"It's not a matter of needing any more of Maggie's input," said Wayne after Loretta had wandered back toward the cash register. "It's a matter of going the extra mile for someone who's put a whole lot of time and effort into a major improvement for the school. It would be a way of thanking her."

"Yeah, I'm sure she'd appreciate my gratitude." One corner of Kelleran's mouth pulled up in a faint half grin. "The same way she'd appreciate knowing you put me up to it. Then again," he added, "it might not be the same at all."

Wayne narrowed his eyes but chose not to rise to the bait.

"Harrison women can be a bit touchy about someone sticking his nose into their business," said Kelleran. "I'd worry about my nose if I were you, Hammond."

"I can deal with Maggie."

"You can, huh?" Kelleran shifted and crossed his arms on the table. "Exactly what's going on between the two of you, anyway?"

"That's between the two of us."

"I figured you'd say that." Kelleran shrugged. "And I figured I'd have to point out that Maggie is kind of my sister-in-law. Living on my ranch. Eating her breakfast at my kitchen table every morning. Almost every morning," he added with a pointed look. "I have to put up with her on a daily basis, and believe me, it's a trial."

"If you're waiting for me to disagree with any of that," said Wayne, "you've got a long wait ahead of you."

Kelleran gave him a quick, companionable grin.

"I just hope I don't have to wait too much longer for you to get to the point," said Wayne.

"My point is that your business with Maggie affects a lot more people than just the two of you." He sighed and scrubbed a hand over his face. "I had to deal with a house full of weepy females last night."

"Maggie was crying?" Wayne's heart squeezed tight. "I knew she'd be upset about the board's decision, but—"

"The crying had nothing to do with that. She was

feeling guilty for putting Jody in the middle of things, and Jody was feeling guilty for getting herself out of them." He exhaled on a long, weary sigh. "Ellie was upset because she's been feeling too poorly to notice that Jody was upset, and Jenna was crying because everyone else was upset."

He took a long sip of coffee. "And Nora was crying because she never saw a scene she didn't want to steal."

"That's a hell of a lot of tears."

"I tell you, it made me want to weep myself."

"Guess things have gotten a little out of hand," said Wayne.

"Any way to stop 'em?"

"Not that I can tell."

"And you're not upset over it?"

Wayne shrugged.

"Good to know you're not going to get weepy on me, too." Fitz took another long sip and set the coffee aside. "Now, back to that point I was trying to make. If this business you and Maggie have got going on between the two of you is what's behind this meeting and this request, then it's not an entirely private affair."

The word *affair* hung in the air between them for a moment, lingering with the sultry tones of Shania Twain and the aroma of Max's chicken apple sausages. Wayne searched for some sign of judgment or challenge on the actor's face, but all he found was sympathy.

"I could say I'm only thinking of the welfare of the school," said Wayne.

"You could say it, but I wouldn't buy it."

"The principal says she's a good teacher. Great with the students, a real asset to the school. She'd like to see Maggie stay on."

"Isn't going to happen." Kelleran shook his head. "She won't be here much longer, you know."

Kelleran's confirmation of Wayne's fears about losing Maggie sent an icy flood of panic washing through his gut. He made sure his hands were steady before he turned one over, slowly, palm up.

Begging.

"Then do it for her now," he said.

"It won't be enough to make her stay."

"That's not why I'm asking."

"I don't buy that, either."

Wayne stared out the window. "This isn't about the money."

"Nope."

"And it isn't about me."

"It never was."

Wayne glanced back at Kelleran and saw the truth in his face. "It can't be about Maggie and me, because there's not enough there to base any decision on."

"I'm sorry to hear it," Kelleran said, and Wayne could see he meant that, too.

"So, this must be about Maggie."

Kelleran studied him for a long moment. "You're in love with her."

Because he couldn't bring himself to deny it, he

was forced to admit the awful, awesome truth. "Yes. Yes, I am."

"God, I'm sorry," said Kelleran, and once again Wayne saw genuine sympathy in his features.

The two men sat in silent commiseration for a few moments, and then Kelleran crumpled his napkin and tossed it on the table. "All right, Hammond. You win."

"You'll double the donation?"

"I'll think about it." He leaned to one side and pulled his wallet out of his back pocket. "Considering that I'm dealing with such an urgent need."

"Thank you," said Wayne.

"Yeah." Kelleran slapped a generous tip on the table and angled out of the booth. "I'll do my part. Now you do yours."

"What's that?"

"Deal with Maggie." Kelleran gave him a loaded look. "If you want her to stick around, you're going to have to do a hell of a lot more than write a check."

CHAPTER NINETEEN

ON MONDAY MORNING, Maggie leaned her forehead on her hands where they clenched the steering wheel, dreading the short walk to the ranch house back porch. She was exhausted, even though she'd played hooky the night before and skipped correcting essays to get a head start on some needed sleep. But in spite of the long, quiet night, hauling herself from bed to face the paperwork at dawn had been torture.

Everything seemed more difficult lately, as if she were swimming through molasses. Maybe she was pushing herself too hard, heaping rehearsals on top of a busy teaching schedule. Maybe the meals she'd skipped lately were taking a toll on her energy level. Maybe she was depressed because of the weather, or the stress, or the lack of nutrition.

Or the fact that an apocalyptic act of God had obliterated her chances of winning this year's windfall funding, in spite of all the hard work everyone was putting into the revue.

And maybe she missed Wayne more than she wanted to admit.

She pushed the door open and winced as a cold, moist wind slapped at her. Her legs seemed to be encased in concrete. She hadn't realized she was so out of shape.

Or maybe, she thought as she moved through the mudroom and the odor of sizzling bacon assaulted her stomach, she was coming down with the flu. That might explain a lot of the symptoms she'd been feeling during the past couple of days.

"Morning, Jody," she said as she dropped into one of the kitchen chairs. The coffeepot seemed a mile away, and she wasn't sure she wanted it enough to make the trip. "Morning, Mom."

Jenna turned from the cooktop and frowned. "What's wrong, Maggie? You look like death warmed over."

"That's how I feel." She leaned an elbow on the table and ran a hand through her hair. "I think I might be coming down with something."

Jody scooted her chair a few inches down the table. "Don't breathe on me," she said. "I don't want to miss Lindsey's party Saturday night."

"Don't worry, you won't catch it that fast."

"I don't want to catch what you have at all."

Nora drifted into the room with good morning greetings and entirely too much good cheer. "Need some help with rehearsals tonight?"

"I want to run through the toga skit with the junior high students," Maggie said. "Want to take back your offer?"

Nora shook her head with a smile. "I think they need all the help they can get."

Maggie listlessly plucked a napkin from the holder on the table and spread it across her lap. She didn't want breakfast, but she knew she should eat something. Maybe some dry toast, something bland to settle the seething inside and help keep up her energy. She had an errand to run on her lunch hour, one last set decorating project to discuss with Janie and tonight's rehearsals with a bunch of squirming, shoving, giggling adolescents. So many things left to do, and not enough days left to do them in. She couldn't waste one on illness.

"I've got to pick up some supplies in town this afternoon," Jenna told Jody as she scooped bacon and eggs onto a platter. "Do you want me to come and get you at three?"

"No thanks," said Jody. "I'll hang out with Chrissy. Her mom's getting her hair done, and we can work on our homework together."

Ellie came down the stairs as Jenna set the platter on the table. She took one look at the breakfast fare and raced through the kitchen, heading for the tiny bath off the mudroom.

"Gross." Jody dropped her toast on her plate. "I hate it when she does that."

"She can't help it," said Nora with a sigh. "Poor thing."

Maggie listened to the sounds of Ellie's morning sickness, and her meager control over her own stomach slipped another notch. She bolted from her place at the table and dashed for the back porch. She gripped the railing and gulped in cold, fresh air as fast as she could manage. It didn't help. Soon she was retching over the edge, shivering in the cold and dizzy with fatigue.

The door clicked closed behind her and her mother's hand settled gently on her back to rub in soft, calming circles, the same soothing gesture she remembered from childhood. "Maggie," she said. "Poor Maggie."

"I'll be okay in a minute." She trembled from the insult to her system, achy and hollow and doubting she could make it to work. Maybe she'd feel better if she rested for a while. That was the answer—a quick morning nap, and she could still handle the afternoon's activities. "I just need to sit down and rest for a while."

"If you say so."

Jenna handed her a warm, moist dish towel. It was heaven against her face. "I'd better call the school and let them know I won't be making it to first period."

"I think that's a good idea." Jenna leaned against the railing. "Then you can call and see about getting an appointment with John Webb."

"Dr. Webb?" Maggie concentrated on folding the towel. "Why would I want to bother him over a case of the flu?"

"Maggie." Jenna sighed and brushed Maggie's hair from her face. "Are you sure it's the flu?"

"What else could it be?"

Jenna tilted her head toward the mudroom with a

smile. "There's more than one reason a woman gets sick in the morning."

"Not for me, there isn't."

But in the next instant, an intense hope and over-whelming reaction rushed through her, battling with logic, threatening to buckle her legs and curl her over the porch railing again. "You know it's impossible."

"I know you've always had problems, even when you were young." Jenna stroked her face. "I know what the doctors told you. But did any of them ever use the word *impossible?*"

"All right. It's possible. Anything's possible, but…"

She gulped in another deep breath and shook her head. She wouldn't do this to herself, wouldn't get her hopes up, not again. Couldn't get her hopes up—she wasn't married, wasn't settled, wasn't ready. *"No."*

Jenna tugged her sweater around her middle and hunched her shoulders against a raw gust of wind. "You'd be a better judge of that than I would be, I suppose."

"I know what this looks like, but I can't—I mean, I don't know if I—"

"Best to find out, then."

Jody stepped out on the porch. "Aunt Maggie? You okay?"

"Yeah." She handed the towel back to Jenna. "Perfectly all right."

Nora appeared behind Jody, silently studying Maggie with those dark, exotic eyes.

"Let's all get back inside, out of this cold." Jenna gave Maggie's arm a squeeze before she turned and shooed Jody into the house. "Finish your breakfast. I'll drive you to school this morning."

Maggie pressed her hand to her middle and waited for Nora to leave, too. "I'll be fine."

"A soda cracker breakfast used to help me get started."

"Soda crackers, huh?" Maggie tried for a cocky grin but barely managed a grimace. "Why do you think that would work for what I've got?"

"I don't know what you've got. But I think you should find out." Nora slid her hand along the railing. "I heard what Jenna said. I'll go with you, if you'd like."

"One single woman holding another single woman's hand?"

Nora smiled and lifted a shoulder in a nonchalant shrug. "One friend lending a little support to another."

Maggie sucked in a deep breath. "Thanks. I could use a little friendly support. I think I'll need it, either way."

It couldn't be true.

But what if it was?

"*God*," she said. "It's just—it's too much to absorb all at once."

Nora smiled and nodded. "It usually is."

"You're right." Maggie shook her head. "But in my case, with my history, the odds are against it."

"You could buy a test."

"At the local drugstore?" Maggie rolled her eyes. "After all the excitement over Wayne's condoms?"

Nora laughed. "I'd forgotten about that."

Maggie groaned and twisted over the railing again. "I think I'd better call Dr. Webb," she said with a gasp.

MAGGIE'S EYES DRIFTED SHUT later that morning as Nora drove through the entrance to Granite Ridge, headed home.

"Are you doing okay?" Nora wrapped her fingers more securely around the steering wheel of the SUV and glanced nervously toward the passenger seat. "You're awfully quiet."

"I've got a lot on my mind." Pregnant. Expecting a baby. Wayne's baby. Maybe if she said it out loud a few hundred times it would all seem more real.

The only thing that seemed real right now was Nora's poky driving and the bumpy ranch road.

"What a mess," she said. "The irony is staggering. There I was, a year ago, trying to get pregnant in some subconscious effort to save my marriage, and then my husband ended it for me by getting someone else pregnant."

Nora shot her a sympathetic glance.

"On top of that," Maggie continued, "I never wanted to spend my life in Tucker, and now I'm pregnant with the child of a man who's tied more closely to this town than just about anyone who lives here."

"Are you going to marry him?" Nora eased over a cattle guard. "If he asks?"

"Oh, he'll ask, all right. Wayne Hammond is a stand-up kind of guy."

"He seems that way to me, too." Nora nodded. "And he sure knows how to keep his cool under fire."

"I'm not planning on going in with guns blazing."

"I was thinking of the dinner scene my first night here."

"Ah, yes," Maggie laughed in spite of her misery. "The infamous stew."

"Everyone else around the table was going through all this emotional upheaval for all these different reasons," said Nora with a smile, "and Wayne just sat there, this calm island in the midst of the tempest, quietly eating his dinner."

"That's one of his most annoying habits."

"Eating through stressful situations?"

"The calm island in the midst of the tempest routine." Maggie closed her eyes and tipped her head back against the seat. "I can just imagine how he's going to take this news."

"Calmly?"

"No, not completely. I'm sure he'll be going through some emotional upheaval of his own. On the inside, anyway." She rested her elbow on the narrow window ledge and rubbed her hand over her forehead, hoping she and Wayne could find some way to hold on to a few moments of shared joy to get them through the pain they'd likely cause each other before this was settled. "It's not exactly a state secret here in Tucker that Wayne wants a wife and a family."

"That sounds encouraging."

Guilt washed through Maggie as she remembered Nora's situation—a husband who'd deserted her when she'd announced she was expecting his child. He'd claimed he'd married a movie star, not a housewife, and he didn't intend keeping his part of the bargain once the situation had changed.

"I guess it does," Maggie admitted.

"You don't sound particularly encouraged."

Maggie drew in a deep breath and exhaled with a long sigh. "I don't want to hurt him. He's a good man."

"But…"

"But it's that calm island thing. He's an intensely private person, always has been. Almost obsessive about keeping everyone at a certain distance. Even me. I don't feel as if he's ever let me in far enough to see the real Wayne."

"The real Wayne?" Nora slowed to make a turn. "Was it the real Wayne or the fake one who made a baby with you?"

"Ouch."

"Sorry. I know you're stressed. Believe me, I've been there." Nora stopped in the middle of the road and turned to face Maggie. "And it's because I've been there that I want to help, to be there for you."

"I know." Maggie shifted out of her slouch. "And I appreciate it."

"Seems to me you know Wayne pretty well. The calm island part of him, the emotional part of him, and plenty of parts in between. You even understand him well enough to recognize the secret part."

Nora leaned forward. "Is that secret part a problem because you're worried what the secret might be, or just because there's one, small part of him he hasn't opened up to you?"

Nora was right—Maggie knew Wayne well enough to understand that his most private self wouldn't be all that different from the self he put on display.

He's a good man.

"Do you love him, Maggie? The real Wayne—not the fake one, or the sensitive one, or the one you think he's hiding from you or the one you want him to be," said Nora. "Do you love *him?*"

"Yes, I do. Oh, God." Maggie blinked hard and fast, trying to fight back the prickle of tears while her throat swelled painfully. "I hate this crying stuff."

"Get used to it." Nora dug through her purse, produced a wrinkled tissue and shoved it into Maggie's hands. "Hormones are another item on the list of things beyond your control now."

"I sure do appreciate you." Maggie wiped her nose. "I don't like you very much right now, but I appreciate what you're trying to do."

"One more piece of advice," said Nora, "and then I'll shut up."

She took her foot off the brake and continued toward the ranch house. "If you think Wayne is throwing up barriers, well, you've just been handed a very important reason to try harder to break through. That baby deserves a chance for a family."

"I know." Maggie rubbed her hand over her flat stomach. Her extremely flat stomach, considering all the meals she'd missed or lost recently. Somewhere down there, deep inside, another person was growing. Someone who would always be a part of her.

And a part of Wayne.

Her hand stilled. "That idea's going to take some getting used to, too."

WAYNE TURNED into his gravel drive on Monday afternoon, running late and worn down by the round trip to Butte. His foreman had met him on the road to inform him that the filter in the pump house was broken and his small grains farmer was relocating to Colorado. Benita had left by now, and snacking on a reheated meal in front of the computer monitor wasn't how he wanted to spend the evening. He wanted to spend it with...

Maggie.

Her car was parked in front of his house. She was there, waiting for him. His system revved up as if he were ten years younger, with not a care in the world, and his heart swelled with anticipation.

He took the porch steps in two leaps and strode into the entry to find her staring at the painting of a street scene in Philipsburg hanging above the carved oak mantel. She wore a simple white sweater and plain brown slacks over practical loafers—no raspberry bouclé or big city black. Her arms were folded across her middle in that familiar, slightly belligerent stance that told the world she was ready to take it on, and her long, graceful neck arched back, just begging to be kissed.

He paused on the landing to imagine brushing his lips along that smooth stretch of soft skin, struck again by how good she looked here in this room, filled with the urgent, overpowering longing to find her here whenever he came home.

He'd done some thinking during the last hunting trip, and he'd decided it was time to do some courting. If he didn't take that chance, he'd sure as hell never have a chance with her.

Swamped with the need to touch her, to hold her and keep her here, to try to explain how she made him feel and how much he loved her, all he could manage was saying her name. "Maggie."

She turned to face him, and her expression was a careful blank that warned of trouble ahead. "Hello, Wayne," she said. "Here I am again, making myself at home."

He slipped his hands into his pockets. "You know I don't mind."

"Yes…well." She rubbed her hands up and down her arms. "I need to talk to you, and Benita said it would be all right if I waited here."

"You don't need a reason to be here," he said, moving to the dining room sideboard to pour them both some brandy. "But if you're looking for one, it's good to see you, Maggie. Good to come home and find you waiting for me."

"Going to make this tough on me, huh?" she asked with a halfhearted smile and a shake of her head, refusing the drink he offered. "You know, sometimes that overly solicitous attitude of yours grates on my nerves like fingernails on a chalkboard."

"I s'pose I could try real hard to be obnoxious once in a while if it would make you feel better." He set the drinks on the sofa table near the glass fish. "Or would that defeat the purpose?"

"See, there you go again, trying to please me." She paced to the long window and stared at the mountains. "You make me sound like a shrew for complaining."

"Sounds like I'm damned if I do and damned if I don't." He moved into the room and knelt to touch a match to the kindling set on the hearth. "Stay for supper, Maggie. You can catalog my shortcomings over one of Benita's casseroles."

She fingered the curtains draped to one side of the pane. "I might not be welcome after you hear my news."

He went absolutely still inside. San Francisco. She'd come to tell him she was leaving.

He rose and squared his shoulders. "Best tell me and get it over with."

"I'm pregnant."

The shock of her announcement was something akin to a physical blow. All the blood seemed to drain from his brain, and he was paralyzed, at first, afraid to move even if he'd thought it was possible. And in the next moment elation surged through him, filling him so full he thought he'd burst.

Maggie Harrison Sinclair, pregnant with his child. A child they'd made together. A precious, wondrous gift.

A miracle.

He tried to speak, but he had to swallow and make a second attempt. "How can that be?"

"I don't think I have to explain the basic facts to a rancher," she said, turning to face him. "We both know when it might have—when it happened."

"Maggie, I…" He couldn't help it, couldn't maintain the appearance of a serious consideration of their situation. His face cracked with a smile so wide he was certain he must look like an empty-headed fool.

A baby. The child he'd always wanted, with this amazing woman he'd come to realize he'd always loved.

Was it a boy or a girl? His eyes dropped to her belly, and he stepped toward her, one hand outstretched.

"No," she said as she shifted back. "Please…don't. Don't touch me."

His smile collapsed with concern. "Aren't you feeling well?"

"No. No, it's not that, it's…" She bit her lip and turned away, edging toward the entry. "I don't know what to say. How to say this. It isn't easy for me."

"I'm sorry for that." He moved to stand beside her, nearly trembling with the need to take her in his arms, to hold her and love her, to show her she had nothing to worry about. "I want to make this as easy as I can. You know I will."

"I knew you'd offer to. And I appreciate that, Wayne. I do, really."

He didn't care for the cool and businesslike sound of her voice. "I'm not just being overly solicitous here."

"Wayne, I—"

"And I'm not going to make a marriage proposal just because it's expected."

She closed her mouth and blinked. "Oh. All right."

He didn't care for her calm acceptance of that last statement, either. "But I am going to make it." He stepped closer. "The proposal, I mean."

"I wish you wouldn't."

He narrowed his eyes. "Why not?"

"Because I won't accept it."

"The hell you won't!" He ignored her jolt of shock and stalked to the fireplace to jab at the logs with the poker. He rarely displayed his temper, but he figured he was entitled to do so at the moment. "That's my child you're carrying."

"It's not a possession."

"I hope you realize that, too." He fisted his hands on the rough rock of the chimney, fighting for control. "I won't let my child be a bastard. I won't let my child be raised without my support."

"I'd never cut you out."

He glared at her over his shoulder. "You better believe I'll hold you to that."

"This sounds more like a threat than a marriage proposal."

He closed his eyes and lowered his head, shutting her out so she wouldn't be scorched by the shame that burned through him. There she stood, alone and frightened and likely feeling ill, bearing the burden of breaking this news, and all he could do was rip and growl at her instead of finding some way to express the indescribable joy fluttering just beneath his rib cage. "I don't suppose you could give me a chance to start over and make this right."

"We can't go back and change things now."

Her words—and the terrible finality of her tone—layered a thick blanket of despair over everything else inside him. No, he couldn't go back. He couldn't go back and change things, the things in his past that kept him from letting people—letting Maggie—see his fears and insecurities, his howling needs. And if he said the wrong thing, did the wrong thing, he could lose both Maggie and his child.

His child. Their child. *Maggie.*

He shoved away from the rock wall and slowly, carefully turned to face her, measuring his every move as if his entire future depended on each play of muscle, each crease of skin. He was too unsteady to find the right words, the right expressions. And he didn't like to be rushed into things, couldn't think straight when he was. So he'd let her go—for now.

"You're right," he said.

"Oh. Well." She stepped to the landing, heading

toward the door. "Thank you for the dinner invitation, but I think it's best if I go."

"Whatever you want."

She pulled a tan wool jacket from his entry closet and slipped into it. "I've got some catching up to do tonight, since I missed school to go to the doctor."

"Have him send me the bill."

She opened her mouth—most likely to argue—and shut it again with a frown. "All right."

"I'll walk you to your car."

"I know the way."

"I know you do." He climbed to the entry landing and wrapped his fingers around her arm. And he was achingly aware, as he touched her, that a life they'd made together was sleeping inside her.

He didn't want to think of letting her go again. But he had to, after he'd escorted her through his front door and steadied her down the rock steps and guided her to her muddy car. He had to let her go, had to step aside as she backed away and watch in silence as she disappeared down the road.

He'd taught himself all too well how to be understanding and agreeable and patient, how to negotiate and compromise. How to retreat. He'd always made it easy for a woman to walk out on him.

But he swore, to himself and to his child, that he'd never let this woman walk out on him again.

CHAPTER TWENTY

MAGGIE SAT AT THE Harrison kitchen table later that night, her hands wrapped around a half-empty mug of cooling cocoa. Half-empty—that was her take on her life at the moment, in spite of all the love and support and happy wishes of her family.

"Remember that calm island theory of mine earlier today?" she asked Nora. "Didn't pan out. Turns out Wayne has a bit of a temper under that quiet exterior."

"Would that be the real Wayne or the fake one?" Nora sipped at her drink and licked the mustache from her upper lip.

Ellie pulled another soda cracker from the box centered on the table. "I could have told you about his temper. I once saw him pull a fence post clean out of the ground in sheer frustration and toss it at least fifty yards."

"Then what happened?" asked Maggie.

"He got all cute and sheepish and planted it back the right way."

"He does have that cute and sheepish act down pat," said Nora. "It's got a certain appeal all its own. Mix in a little heat, and you've got a pretty attractive package."

"You don't have to sell me on the package," said Maggie. "I'm already head-over-high-heels in love with the man. The real one," she added.

"Then why are you sitting here with us, drinking warm milk and eating soda crackers, instead of over at his house, enjoying a warm bed and something more appetizing?" asked Nora. "It's obvious to anyone who manages to catch a glimpse of his face—when he's not pointing it at the floor—that he's head-over-boot-heels in love with you, too."

Maggie sighed and shoved a hand through her hair. "You should have heard him. It wasn't just the temper that got to me, it was the way he sounded. Authoritative, demanding. Completely controlling. 'I'm not asking you to marry me, I'm telling you to. No child of mine is going to be a bastard, and that's the end of it.'"

"Not exactly romantic," said Ellie.

"It was like listening to Alan at his—*oh*." Maggie covered her mouth with a hand, remembering some of what she'd said to Wayne when they'd gone riding. *And then I thought I might be pregnant, and he asked me to marry him.*

"He's been controlling, all right," said Ellie. "I heard he's been sneaking around behind your back, forcing people against their will to help you with your revue, threatening poor Benita into sewing your costume. And didn't he loan you his air compressor just so he could keep you under his thumb?"

Maggie slowly lowered her hand. She was remembering, too, how much Wayne hated to be rushed into anything.

Poor Wayne. Unexpected fatherhood was as big a rush as a man could get.

"I like a man who takes control," said Nora.

"You'd like a man with one eye in the middle of his forehead and his knuckles dragging on the ground right now," said Fitz as he came down the stairs. "You can't help it—it's hormones. I've been reading up on it."

"God," said Ellie. "Not this again."

"Come to bed, wife." Fitz lifted her out of her chair and carried her toward the stairs. "You know how horny I get when I read about hormones."

"Wait," said Ellie, squirming in his arms. "I need to tell Maggie something."

"God," said Nora. "Not this again."

"You've already told me a dozen times," said Maggie.

"Two dozen, at least," added Nora.

Fitz paused on the first step. "I want to hear it again."

"I have to say it for Mom, too," said Ellie, "since she's already gone to bed and isn't here to say it again for herself." She smiled at Maggie. *"I told you so."*

"She forgot the crackers," said Nora when Fitz and Ellie had gone.

"He took a box upstairs earlier." Maggie sighed and rested her chin on her hand. "I want what they've got."

"You can't have what they've got. Only they can have it." Nora took another sip and licked at her lip.

"You can have something else. And people like me will sigh over you when you get it."

Maggie bit into a cracker. "How did you get to be so smart?"

"By making so many mistakes." Nora glanced at Maggie over the rim of her mug. "How many more are you going to make before you're finished?"

"I don't have a lot of time left to waste on mistakes," said Maggie with another sigh. "I have to make a decision about that job in San Francisco by the end of next week."

INTERMISSION ON THE NIGHT of the revue brought a welcome break in the chaos backstage as most of the actors left to mingle with the audience and stuff themselves with cookies and punch.

Maggie ducked into the wings near the electrical panel. "Where's Jody?" she asked Lizzie Bardett.

"She might be in the dressing room."

"Why would she be in there?"

"Mr. Kelleran is in there."

"What's he doing in there?"

She didn't wait for Lizzie's answer. She stalked across the stage, tossing out harried instructions to the students setting up for the next scene, heading toward the crowd gathered at the narrow dressing-room doorway. "What is that man up to now?" she muttered under her breath.

The famous movie star was asking for autographs.

If she hadn't already understood why her sister-in-law had fallen in love with this man, she would have figured it out at that moment.

He looked up and saw her standing there and nodded with a smile. "It's the director."

"It's the audience," she said. "Backstage."

"I know it's probably off-limits, but I couldn't resist." He shoved his wrinkled program at Tanya Wolf and asked her to sign it, right there by her name, and told her he'd been impressed by the way she'd made eye contact with the other actors on the stage. Tanya's cheeks flamed bright pink, and she stuttered her thanks as she returned the paper.

"I suppose I can make an exception in your case," said Maggie.

"I'm an exceptional kind of guy," Fitz said with a wink.

"That's my line."

His eyes narrowed with suspicion. "What brought that on?"

"Nothing in particular."

She reminded the students that only those in the first two skits of the second act should be in the room, and then she stepped aside to let the others leave. "Curtain in ten minutes," she announced.

"Got a moment?" Fitz took her arm and led her into the dim, dusty space behind the backdrop. "There's something I want to discuss with you."

"This really isn't a good time." She heard a crash and squeezed her eyes shut with a prayer that the Victorian set door hadn't fallen off its frame for the one hundredth time. "I'm sort of busy right at the moment."

"I can see that." He smiled and leaned closer. "But I think you're going to like what I have to say."

"Oh?" She managed a weak smile. "Well, in that case, I think I can spare a minute."

"The early reviews are in, and you've got yourself a smash hit here."

"Thanks." She brushed the back of her hand against a stray wisp of hair. "I was pretty sure the applause I heard was edging past the polite range toward genuine approval."

"They love it." He cocked his head to one side. "You've accomplished everything you set out to do."

"Everything? Yes, I suppose I have."

And none of it seemed to matter. Nothing seemed to register without Wayne in the audience, observing everything in his quiet, patient way.

Where was he? He'd been missing for days—and he hadn't gone hunting.

"I'm damn proud of you, sis." Fitz pulled her into his arms for a quick, gentle hug. "So proud."

She swayed against him, wishing it were Wayne holding her, supporting her. "Thank you."

He stepped back with a wide grin. "I came back here to tell you that I've decided to donate enough money to do whatever you want to do here. A separate fund, just for the stage. The sky's the limit."

She closed her eyes and sucked in a deep breath to battle back an untimely wave of nausea. "That's wonderful news, Fitz. Thank you."

"What's wrong, Maggie?" He reached out and traced a finger down her arm. "Aren't you feeling well? Pregnancy acting up?"

"I'll be all right." And she was feeling better—a little better—knowing that her plans for the stage were going to become a reality.

"You wish Wayne was here tonight, don't you?"

To her horror, her throat closed up and a hot, fat tear slid down her cheek.

"Oh, hell. Not again." Fitz took her by the arm and pulled her deeper into the shadows behind the backdrop. "Here," he said, pulling a bandana from his back pocket to carefully dab at her face. "You're going to ruin your makeup."

"I don't know why I'm doing this," she said, snatching the bandana to blow her nose. "And don't start in again about hormones."

"Hormones? Me?"

"You're right—I've got everything I wanted. The money for the stage, a wonderful job offer in a fabulous city, a family that loves me, a baby I never thought I'd have—"

"There's a husband missing from that list."

"Yeah. Well." She sniffed hugely and gave him a watery smile as she tried to return the bandana. "I didn't have time to proofread it."

Fitz shoved the bandana back toward her. "I don't want that thing, now that you've honked all over it."

"I'd better go check on things before the end of intermission." She gave him a tight hug. "Thanks, Fitz."

"Maggie," he murmured against her hair.

"Mmm?"

"About that family that loves you…"

She pulled back and gazed up into his face. "Yes?"

"I do, you know." He gently patted her stomach. "Both of you."

"I know. We love you, too."

She took a deep breath and stepped out of the shadows behind the backdrop, and then turned to face the next act.

"THIS IS MY FAVORITE scene," Jody whispered over her shoulder to the tall, shadowy form that had appeared behind her in the wings.

Across the stage, Aunt Maggie took her place on the settee Nora and Mrs. Bardett had dragged out and signaled for Jody to open the house curtain.

"Are you ready, Mr. Montgomery?"

"I'm not Mr. Montgomery." Lucas Guthrie moved into the faint glow of the prompting light beside her. He bent down close to her ear, and his breath tickled the side of her neck. He smelled like chocolate and punch.

"Nora said I could watch from backstage during the second act," he whispered. "She said I could help pull the curtain."

"Where's Mr. Montgomery?"

"He's not here," said Lucas. "Mr. Hammond told me to tell you he's going on instead."

"What?"

Out on the stage, Aunt Maggie lifted her head from her pose and motioned again for Jody to open the curtain.

Jody peered around the tormentor to see Mr. Hammond standing in the shadows, staring at Maggie. He wore a fancy shirt and string tie and held a big bunch of red roses.

"What's going on?" asked Jody in a panic. She was the assistant stage manager for the entire second half of the revue, and if anything went wrong, it would be partially her fault. "Where's Mr. Montgomery?"

"He said to let Mr. Hammond go out first."

Lucas put his hand over hers on the rope pull. His hand was warm and moist, and a little sticky from the intermission refreshments, and the feel of it on hers made her throat close up.

"We're supposed to pull it real slow," he said.

"I can't do this."

She tried to free her hand from his, but he squeezed her fingers.

"Yes, you can," he whispered, right in her ear. "If you think you're brave enough. I know I'm feeling a whole lot braver about a lot of things tonight."

He reached above her head with his other hand for a second grip on the rope, and together they slowly pulled the curtain open.

I CAN DO THIS. All I have to do is put one foot in front of the other and aim for Maggie until I reach her. Concentrate on Maggie. Concentrate on reaching her. Reaching her, wanting her, winning her. I want her so much, I need her enough to do this.

So do it. You can't wait behind this curtain all night. This musty, ragged curtain—she was right, this curtain needs to go. She was right about all of it, everything. Go to her, tell her. Take a deep breath and move just one foot. Now another.

Something stabbed his hand—the roses. He loosened his grip so he wouldn't crush and ruin them before he could give them to her. They smelled so good, so rich and sweet, so different than all the rotting, ruined things backstage and the sweating actors.

God—maybe I'm one of the sweaty, smelly things, too.

Lift the flowers, suck in the sweet rose scent and forget about the rest. Keep moving.

The lights were blinding, blocking out everything but faint forms in the front seats, rows of legs and shoes fading to indistinct black beyond.

Don't look in that direction, don't look beyond the stage edge and adjust to the darkness. Let the lights do their work, the colored rows of fat, sun-like bulbs. So bright, so hot.

So hot the first drop of sweat trickled between his shoulders, sliding down his backbone to dive into his waistband.

It doesn't matter, not really. Keep moving. Don't let

them know I'm sweating, terrified, my heart pounding so hard I'm afraid I'm going to die out here.

She glanced up and stilled, a dream of a woman dressed in a sapphire blue gown, leveling her sapphire blue eyes on his. He knew how to read just about everything on that beautiful face now. She looked behind him, and he could see the wheels turning.

I love that about her. I always have. She's wondering what she'll do, how she'll play this scene. Don't let her think too hard, don't stop—keep moving.

The audience's murmurs were getting louder, spreading unease like a river, sprouting whispers and words from that mass of humming sound. Men, women, children, all wondering what he was doing.

"Wayne! Hey Hammond—you're not on the program."

Laughter.

Pull in, pull in. Steady. This shirt's nearly soaked through with sweat— but it doesn't bother me, it doesn't matter. Breathe, swallow, walk.

Keep moving. You're halfway there.

Aim for Maggie, sitting on that sofa, staring down at her hands and trying so hard to figure out what to do. What to do about me. About us. At least I'm moving, getting closer to the answer, getting closer to something to hold on to.

Aim for Maggie. Tell her you love her. Tell her you want another chance, that you mangled the last one because you were desperate, afraid of losing her. You're willing to beg, if that's what it takes.

You've done it before, you can do it again. You have no pride where she's concerned.

You'll let her see inside you, see everything. Nothing matters but Maggie. Nothing matters but loving her.

That's the only thing that's real.

MAGGIE WATCHED Wayne walk across the stage, heading right for her, squeezing that silly bunch of flowers so tightly in his big hands she was certain the thorns would draw blood before the stems snapped and fell to the stage floor. She saw the strain of the stage fright in his tightly pursed lips and the undiluted panic in his all-or-nothing gaze, and she felt each stiff twitch in his gait as if it were a knife thrust clear through her.

If she could have risen from her set chair and shoved him out of the line of fire, she would have done it. But she was rooted to her spot, trapped in the rainbow glare of the footlights, stunned by the rapid murmurs and the sudden hush of the crowd in the inky gap beyond the stage apron.

Her mind raced through a dozen lines that might cover the mistaken cue and rescue them both from making a bigger scene than the one described in the program, but she was afraid he might break and ruin whatever chance he had of getting through this in one piece. She held her breath, as panicked as he, and waited to see what would happen.

"Maggie." He cleared his throat and worked his jaw, struggling to get the next words out. "I've come to ask you a question."

"Why, Mr. Hammond," she said, staying in character, sticking to the lessons she'd taught her students. She swept a hand toward the empty spot on the settee. "What a lovely surprise. Won't you join me?"

She leaned forward, peering past his long legs, hoping to send some signal to Jody at the curtain pulley, but the shadowy figures in the wings ducked out of sight.

"This isn't an act, Maggie," he said. "I'm not playing a part."

No hope, then, of salvaging the scene.

She smoothed her hands over her skirts, wishing she could make them stop trembling. "What are you doing, then?" she asked.

"I said I've come to ask you a question."

He dropped to one knee, and someone in the audience gasped. Another wave of murmurs rose and ebbed.

"You don't have to do this," she said, but he extended his hand with the roses.

"Yes, I do."

"No, you don't, Hammond," called Boot Rawlins from the back of the auditorium, and the crowd laughed again.

She took the flowers, tempted to bury her face in them, to hide in them, to stand and run into the wings and close the curtains on her shame. What misbegotten, selfish part of her had brought him to this? Dragged this deeply private man out on a stage, in spite of his dread of public exposure, to kneel before her and beg?

How could she say yes when he asked her his question? She didn't deserve him. She didn't deserve the love she could see in those deep brown eyes that were locked on hers, drawing her in with hope and promising her heaven. Had she once thought she was too special to stay in Tucker, too special for anything and anyone this town could produce? She'd been such a fool.

But she wouldn't desert him on this stage. She wouldn't leave him, she wouldn't abandon him like so many other women in his life.

She laid the tissue-wrapped stems on the settee beside her and met his gaze. "Go ahead, then."

"I want your promise to consider my proposal with an open mind."

Oh, dear. The dear, *dear* man. Sentimental tears stung her eyes, and she clasped her hands in her lap, thinking back to the bargain they'd made so many weeks ago in the school parking lot. This was the real Wayne—a man who wouldn't be rushed, a man who cared enough about the special, finer things in life to take this kind of care with a proposal. A man who'd walk through fire—or across a stage—for her.

What was her next line? "I'll consider your proposal, if—"

She stopped and smiled as she remembered the rest. "If you'll consider the possibility that my mind was open to it in the first place."

"All right," said Wayne. He placed his hand over hers. "That's something I think we can work with."

He cleared his throat. "Maggie Harrison Sinclair, will you marry me?"

She gave him a private smile to let him know her answer, and then she paused for dramatic effect. More than a few sniffs could be heard in the crowd. The good people of Tucker were getting their money's worth tonight.

"Yes, I'll marry you," she said.

The curtain closed in rapid, jerky, swaying swishes.

WAYNE COULDN'T STOP grinning as Maggie tugged him behind the backdrop a few moments later. He pulled a little blue box out of his pocket and handed it to her.

"Where did you get this?" she asked.

"I thought a woman like you would recognize the wrapping."

"I do. It's from Tiffany's." She took the box with a suspicious glance. "Where did you get it?"

"In New York."

"When did you go to New York?"

"Two days ago."

"You went to Butte." She narrowed her eyes at him. "Benita told me."

"I did go to Butte. That's where I caught the plane to New York."

A slow smile spread across her face. "You've done this before, haven't you? Told people you were going to Butte and then gone somewhere else?"

"It's not a lie." He shrugged. "I do go to Butte."

"*Wayne.*"

"I like the sound of that *Wayne*," he said, drawing her into his arms. "It's got a nice, threatening ring to it. A wifely kind of sound."

"You'll be hearing a lot more of it if you don't open up and answer my questions."

"All right." He leaned down to skim his lips along the side of her neck. "Sometimes I catch a plane to New York when I go to Butte. I like it there. I even like the theater—as long as I'm in the audience."

"You go to the theater?" She shook her head in amazement. "What else do you do on these little jaunts?"

"Visit museums. Some galleries. I like looking at art. I've picked up some nice things here and there."

"You mean those prints and paintings on the walls in your house are—"

"Worth a bit more now than when I bought them." He brushed her hair from her eyes, loving the silky feel of it against his fingers. Maybe she'd let him brush it again later tonight. "I've been following the progress of a couple of those artists. They're doing pretty well for themselves."

"I don't know what to say." She shook her head with a laugh. "There is a fake Wayne."

"What?"

"Never mind." She looped her arms around the back of his neck, and the box poked at the side of his face.

He reached up and took her hands and pulled them between them. "Aren't you going to open it?"

She untied the pretty white ribbon bow. "Look at me," she said with another laugh. "My hands are shaking."

"That's my cue." He took the velvety box from her and pried back the lid. "I hope you like it."

"Oh, my," she said with a gasp. "What's not to like?"

He pulled out the ring with three large, glittering emerald-cut diamonds and slipped the classic platinum band over her finger. "I thought this looked like you," he said. "Different. Kind of classy. And they didn't have anything in raspberry bouclé."

"It's perfect, Wayne." She raised her hand, admiring the ring. "It's exactly what I would have chosen for myself."

"That's a relief." He slid the container back into his pocket. "It would have been a lot of trouble to take it back."

"I love it. I really do." She wrapped him in a tight hug. "And I love you, too."

"I kind of figured that might be the case, even though you've been trying your best to convince yourself otherwise."

"Why do you put up with me?" She rested her face against his chest with a sigh. "Why do you want to put up with me?"

"Who else is going to bother?" He lowered his forehead to hers and closed his eyes. "And besides, I love you, too."

He slid a hand between them, over her middle. "And I already love this person, whoever he is."

"She."

"It doesn't matter to me."

Maggie edged away with a worried look. "I know this is all happening way too fast, and—"

"And I don't like to be rushed into things." He tipped her chin up on his knuckle for a slow, sweet kiss. "But I've been waiting for this for most of my life."

"I have more news," she said. "Fitz is donating the money for the stage. All of it, everything I want."

He swept her up and spun her in an awkward circle, knocking over an ugly lamppost with a crash.

"Wayne."

"Sorry," he whispered. "I knew Kelleran would come through."

"You did?"

"We'll discuss it later." He set her down with a sigh. "We'll discuss everything later."

"I have to go," she said, and for the first time, those words didn't bother him at all. "I need to check on the next scene."

"That's all right." Wayne grinned at her. "The show must go on."

* * * * *

Happily ever after is just the beginning...

Turn the page for a sneak preview of
A HEARTBEAT AWAY
by
Eleanor Jones

Harlequin Everlasting—Every great love
has a story to tell. ™
A brand-new series from Harlequin Books

Special? A prickle ran down my neck and my heart started to beat in my ears. Was today really special?

"Tuck in," he ordered.

I turned my attention to the feast that he had spread out on the ground. Thick, home-cooked-ham sandwiches, sausage rolls fresh from the oven and a huge variety of mouthwatering scones and pastries. Hunger pangs took over, and I closed my eyes and bit into soft homemade bread.

When we were finally finished, I lay back against the bluebells with a groan, clutching my stomach.

Daniel laughed. "Your eyes are bigger than your stomach," he told me.

I leaned across to deliver a punch to his arm, but he rolled away, and when my fist met fresh air I collapsed in a fit of giggles before relaxing on my back and staring up into the flawless blue sky. We lay like that for quite a while, Daniel and I, side by side in companionable silence, until he stretched out his hand in an arc that encompassed the whole area.

"Don't you think that this is the most beautiful place in the entire world?"

His voice held a passion that echoed my own feelings, and I rose onto my elbow and picked a buttercup to hide the emotion that clogged my throat.

"Roll over onto your back," I urged, prodding him with my forefinger. He obliged with a broad grin, and I reached across to place the yellow flower beneath his chin.

"Now, let us see if you like butter."

When a yellow light shone on the tanned skin below his jaw, I laughed.

"There…you do."

For an instant our eyes met, and I had the strangest sense that I was drowning in those honey-brown depths. The scent of bluebells engulfed me. A roaring filled my ears, and then, unexpectedly, in one smooth movement Daniel rolled me onto my back and plucked a buttercup of his own.

"And do *you* like butter, Lucy McTavish?" he asked. When he placed the flower against my skin, time stood still.

His long lean body was suspended over mine, pinning me against the grass. Daniel…dear, comfortable, familiar Daniel was suddenly bringing out in me the strangest sensations.

"Do you, Lucy McTavish?" he asked again, his voice low and vibrant.

My eyes flickered toward his, the whisper of a sigh escaped my lips and although a strange lethargy had crept into my limbs, I somehow felt as if all my nerve endings were on fire. He felt it, too—I could see it in his warm brown eyes. And when he lowered his face to mine, it seemed to me the most natural thing in the world.

None of the kisses I had ever experienced could have even begun to prepare me for the feel of Daniel's lips on mine. My entire body floated on a tide of ecstasy that shut out everything but his soft, warm mouth, and I knew that this was what I had been waiting for the whole of my life.

"Oh, Lucy." He pulled away to look into my eyes. "Why haven't we done this before?"

Holding his gaze, I gently touched his cheek, then I curled my fingers through the short thick hair at the base of his skull, overwhelmed by the longing to drown again in the sensations that flooded our bodies. And when his long tanned fingers crept across my tingling skin, I knew I could deny him nothing.

* * * * *

*Be sure to look for A HEARTBEAT AWAY,
available February 27, 2007.*

*And look, too, for THE DEPTH OF LOVE
by Margot Early,
the story of a couple who must learn that
love comes in many guises—and in the end
it's the only thing that counts.*

HARLEQUIN® *Romance*®

From reader-favorite

MARGARET WAY

Cattle Rancher, Convenient Wife

On sale March 2007.

**"Margaret Way delivers…
vividly written, dramatic stories."**
—*Romantic Times BOOKreviews*

---

*For more wonderful wedding stories,
watch for Patricia Thayer's new miniseries
starting in April 2007.*

Rocky Mountain
BRIDES

EVERLASTING LOVE™

Every great love has a story to tell ™

Save $1.⁰⁰ off

the purchase of any Harlequin Everlasting Love novel

Coupon valid from January 1, 2007 until April 30, 2007.

**Valid at retail outlets in the U.S. only.
Limit one coupon per customer.**

RETAILER: Harlequin Enterprises Limited will pay the face value of this coupon plus 8¢ if submitted by the customer for this product only. Any other use constitutes fraud. Coupon is nonassignable. Void if taxed, prohibited or restricted by law. Consumer must pay any government taxes. Void if copied. For reimbursement submit coupons and proof of sales directly to: Harlequin Enterprises Ltd., P.O. Box 880478, El Paso, TX 88588-0478, U.S.A. Cash value 1/100¢. Valid in the U.S. only. ® is a trademark of Harlequin Enterprises Ltd. Trademarks marked with ® are registered in the United States and/or other countries.

5 65373 00076 2   (8100) 0 11302

HEUSCPN0407

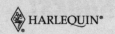

EVERLASTING LOVE™

Every great love has a story to tell™

Kristi Gold

Save $1.⁰⁰ off

**the purchase of
any Harlequin
Everlasting Love novel**

Coupon valid from January 1, 2007
until April 30, 2007.

Valid at retail outlets in Canada only.
Limit one coupon per customer.

RETAILER: Harlequin Enterprises Limited will pay the face value of this coupon plus
10.25¢ if submitted by the customer for this product only. Any other use constitutes
fraud. Coupon is nonassignable. Void if taxed, prohibited or restricted by law.
Consumer must pay any government taxes. Void if copied. Nielsen Clearing House
customers submit coupons and proof of sales to: Harlequin Enterprises Ltd. P.O.
Box 3000, Saint John, N.B. E2L 4L3. Non–NCH retailer—for reimbursement submit
coupons and proof of sales directly to: Harlequin Enterprises Ltd., Retail Marketing
Department, 225 Duncan Mill Rd., Don Mills, Ontario M3B 3K9, Canada. Valid in
Canada only. ® is a trademark of Harlequin Enterprises Ltd. Trademarks marked with
® are registered in the United States and/or other countries.

52607370

HECDNCPN0407

REQUEST YOUR FREE BOOKS!
2 FREE NOVELS PLUS 2
FREE GIFTS!

HARLEQUIN ROMANCE®

From the Heart, For the Heart

YES! Please send me 2 FREE Harlequin Romance® novels and my 2 FREE gifts. After receiving them, if I don't wish to receive any more books, can return the shipping statement marked "cancel." If I don't cancel, I will receive 4 brand-new novels every month and be billed just $3.57 per book in the U.S., or $4.05 per book in Canada, plus 25¢ shipping and handling per book and applicable taxes, if any*. That's a savings of over 15% off the cover price! I understand that accepting the 2 free books and gifts places me under no obligation to buy anything. I can always return a shipment and cancel at any time. Even if I never buy another book from Harlequin, the two free books and gifts are mine to keep forever.

114 HDN EEV7 314 HDN EEWK

Name _____ (PLEASE PRINT)

Address _____ Apt. _____

City _____ State/Prov. _____ Zip/Postal Code _____

Signature (if under 18, a parent or guardian must sign)

Mail to the **Harlequin Reader Service®**:
IN U.S.A.: P.O. Box 1867, Buffalo, NY 14240-1867
IN CANADA: P.O. Box 609, Fort Erie, Ontario L2A 5X3

Not valid to current Harlequin Romance subscribers.

Want to try two free books from another line?
Call 1-800-873-8635 or visit www.morefreebooks.com.

Terms and prices subject to change without notice. NY residents add applicable sales tax. Canadian residents will be charged applicable provincial taxes and GST. This offer is limited to one order per household. All orders subject to approval. Credit or debit balances in a customer's account(s) may be offset by any other outstanding balance owed by or to the customer. Please allow 4 to 6 weeks for delivery.

Your Privacy: Harlequin is committed to protecting your privacy. Our Privacy Policy is available online at www.eHarlequin.com or upon request from the Reader Service. From time to time we make our lists of customers available to reputable firms who may have a product or service of interest to you. If you would prefer we not share your name and address, please check here. ☐

HR07

Super Romance®

COMING NEXT MONTH

#1404 THE SISTER SWITCH • Pamela Ford
Singles...with Kids
Against Nora Clark's better judgment, she agrees to switch places with her twin. And the havoc this creates wouldn't be so bad if only her sister's new client was someone other than Erik Morgan, a doctor at the hospital where she works. Or if her son had decided Erik would be perfect as his new daddy. Or if Nora could let go of her late husband and let herself love again.

#1405 FIRST COMES BABY • Janice Kay Johnson
9 Months Later
Laurel Woodall and Caleb Manes aren't going about things the "right way." They've been friends since college, but never lovers. Still, when Laurel needs a man to make her dream for a child come true, Caleb is the one she asks. Will love come later?

#1406 THE LAST COWBOY HERO • Barbara McMahon
Home on the Ranch
For ten years Holly and Ty each thought the other guilty of betrayal. When Ty moves back home, he discovers Holly is still living right next door. To complicate matters, someone is sabotaging both ranches. Working together, can they find a spark of the love that was once so strong?

#1407 TEMPORARY FATHER • Anna Adams
Welcome to Honesty
Honesty, Virginia, is just a rest stop for Aidan Nikolas. He doesn't plan on staying, though he can't deny it has its charms—especially Beth Tully and her son, Eli. But how can he get involved with Beth when what Eli needs is a man who can become a permanent father?

#1408 A READY-MADE FAMILY • Carrie Alexander
North Country Stories
A ready-made family is just right for Jake Robbin. And when one appears on his doorstep—in the form of Lia Howard and her three children—he thinks it might be time to take advantage. But there's something that Lia isn't telling him....

#1409 HOUSEFUL OF STRANGERS • Linda Barrett
Single Father
Take a fifteen-year-old runaway, a widow who's just lost her child, a single dad with ten-year-old son and a very wise mother, put them all under the same roof—and watch a family come to life.